DISCOVERING HER EARL

Scots and Scoundrels, Book 2

Allison B. Hanson

ARE YOU SIGNED UP FOR DRAGONBLADE'S BLOG?

You'll get the latest news and information on exclusive giveaways, exclusive excerpts, coming releases, sales, free books, cover reveals and more.

Check out our complete list of authors, too!

No spam, no junk. That's a promise!

Sign Up Here

www.dragonbladepublishing.com

Dearest Reader;

Thank you for your support of a small press. At Dragonblade Publishing, we strive to bring you the highest quality Historical Romance from some of the best authors in the business. Without your support, there is no 'us', so we sincerely hope you adore these stories and find some new favorite authors along the way.

Happy Reading!

CEO, Dragonblade Publishing

**Additional Dragonblade books by
Author Allison B. Hanson**

Scots and Scoundrels Series
Winning Her Duke (Book 1)
Discovering Her Earl (Book 2)

CHAPTER ONE

London, May 1812

CLENCHING HIS FINGERS in his hair, Julian Huntly, Earl of Melville, paced the length of his solicitor's office for the sixth time.

"How is this possible? The bloody arse has been gone *five years*. How can he still be making demands of me from beyond the grave?"

The thin man who'd been hired by Julian's father years ago was wise to look worried. He was no doubt familiar with the saying about what came of messengers. And since the late earl wasn't alive, Mr. Reeves was the only person left to bear Julian's anger with his meddling sire.

"The late earl was very clear in his wishes, my lord. This document was not to be opened until the year before your thirtieth birthday. You see the date it was to be opened—"

"Aye, I see the bloody date!" Julian pressed his hand to his temple and made another lap in the small, cluttered office filled with the scents of paper and dust. Anger caused his brogue to worsen, not helping with Mr. Reeves' nervous condition.

Julian had been free of his father's demands since he'd been four and twenty, yet he could still hear the man's voice in his head. The constant judgement and disappointment.

Julian's mother had died when he was eight. Afterward, his

1

father took his only son's upbringing upon himself. Unfortunately, Julian was never smart enough, strong enough, fast enough, or brave enough to win even the smallest amount of praise from his disapproving father.

At some point in his youth, Julian had simply given up trying to impress the man, and instead grasped onto something he felt he was good at.

Assuring that anyone *not* related to him, liked him.

When he made someone laugh, he felt as if he were twenty feet tall, instead of the six feet four inches he truly was. He relied on his charm to earn him acceptance, and it felt good. As if he'd been walking the desert his entire life and someone had offered him a glass of water.

He'd attended George Heriot's School in Edinburgh and made friends he still had to this day. When they'd reached adulthood, the three of them descended on London. Three large Scots that had planned to own the Town. And now this.

Poor Mr. Reeves cleared his throat.

"You'll have the rest of this Season and most of next to find a bride in time to marry before your birthday next year at the end of May," the solicitor pointed out.

"Except I don't wish to marry."

But even as he said it, he knew his statement wasn't exactly true.

Julian wasn't completely opposed to the idea. His good friend Hale had married last year and seemed quite content with his choice. But Julian didn't want to marry because he felt yet again that his father was trying to control him.

His sire had forced his will on Julian for as long as he could remember and by God, Julian wouldn't allow it now that the man was dead.

"There must be another way. This document would have been drawn up in Scotland, have ye reviewed Scottish laws?"

"I'm sorry, my lord." The man shook his head. "Regardless of it being signed in Scotland, it clearly states that if you are not married to a proper lady by the eve of your thirtieth birthday all unentailed properties will be handed over to Lord Osborne."

"Lord Osborne? That makes no bloody sense. My father didn't even get on with Lord Osborne."

"Perhaps he thought it an effective motivator."

Julian didn't have an issue with Lord Osborne one way or the other, but he couldn't allow the man to take his unentailed properties. Specifically, the two lucrative mines passed on to Julian through his mother.

The revenue from the mines was his main source of income. His estates in Scotland and England were managed well, but he invested the monies from them back into the properties, equipment, and upkeep on his tenants' homes. Julian couldn't stand to take from his tenants to cover other expenses. Including his own lifestyle.

He didn't play deep in the pockets at the tables or wager too much at the tracks. He didn't even overindulge on clothing or mistresses.

Still, the mines gave him freedom. But that wasn't the only reason he couldn't afford to lose them.

When he'd first visited the mines, a few months after his father's death, he'd been appalled by the state they were in.

Men and young boys—children too young to manage the duties they'd been forced into—working in unsafe conditions for little pay. Their shabby homes were falling down around their ears and they seldom had a decent meal.

It had made Julian sick to know he'd lived in luxury while those people had suffered so.

He'd made immediate changes. Including removing the children from the mines and setting up a school. He'd invested in safety measures, repaired their homes, and raised the workers' salaries which in turn made the mines more profitable than they'd ever been before. Healthy workers were more productive workers.

And now, they could end up with Lord Osborne who ran his

mines in the same fashion Julian's father had. He couldn't allow the miners and their families to go back to that life.

"You could pull more income from the other estates to cover your expenses," Mr. Reeves offered as if he had no issue with taking money from the people who had rightfully earned it.

But thinking of his estates did give him an idea.

"Haverdale and Wellfrey. They aren't entailed. I could sell them and—"

The solicitor was shaking his head before the sentence was out.

"No. You cannot sell them. You never could."

"Bloody bastard." It seemed his father had thought of everything. Of course, the bugger had seen fit to force his will on Julian yet again. Years after Julian had been free of the wretched man.

"It isn't unheard of for a father to want his son to ensure the line by your age."

Julian answered that comment with a hard glare, and a Scottish curse that had sturdier men shaking in their boots. Julian turned back to read over the letter again. He pointed at a section near the end.

"What does this mean here?" He tapped the parchment. "Someone must *approve* my wife? Who?"

"I don't know. That is only to be disclosed after you choose a lady to wed."

"Then it's possible I could go along with this insanity and marry someone I think is proper enough for the blighter, only to have some unnamed person come along and deem her unfit? I could still lose my mines even if I did his bidding?"

"Yes, I suppose that is possible. But I imagine your father prepared this person to approve a wife who would make a suitable countess. Otherwise, I would think he would have stipulated his specific requirements in the document. He was quite thorough on everything else."

Julian pointed at the stacks of books on every flat surface of the room.

"You dig through every one of these bloody books and confer with my solicitor in Scotland. You find a way to get me out of this. There has to be a law against such things. And if you can't find something, get a second opinion, and a third, and a six hundred and forty-seventh opinion, until someone figures out how to save my mines."

"You have the ability—"

"Do not tell me I can save the mines myself. I will not be forced into marriage by a man who imposed his will on me every second of my youth. I was free of him when he died. He will not manage me from where he rots in the ground. Find another way."

With that, Julian left.

When he'd walked to his solicitor's office earlier, he'd been wearing a smile on his face despite the gray clouds above. Now, he didn't think he could remember how to smile as he stormed home in the frigid downpour. It had been unseasonably cold so far this spring, and this day was another unpleasant day for late May.

Maybe he would catch a chill and it would end the whole matter as it had for his mother. Julian's death would certainly thwart his father's ridiculous plans. Though Julian wasn't close to giving up yet.

As he walked, he thought of the ways he could economize his lifestyle if it came to that. He didn't need to have quite so many books. His yearly donation to the Darlington Expedition would have to go, though he did love seeing the Egyptian artifacts that were exhumed with the aid of his contributions.

Julian rarely entertained, so he could surely get rid of the silver and elaborate place settings in the formal dining room.

He was considering other things he might be able to do away with rather than kneel to his father's wishes as he entered Melville House.

Spencer, the butler, fretted as Julian dripped through the foyer.

"Should I have a bath drawn, my lord?"

So much for Julian's plans to catch a deathly chill. No, he wouldn't let his father win at this. His reign had ended when he'd died. Julian had been free of his oppressive rule for the last five years, he'd find a way. He had to.

Besides, on the off chance he ended up in the same place as his father in the afterlife, Julian was in no hurry to see the bastard anytime soon. A bath, and dry clothes were a brilliant idea.

"Thank you, Spence. I would appreciate it."

While that was being seen to, Julian went to his study to pour a whisky. It may not be noon yet, but it was well-earned.

Wanting something else to do to keep his mind off of his dilemma, he decided to go through the mail that had arrived while he was out.

He flipped through the pile of invitations and pulled out a letter from his dear friend Hale who had moved home to Scotland with his wife. While neither Kit nor Graham, his other friends, had any immediate plans to marry, Julian didn't want to end up becoming the sole bachelor of the group. Another reason why finding someone to marry was not so disagreeable. That was until his father had demanded it.

And he was back to thinking about his plight.

Setting the letter aside, he continued through the stack until he found one that stood out from the others because of the hieroglyphics drawn on the side of the envelope.

He knew what it was before opening it since he had gotten an invitation like this each year at this time.

The Darlington Expedition Ball.

Lord Darlington invited contributors to his home every June near the end of the Season. He solicited funds to cover his expenses and the benefactors were ensured their names would be assigned to the artifacts collected when they were displayed in the British Museum.

Julian didn't care so much about the recognition as he did the excitement of being the first to see what was found during the exploration of the tombs. He and the other contributors were able to view the artifacts before they were put on display. Julian had always been interested in adventure and discovery in other lands even if he'd only had the opportunity to visit the continent briefly.

His father had forced Julian to read books about agriculture and business, which had certainly come in handy. But when he was permitted to read for pleasure, he always chose books about adventure. Something his father deemed a waste of good paper.

"My lord, your bath is ready."

"Thank you, Spence."

Julian went up to his rooms to meet his valet. Bentley frowned as he peeled the wet garments from Julian's body.

"Sorry, old chap. I should have called for a hack, but I needed to walk to expel some pent-up energy." The older man had always been kind to Julian, even when he'd been his father's valet when Julian had been a boy.

"It's of no matter, my lord. I will have them replaced."

"Replaced?" Julian asked. Surely, that wouldn't come cheap.

"There is no saving this jacket," Ben assured him.

"Very well." Julian let his head fall back in the tub as the man left him alone to wash. And think.

No matter what expenses Julian managed to cut, he worried it wouldn't be enough. And it wouldn't help the men who worked in his mines and their families if Julian ran out of blunt. What would become of them?

And what would happen when he did decide to marry and have children? How would he provide for the family he was avoiding now, after he'd allowed the unentailed properties go?

And if he was planning to have a family anyway, why not just do it now?

Simply because he wanted to defy his father, who wasn't even here to know? He would be punishing himself, his future family, and the people who depended on him with his stubbornness.

By the time he had dressed and returned to the study, it was clear he had no other option than to go along with this ridiculous scheme.

It shouldn't be that difficult for him to find a proper bride. Not that he thought of himself as some great catch, but he had a title. A rather impressive one at that. There would be some women who refused to wed a large Scot, but his title would be enough to make many of the mamas gather their daughters to jump at the chance to be countess. And he'd have his choice of the lot.

He picked up the invitation to the Darlington Ball and smiled as an idea grew into a plan.

If he was going to marry, he was damn well going to make sure he had a bit of fun before conceding. He wouldn't miss this last chance at adventure.

CHAPTER TWO

M ISS ELAINA BANTHAM held tight to the bedpost as the housekeeper—currently acting as her lady's maid—tugged on her corset. It wasn't as if Elaina wasn't already too tall for society's standards, but she also had curves that needed to be squeezed into submission.

Statuesque, her Aunt Rose would say. Her Uncle Henry would agree by claiming her *lovely.*

Lainey loved them both for taking her in after her parents died. It had been comforting for an eleven-year-old to have her aunt, who so reminded her of her mother; it was as if she still lived.

Aunt Rose and Lainey's mother had been only a year apart, and many people thought them to be twins because they were so much alike. The three of them had been close and when Lainey's mother passed, Lainey and Aunt Rose had both shared an excruciating loss which strengthened their bond as well.

Her Uncle Henry, Viscount Darlington, had always treated her as his own, despite there being no connection by blood. He'd also included her in their extensive adventures.

While most young women only read of such places as China or Egypt, Lainey had been there. She'd seen amazing things and met interesting people.

Which made tonight's ball seem that much more insufferable.

The *ton* claimed very few interesting people.

If she had her choice, she would much rather be wearing breeches while digging in the dirt than face a room full of gossiping ninnies and boorish dandies.

But her aunt and uncle had once again asked her to attend their annual ball, and she didn't want to disappoint them.

It wouldn't be the jungles of the Amazon that made her sweat, or being chased by a baboon that made her heart race tonight. It would be a ballroom stuffed with people who would cause her plenty of discomfort this evening.

Lainey remembered all too well the failure that had been her come out and the person who had ruined all her dreams of a happy ever after. And she was sure he would be in attendance tonight.

"Look at you," Aunt Rose startled Lainey as she glided into the room. "So statuesque. I wish I had your height, it would rather even out some of this middle." She pointed to her waist.

"You are beautiful, auntie."

"As are you. We women spend too much time wishing for attributes we don't have, all while the ones who do have them often find them a bother. It is the curse of being a woman I suppose." She fussed with Lainey's red-blonde curls that had been fashioned by her ears, and cocked her head.

"Apparently these are all the rage this Season. Of course, what would I care about being fashionable for a bunch of stuffy aristocrats?"

"You may not care, but they suit you." She tilted her head the other direction and Lainey knew what she would say next before she opened her mouth to speak. "This might be the year the right man finally notices what a catch you are and sweeps you off your feet."

Lainey refrained from sighing. At three and twenty, Lainey was considered a spinster and perfectly fine with her status. Men didn't like women who were taller than them, which meant Lainey's five feet ten inches frightened off the majority of the men in attendance.

Her unfashionable hair and freckles didn't help matters either.

But rather than argue with her aunt, she offered a smile and nodded.

"We shall see."

With their arms linked, they descended the stairs to find Uncle Henry waiting.

"How lucky I am to have the loveliest ladies in London by my side as we greet our guests tonight. The men won't stand a chance when they see you, they shall want to donate enormous sums for the opportunity just to be near you."

Lainey couldn't help but roll her eyes.

"I saw that, Elaina," he scolded with a wink. "Let's ready ourselves to charm the britches off the *ton*."

With a laugh, Lainey followed her aunt and uncle to the edge of the ballroom where they would wait for their guests to arrive. There they would greet each one pleasantly, all in the hope they would want to donate funds toward the next expedition that would be starting at the beginning of the following year.

Their most recent artifacts were ensconced in glass cases along the wall where previous donors were honored for their gifts. Not that they had dug them out of the dirt themselves, but they'd paid for the trip, and seeing their name associated with an artifact made them happy.

It was all about making the donors happy. Which was why she pasted a smile on her lips and went out to greet the *ton*, even though she'd much rather face a Nile crocodile.

An hour later, Lainey's feet hurt and she worried her cheeks would be pulled up forever in the strained smile that had taken over her face.

Fortunately, she was given a reprieve when Lord Melville entered the ballroom. If she'd ever had a reason *not* to smile, it was him. Ever charming, he stood well over six feet, putting him in the small group of men that wouldn't be intimidated by her height.

But despite his meeting any physical requirements, the large

Scot was completely unacceptable. His arrogance was enough to dismiss him. Not that she would be granted the opportunity to dismiss him. He could never claim enough of an interest in her to be dismissed.

This was her cue to leave the receiving line and go find refreshment.

"Excuse me, aunt. I'm parched. Would you like me to bring you something to drink as well?"

"Yes, dear. How sweet of you."

Lainey only suffered the slightest twinge of guilt as she rushed away, just before the man had stepped up to their group. She only needed to delay long enough that he offered his greetings and moved along. Then she could return to her aunt's side with a cup of lemonade, and no one would think anything of it.

She stood at the edge of the room, watching as the guests, dressed in colorful gowns and black eveningwear, perused and pointed at the artifacts with excitement.

Her aunt had done a beautiful job of incorporating the splendor of their London townhouse with hints of Egyptian décor. Even the underlying scents of cinnamon and myrrh made her think of her home away from home. Egypt.

She may not have to worry about sand or scorpions here, but there were plenty of other dangers.

She glanced over at the biggest one, who was still speaking with her uncle. She'd finished the first glass of lemonade, and started on the second, determined to wait him out.

She kept her smile in place as she nodded to the few guests who acknowledged her where she hid behind a potted palm. She wasn't comfortable with people. She didn't know how to start a discussion or keep it going. Unless someone asked about antiquary or archaeology, she was rather lost.

But when she was engaged in conversation on her favorite topics, she often forgot to stop talking about dirt until the other person began searching for some way to escape her ramblings.

Because of that, it was best if she stayed clear of conversation altogether.

Glancing over to her aunt and uncle, she realized her plan wasn't working as it had in years past. Lainey had finished her second cup of lemonade as well as the one she'd retrieved for her aunt. However, the earl still stood next to her uncle chatting with him, while her aunt was now searching around the room.

Most likely for her.

Any second now, Aunt Rose would spot Lainey hiding by the wall behind her and wave her over. She might have taken refuge outside, but it was terribly chilly out, despite it being June.

"Good lord," Lainey muttered when the inevitable happened and she was found. Getting another cup of lemonade, she returned to her aunt, hoping to hide. But due to her aunt's small stature, it was like a rhinoceros hiding behind a shrub.

"There you are, dear," her uncle said when she was close. "Let me introduce you to Lord Melville. Lord Melville, our niece, Miss Bantham."

As if she had not been introduced to him at several balls in the past. She needed no introduction, but as she curtseyed, he bowed and said, "It is a pleasure to meet you." Just as he had every other time they'd met. His rumbling brogue did odd things to her stomach.

"Your aunt and uncle have told me what an asset you are in the field. I hope to learn much from ye when I join the expedition next year."

Lainey blinked as her mind struggled to piece his words together in a way that made sense.

"Isn't it wonderful? Lord Melville will be joining us in Egypt," her aunt explained as if Lainey hadn't come to that conclusion on her own. And maybe it was taking longer than it should have, but the thought was preposterous.

Wonderful? No, it wasn't wonderful at all. It was impossible.

Before she had the chance to consider her response, panic took over and she uttered words that made her aunt and uncle gasp as the earl flinched.

"You can't possibly allow this bored dandy to accompany us on an active expedition. He's untrained and will only injure himself or someone else. He'll no doubt wish to come home minutes after we've disembarked because the heat is intolerable." And even the heat wouldn't be as intolerable as having this man spend more than a minute in her presence.

Her rant had gone wide from the rule of keeping the donors happy, but she could not allow this man to join them, for she hated him with her entire being.

All these years, and he probably didn't even realize how much she despised him. But the cat was rather out of that bag now.

⟫⟫⟫⟪⟪⟪

JULIAN STOOD STILL in the awkward silence following the woman's outburst. He'd seen her at these functions in the past but had never spoken to her. For whatever reason their paths had never crossed.

He'd always thought her quiet and shy, but he realized now he'd been quite wrong on both counts. She'd practically yelled her disapproval, and the way her brown eyes blazed at him in anger, he knew she was not so shy she wouldn't take a step closer and plant him a facer.

He was glad her aunt had placed a calming hand on Miss Bantham's arm to keep that from happening.

Lord Darlington looked around and smiled at the people closest to them who had turned curious gazes in their direction while Lady Darlington offered a strained laugh.

"Oh, Lainey, you are too funny."

Julian studied the taller woman hoping to see some sign that she was indeed joking, but her glare had not wavered as she stepped toward him with her fingers clenched into fists.

"You can't do this. You won't ruin this too." With that, she turned and rushed away.

Though the situation had been quite unpleasant, he barely fought the urge to follow after her and... do what exactly? Ask her why she was so angry with him? Or angry at the world in general?

Not exactly. As he considered the flutter in his stomach, he realized he suffered an entirely different reaction than what the situation warranted. He briefly imagined kissing her, exploring the passion she barely reined in.

Absurd.

Passion came in all forms and was closely related. Anger was just the opposite side of the coin from desire. Though she was making an argument that perhaps some coins had only one side. All he'd seen was anger sparking from her eyes. He would be better served to find another adventure and stay clear of the woman.

But he wouldn't. Or perhaps, it was that he *couldn't.*

Julian blamed his father's constant disapproval for his need to be accepted by every other person. After spending so much of his life not being good enough, he couldn't tolerate anyone rejecting him now. It was ridiculous and clearly the reason for his surprisingly lustful reaction to the harpy.

She was pretty, with luscious curves that called for a man's hands to trace them. He wasn't sure how he'd had time to notice that when he feared she would pummel him, but he had. Call it a gift.

"I apologize for my niece," Lord Darlington said. "She is usually quite pleasant. I'm not sure what caused that reaction. I'm certain she will come around and will be more than happy to welcome you."

The man was unexpectedly generous after Julian had basically forced the man into an ultimatum. To allow Julian to join the expedition to Egypt or he would withdraw his funding.

It was a drastic measure, but he couldn't afford to be turned away. This was his last chance for adventure, and he had done what needed to be done to secure his place. Or rather the place he'd taken under duress.

"It seemed she was quite concerned with my lack of training and the risk I might bring to the team. If there is anything I can do to reassure everyone I'm willing to learn, I would be happy to do so. I understand I know nothing, but if someone would only teach me, I promise, I'm a fast learner."

And he *was* a fast learner in the sense that it took him only seconds to find a way to appease anyone in his presence. Even the woman who'd run off would have to agree he was willing to put her mind at ease.

Why hadn't she liked him? He found he still wanted to track her down, though now that his unsolicited attraction had abated, he only wanted to find out why she'd seemed to loathe him. No one loathed him. He made certain of it.

The Darlingtons exchanged a look that seemed to contain an entire conversation. One that hadn't needed to be spoken for them to understand each other. He'd seen Hale and his duchess communicate in a similar fashion many times and thought it proof that perhaps witchcraft was a real thing.

The devilish twinkle in Lady Darlington's eyes and the crooked grin on Lord Darlington's face gave Julian pause. He couldn't help but feel he was about to be tossed into shark infested waters.

"There is a small expedition leaving in two weeks to the Highlands. It's only the ruins of a castle, but it is said the castle was abandoned hastily which means there could be artifacts of value on the grounds that have been left behind. Even if there are no treasures to be found, it would still give you an opportunity to learn the techniques and determine if you are interested in digging about in the dirt. As well as give us the chance to evaluate your suitability for the larger expedition leaving in January. I believe you have an estate nearby which would be convenient."

While Scotland didn't have the same allure as Egypt, because Julian had already spent most of his youth in Scotland, he wouldn't turn down this chance to prove himself worthy of his place on their team.

"I would be honored for the opportunity and to host the team at my home."

"Very well. You should be ready to leave the first week of August. That will give you plenty of time to gather supplies."

He offered a winning smile even if inside he felt the first flutter of panic.

Supplies? He didn't have the first idea of what supplies he would need for an expedition. He gave a casual nod. He wouldn't let the things he didn't know stop him from taking advantage of this opportunity.

He would figure it out. Until then, excitement filled his veins.

He was going on an expedition. One that would lead him to the adventure of a lifetime. It would have to. He would only have this one opportunity to make enough memories to satisfy his thirst for excitement.

For when the expedition was over and he returned to England, he would choose a proper bride and marry.

Just as his father required.

CHAPTER THREE

As Julian gazed around the room, he hated to admit even to himself that he was looking for her.

Miss Bantham.

Why hadn't she succumbed to his charms? Everyone liked him. He went to great lengths to make sure of it.

Whatever it was, she most certainly didn't like him and an hour later, he found it bothered him to the point of distraction.

He hadn't even been given a chance to captivate her with his wit. She'd merely been introduced to him and decided from that short exchange she disliked him. Perhaps she was too English to accept his plaid sash and brogue. Except she had called him an arrogant dandy, not an uncivilized barbarian.

Meanwhile everyone else he'd encountered had been *pleased* to speak with him. Perhaps there was something wrong with *her*. He had to know.

Seeing Lady Archer and Lady Foxley across the room, he made his way to them. If anyone would know anything about anybody, it would be the two biggest gossips of the *ton*.

"My ladies, it is so good to see you this evening. I dinna realize we shared an interest in antiquary."

"Oh, yes, my lord," Lady Archer gushed excitedly. "Lord Archer and I have been continued supporters and have many artifacts attributed to us in the museum."

"I generally prefer living specimens of a zoological nature,"

Mrs. Foxley commented.

"But certainly, you can enjoy an interesting rock now and then?" he said, making the women laugh. As women often did in his presence. Except Miss Bantham.

The more he considered the puzzle the woman was, he was more convinced there was something wrong about her rather than a defect in himself. That had to be it.

"I hope to join the expedition myself. I am most looking forward to meeting new people."

"That does sound exciting, my lord." Lady Archer gave an approving nod.

"I wonder, what do you know of Lady Darlington's niece?" As casual segues went, that wasn't his best example, but this was the only question he needed an answer to. And his question was all it took to launch the women into a thorough accounting.

"Oh, the poor girl. As if her height wasn't enough, she is cursed with that red hair."

He followed their gazes and there she was. Miss Bantham. He found her hair to be a lovely shade between blonde and red. It reminded him of sunshine.

He shook his head. What the devil did sunshine even look like? It was much too bright to stare into the sun, not that it had been out much recently.

"Apparently they don't allow bonnets in China and Egypt for she bears the marks of the sun." This was said with a tut of disapproval from Lady Foxley whose skin was pale and almost waxy.

It took him a second to realize they were speaking of freckles, not large scars as she'd made it seem with her dramatic gasp.

Lady Archer leaned closer to whisper to their small group. "I've heard she took a lover in Morocco."

"Morocco?" Lady Foxley challenged. "No. I heard it was Singapore."

A lover? Miss Bantham? Not that he was judging, he'd had many lovers over the years. But the word *lover* indicated affection, not something he imagined her capable of after his brief interaction with the woman.

When she'd confronted him, he'd envisioned wild passion; nails digging into his skin, the nip of her teeth on his neck.

"Do you know if she takes to fits of anger? Or is slightly mad?" he asked, wanting to get to the more relevant information.

"No. Why? What have you heard?" Lady Archer practically drooled with interest.

"Nothing. Nothing at all." It wouldn't do to start up gossip. "I only like to be prepared."

"She has always seemed pleasant when we've conversed. She tends to speak at length on things ladies shouldn't discuss, but then she is the daughter of a vicar and is only in Society because she was fortunate enough to be raised by her uncle, the viscount."

Julian didn't know if Miss Bantham would call herself *fortunate* to have been orphaned at a young age, but he didn't say so.

"I understood from Lady Darlington that Miss Bantham's mother was her sister. Therefore, Miss Bantham would be the granddaughter of a duke on her mother's side, is she not?"

Lady Archer's eyes flared with intrigue.

"The late duchess was known to seek out other entertainments after the heir was born. The youngest daughter, Miss Bantham's mother, was said to be a result of a liaison between the duchess and a painter." She frowned and placed her fan on Julian's arm before adding the required, "God rest her soul."

"I see." And he did see. There seemed to be quite a bit of scandal swirling around Miss Bantham. Perhaps this was the cause of her bitterness, which meant her unpleasant demeanor had nothing to do with him but with the peerage in general.

He caught sight of her across the room again. But watched in confusion as she smiled in what seemed to be pleasant conversation with an older couple. She seemed quite the opposite of bitter at the moment.

Still, whatever the reason for her earlier outburst, it couldn't have been his fault. Everyone liked him.

Everyone.

"YOU CAN'T POSSIBLY be serious," Lainey said when the ball was over and she was alone with her aunt and uncle, currently known as the traitors who'd raised her.

She'd hardly been able to wait until the last guest had left so she could broach the subject of Lord Melville again. She'd planned to point out all the ways he wasn't suited for such a voyage, but her pleas went unsaid when Uncle Henry cut her off with his counterattack.

They couldn't really mean for her to accompany the man to Scotland. It was preposterous.

"Oh, but we do," her uncle said with a steely look. "You will oversee the earl's training in Scotland."

She shook her head, unsure of how she ended up in this situation.

"Please." She had resorted to begging, it seemed. Not a noble trait, but if it worked, she would continue until she was free from this madness.

"I see now, I was out of line," she continued. "I will… apologize to Lord Melville for my behavior and everything will be put to rights." Apologizing to that rotter would possibly make her ill, but she'd do it if it meant getting out of this impossible situation. The lesser of two evils was an apology.

"You *will* apologize to his lordship *and* accompany him on the expedition to Scotland," her uncle said. "You are the one who challenged his fortitude and questioned his abilities to learn the skills needed. It will be you who teaches him and reports back whether or not he is permitted to join us on the larger voyage to Egypt."

"If it's my decision, I can say now, he can't go. There. The matter is settled."

"Do you think that is the fair thing, Lainey?" her aunt questioned, causing guilt to twist in Lainey's stomach. "Is there a reason you dislike the man?"

She couldn't bear to talk about the reason she despised the earl. How embarrassing that conversation would be. Even with the woman who was like a mother to her.

"Is it because he's a Scot?" her uncle asked.

"No. Of course not." She let out a breath. "But do I need a reason? It's clear he's a rake and a scoundrel. Everyone knows it."

"Because the gossips say so?" her aunt asked skeptically. "You are too smart to believe what people say. You are a person of facts, and always insist on getting information first-hand. You must give the earl the chance to prove himself. If he fails as you expect, he will most likely bow out of the larger expedition. But if he prevails, then you'll be reassured he is able to handle himself in Egypt."

Their request was more than fair, but she still didn't like it. She couldn't spend a minute with the man let alone a month in Scotland.

Alone… She quickly grasped onto a possible way out of this.

"For propriety's sake, I can't travel alone with a man. I will be ruined."

Her aunt and uncle exchanged a look and then laughed.

Laughed at her very viable excuse.

"I'm sorry for laughing," Aunt Rose was the first to recover from her mirth. "It's just that you spend your time wearing men's clothes and digging in the dirt. You refused a lady's maid when we offered to have one assigned. You have never whispered a word about your reputation and now all of a sudden it's a matter of great concern?"

"I should have forced a marriage with that maharajah who helped you climb up on the roof, or the emperor's youngest son you convinced to go swimming with you," Uncle Henry said, with an amused smile.

"Don't forget the comte," her aunt mentioned unhelpfully.

"Of course, the comte, you've surely been alone with him numerous times over the years."

"Very well, you've both made your point, but you can't mean to have me travel with a suspected rake." Lainey held up her finger to stop her aunt's retort and continued. "I said *suspected*. As you pointed out, until I ascertain whether he is or isn't guilty of his reputation it doesn't seem wise to put me at risk of his wiles.

"Very well. We will obtain a chaperone to accompany you."

"A chaperone?" Lainey frowned. "Never mind. I don't require a chaperone."

"But your reputation!" Uncle Henry declared in a mocking tone.

Lainey was glad they were amused by her distress.

"I do believe she has recalled her time with Mrs. Kirkpatrick." Aunt Rose chuckled while Uncle Henry practically hooted with laughter.

"I am so glad my misfortune entertains you so."

Mrs. Kirkpatrick had been positively awful. She'd tried to contort Lainey into a proper young lady and pointed out every little thing Lainey managed to do wrong, which was basically everything. Including breathing.

Lainey truly didn't know how she could do something as simple as breathing incorrectly, but she'd managed to and the woman was quick to point it out.

Her aunt patted her shoulder and offered a kind smile.

"We are sorry for making sport of your concerns. You will be pleased to know we didn't plan to send you off with the earl alone. Lord and Lady Leighton will accompany you."

Lainey didn't have anything to say to that. Lord and Lady Leighton were wonderful people and would be suitable chaperones during their travels.

"Very well," Lainey conceded, because what else could she do? "I will do as you wish and see the earl to Scotland to evaluate his abilities." She offered a beaming smile and kept it there more naturally when their humor faded into genuine concern. She'd learned a few years ago that when she smiled like that, they grew worried that she was hatching a plan.

In this case she wasn't, at least not yet. But it didn't hurt to allow them to think she was up to something. In truth, she didn't see a way out of this insanity.

At least she wouldn't need to worry about being in his presence longer than the trip to Scotland. She had only to prove he couldn't handle an archeological dig, and he would go back to the gaming hells and clubs for his entertainments and be out of her life for good.

"Why do you look so worried?" It was her turn to laugh now. "I will see him to Scotland and teach him the techniques as you ask. But you should not be surprised when it turns out I am right about him."

"We trust you and will honor your recommendation. If it turns out you are correct about him, and you write to confirm he is not up for the journey, then he will not be permitted to join us in Egypt." her uncle promised.

"Then I will prepare to leave next week."

She was going to Scotland with the man who had destroyed her future years ago.

Perhaps she should embrace this opportunity. After all, she now had his fate in her hands, and revenge would be well within her grasp.

Lord Melville would pay for his cruelty.

Chapter Four

JULIAN LOOKED DOWN at the message in his hand and back to the street where he was to meet Miss Bantham.

Was this a trick?

He worried he'd be rolled for his watch on this street. Surely a lady of good breeding would not be meeting him in a place like this. It would be like her to send him to his demise as a prank. Or to do away with him altogether.

Before he had the chance to get back into his carriage, another conveyance pulled up behind his and the lady in question hopped down on her own without any assistance from the coachmen.

She was dressed in a simple gown of sage green that suited her coloring. If the woman wasn't scowling every time he saw her, she might be considered pretty. As it were, she was interesting, verging on daunting with the pinched glare on her face.

"Good day," he said, planning to pretend he came to this part of London every day and wasn't the least bit apprehensive for their safety.

"Good day to you, my lord." She pressed her lips together and tugged at her glove before looking him in the eye. "I must apologize for my behavior at the ball."

He couldn't help the grin that pulled up one side of his mouth. She had worded it intentionally, probably hoping he was too daft to notice.

"You said you *must* apologize, not that you wished to. It leads me to believe you are being forced to make the apology and do not actually mean it."

Her eyes went wide, and her mouth fell open, either with surprise that he had figured her out, or offense. With a huff she closed her eyes and spoke.

"Very well. I apologize for my behavior."

"Why do I feel you are struggling not to utter the word '*but*' after that?" He pointed at her. "You are thinking it, aren't you?"

"Are you going to accept my apology or not? It will be the last one you get from me, my lord."

"Fine. I will accept." He glanced around hoping that if he agreed quickly, they could move on with their task and get off the street before they were assaulted. Even someone of his size and stature was unnerved.

"Good. We have much to do before we leave. You need to be fitted with the proper tools and such. I am here to assist."

Julian silently wished Lord Darlington would have accompanied him on this mission rather than his salty niece. It was clear she saw their outing as a punishment. But it didn't seem fair that he be punished as well.

Still, he followed her into a nearby shop without a word.

"Good day, Mr. Davies, my friend is in need of some tools for our next dig. We will be leaving in a week which won't give us time for any custom instruments."

"Not to worry, miss. I always keep a few extras of what you need on hand in case you come calling."

"Smart man." She tapped her temple and waited for the man to pull a few things from behind the counter.

Julian knew he was already in danger of being expelled from the expedition, for he didn't know the names of these items let alone know how to use them.

She picked up a few of the items and weighed them in her grip for a moment before moving on to the next tool.

She waved him over. "Which of these handles feels more

comfortable?" She held the item out with the wooden handle facing him. Actually, she pointed it toward his hand. His *left* hand.

How could she have known?

Rather than make a big deal over the matter, he simply gripped the two options and made his selection.

For a moment, he thought she might select the one he *didn't* prefer instead of the one he did, but after the smallest hesitation, she placed his choice to one side with a few other items she'd already selected. A number of brushes and an item he knew to be a small pick.

He'd purchased many of them over the years for his mines, so he knew what they were at least.

When she seemed satisfied with her pile of items, she nodded to the man.

"And a box to hold everything."

"Very well. Do I send the bill to Darlington House?"

"No. Lord Mel-villain—apologies, *Melville* will see to the bill."

He let out a breath and nodded in agreement before taking the wooden box with the integrated handle and following her out of the shop.

If he hadn't already been sure her slip of the tongue with his name was intentional, the smug smile on her lips would have proven it. And for a moment too long he stared at those lips. The tiny freckle that rested on the bow of her upper lip. It seemed to be taunting him.

He cleared his throat and looked away as if anything else was more interesting.

When his mind had cleared somewhat, he recalled the other thing she'd said to the shop owner. The matter of the bill for the tools.

If he was facing the loss of his mines, he didn't need additional bills. While he had made peace with the fact he would marry someone proper to meet his father's requirements, there was no guarantee his version of *proper* would meet his father's conditions.

That would be the worst possible scenario, to submit to his

father's plans only to still lose everything. His father must be having a great laugh at how well he'd managed to contort his only son to do his bidding.

Well, Julian wasn't shackled yet. Until the time came, he would enjoy every moment of his freedom. So long as he didn't get his throat slit in the dregs of London where she was leading him to another shop close by.

This one was a tailor, though not for evening clothes. The finest thing the man had in his window was a solid, blue waistcoat made from a sturdy fabric rather than the silk one Julian was currently wearing. Everything else seemed to have been made for a purpose beyond that of avoiding dances at society balls.

"You'll want loose-fitting clothing to allow movement," Miss Bantham explained.

It felt rather odd having a woman helping him with his clothing. Perhaps even intimate. When Julian selected a wife, would she accompany him to the tailor?

Miss Bantham looked him up and down, no doubt assessing his size, but he felt an undercurrent of excitement at being the object of her appraisal. He also felt as if he had been given the right to appraise her right back.

She was tall, which he'd known already, but now that she was standing so close, he was able to see exactly how tall she was. Taller than any other woman he'd ever known.

Was this the reason she wasn't married already?

He knew how some men got flustered in his presence when he towered over them. Their insecurities pricked. He imagined a short man, or even one of average size would be intimidated by a woman who looked down at them.

He thought it ridiculous, but then he wasn't in their position, so who was he to say how he might think if he'd matured to be short of stature rather than the giant he was.

While she was taller than many men, she was quite clearly a woman. There would be no mistaking that. Her breasts filled out the neckline of her serviceable green gown. While the waistline was elevated, it hinted at her narrow waist before sloping outward again to caress her hips and luscious backside.

And, of course, he was now thinking about her backside. Isn't that where his thoughts always strayed?

At the sound of her throat clearing, he snapped his gaze up to find her scowling as always, but with a hint of confusion this time.

Good. He'd baffled her. It was only fair because she had certainly perplexed him.

He didn't know what it was about her that both intrigued and irritated him, but it was no matter. She was merely a means to an end. He needed to get through her to earn his place on the expedition to Egypt.

He would charm her into agreeing. He was charming after all. He only had to make sure she noticed.

How difficult could it be?

⇶⇷

LORD MELVILLE MADE Lainey want to growl, but she didn't wish to frighten poor Mr. Harper. The tailor was already wary of her since she was possibly the only lady to come into his shop to purchase clothing for herself.

But today's visit was not for her.

"Mr. Harper makes the finest clothes for everyday work. Over the years he has modified a few things for warmer climes." Not that Lord Melville would be needing those, because he would not be going to Egypt. So far it had been a cool spring, and Scotland was sure to be even cooler in the North.

"Lord Melville needs clothing for working outside. We will be working on a site in the Highlands. We leave next week. Can you outfit him properly by then?"

"Of course, miss." The man looked Melville up and down and swallowed. "Don't know that I ever had a right lord in my shop afore."

"I assure you he is no one special," she said, earning a smirk from Melville.

"I am built the same as other men, I assure you." Melville held out his arms as if to prove his statement, and then added, "Just much larger in every way."

He quirked a brow at her which made her think he'd made some jest, but she couldn't be sure. What he'd said was true. He was larger than any other man she knew. But he was also wrong. He wasn't the same in any way.

She'd noticed he was tall years ago. It was the reason he had first caught her attention. But now she knew it was more than his height that made him different than other men.

He'd no doubt never worked a day in his life, yet his shoulders were broad, his chest wide. His stomach was without the swell or softness other lords covered with straining, brightly-colored waistcoats.

She conducted her evaluation of his frame with quick glances rather than staring as he had done to her. Whatever had he been looking at when he'd watched her walk away? Perhaps he sought evidence of a pointed tail to match her evil behavior when it came to dealing with him.

Standing by the door, she watched quietly as Mr. Harper took Melville's measurements. With the lord's gaze turned away from her, she was able to study him more closely. Without fear of him knowing.

His near-black hair was short. It no longer touched his collar as it had five years ago. Perhaps this was part of his disguise to seem less like a rogue and more respectable. She would not fall prey to that trick.

She looked up from the enticing way his buttocks sloped at the sound of a chuckle and found him watching her in the reflection of the looking glass.

Instantly her cheeks went hot, the heat quickly rushing down her neck and chest. He'd caught her looking at his…

Just as she'd caught him.

However, her reaction was completely different than his. While she had glared at him, he seemed to preen in her attentions. His blue eyes flared in excitement.

Men were strange creatures. Lords even more so, apparently. This one, clearly the strangest of all. He made her equal parts angry and fascinated.

When he winked at her she decided it was perhaps not quite *equal* parts. And she was appalled to find the spark of excitement meant she was more fascinated with the man than angry.

What she should be focusing on was getting her revenge. She considered having Mr. Harper make his clothing too small, but he didn't know if Lord Mel-villain would withhold payment.

If she knew the man had any interest in her physically, she might feign an attraction on her part, but she would surely get in over her head in such a ruse.

For now, she would have to shore up her defenses. There was no way she would allow him to go with them to Egypt. He was far too distracting.

She'd fallen for his charms years ago. She'd not let it happen again.

CHAPTER FIVE

WHEN THE DARLINGTON carriage stopped in front of Julian's home the following week, he took his single bag from Spencer and descended down the steps. The rest of his luggage had been sent ahead on his own carriage with Ben.

He hadn't wanted the rest of their group to think him a dandy for needing a valet for an archaeological dig.

The footman opened the door and Julian hesitated for a moment when he found only Miss Bantham waiting inside.

After he'd caught her appraising him at the tailors, he knew she was not so unaffected by him as she let on. But he shouldn't have let his amusement get away from him. Had he kept the knowledge to himself he might have used it to his advantage. Instead, he'd laughed and then watched as her icy walls grew higher and thicker.

It was a foolish thing but he'd been so relieved to see that she did, in fact, like him. If only in the physical sense. It was something. Or had been. Now she wouldn't even look at him.

With a resigned sigh, he took the seat opposite her and waited for her to acknowledge him in some way.

"Good day to you, Miss Bantham."

"Good day, my lord," she fairly mumbled with only a darting glance in his direction.

He was quite under her skin. It was as good a place as any to start. A few moments alone with her and he might win her over.

At the thought of being alone, he moved his gaze from her to the otherwise empty carriage.

"Are we to make another stop to get the rest of our group?" he asked.

"No. It is just me."

He put his foot out before the footman could shut the door, otherwise sealing his fate with this woman.

"I was to understand the Leightons would be joining us."

"They received word yesterday morning their first grandchild was born. They went ahead to visit. They will meet us in Scotland after they've met their grandson."

"And your maid?"

She looked at him then, and he wondered why he'd wished she would have looked at him earlier. Her brows were pinched together and her usually warm, brown eyes were shooting sparks.

Ah. The glare was back.

"I have no maid."

"A chaperone?" His voice had taken on a begging quality.

For whatever reason that suggestion earned him a shiver of distaste, but she only answered curtly, "I need no chaperone."

He swallowed as panic rose in his throat.

Alone with her the entire trip to Scotland?

It wasn't that he feared he would do something inappropriate. He was a gentleman despite his reputation. He was in no danger of losing his wits and doing something disreputable. Especially since it was quite clear she wouldn't welcome his attentions.

But her reputation…

"But you are a young lady." He gestured to the otherwise empty carriage to make his point.

"Not so young," she muttered, clearly not comprehending the issue.

"We cannot travel alone to the end of the block let alone all the way to Scotland. Your reputation would be ruined." He couldn't believe he, of all people, needed to explain such things to a woman of gentle birth.

She laughed, and though it was brittle and cold, it brightened her face and drew his attention to her full lips. She was quite lovely when she wasn't scowling at him like a wet kitten. He found that he wanted to hear the sound of her laughter without the cynical edge.

"What would someone like you know or care about a woman's reputation except for how to ruin it?" She shook her head and continued her intense inspection out the opposite window. Did she plan to look out that window the entire time? She'd get a terrible crick in her neck if so.

Not that he cared about her neck or anything else of hers. She was nothing but a bitter harpy and he dreaded being with her almost enough to call off the trip. But he wouldn't.

As much as he didn't want to spend another minute with Miss Elaina Bantham, he couldn't give up his dream of a final adventure. For that reason alone, he would endure.

He frowned back at her, dropping his usual smile others found charming.

"I'll have you know, I have never so much as shaded the reputation of an innocent. Yes, I might dally with women who are interested in the same, but I do not prey on young misses and seduce them to ruin."

He'd sounded rather snappish in his defense, but rather than be cowed, she rolled her eyes and made a sound that could only be described as *pfft*.

"You don't believe me?"

She waved dismissively in his direction which only irked him more.

"I assure you whatever I believe doesn't matter. What matters is that I am not intimidated by you. There is nothing you could ever do that would risk my reputation. Mostly because I don't find you appealing or the least bit charming."

Lies. He could tell by the way she'd glanced away when she said it. He wouldn't mention the way she'd gawked at him lasciviously at the tailors. And if the word lascivious was not quite accurate, there was no harm in a bit of embellishment.

His lips crooked up slightly at the memory. She was lovely with a blush on her cheeks. That moment before fiery anger returned to her eyes, he could almost envision how she would look up at her lover with desire in those brown pools of melted chocolate.

He cleared his throat and shook off the thought. It wouldn't do to be caught up in a fantasy when facing down an opponent as cunning as Miss Bantham.

However alluring she might be in his mind from the tiny snippets he'd seen when her walls were down, he couldn't be distracted. He knew himself well enough to know it was only the fact he wasn't able to win her over that made her interesting at all. If she'd smiled and batted her eyelashes at him, he would have been satisfied and could have moved on without another thought.

It was only that she obviously disliked him and he didn't know why that made her a mystery he couldn't let rest. But he needed to. Why should he care about her at all?

If she didn't care about her reputation, then why should he? He allowed the door to be shut and settled in for the duration.

Oddly enough, he didn't feel confined as he usually did when traveling in a carriage. Travel was usually uncomfortable for someone of his size, but he found he had ample room. His knees were close to hers, but not touching. Clearly the carriage had been made for someone of their stature in mind.

At least he would be comfortable physically if mentally he was trapped.

Trapped…

He lurched forward to look into her startled eyes. Seeing her reaction piqued his anger even more. Did she honestly think he would thrust himself on her? Before they were even out of Town?

"You don't plan to trap me into marriage, do you? For I tell you that plan will not work. It cannot." He needed to marry a proper countess. Not the feisty daughter of a vicar who didn't even have a lady's maid.

If he'd thought he'd wanted to see her laughing, he'd been granted his wish. The woman practically rolled off her seat for laughing so much. Twice she attempted to speak and couldn't for getting caught up in another fit of mirth.

He straightened his coat while he waited. The idea wasn't that ridiculous. Plenty of women would jump at the opportunity to coerce an attachment to an earl. Perhaps not him specifically since it had not happened to date, but still, he had a title and his teeth, and…

Good God, this is what the woman had reduced him to?

By the time she was done, she seemed exhausted, but the smile remained.

"My, I haven't laughed like that in a very long time."

"Might I say that despite it being aimed at me, I find your laughter delightful."

And the smile was gone instantly.

"We will be in each other's company for the next two months. Perhaps we should come to an agreement, so the time is not spent in immense irritation," she offered with a tilt of her head.

"I have been the very picture of gentlemanly behavior." When the scowl returned with a vengeance, he quickly backtracked in the hope she wouldn't bury his body on some muddy road on the way to Scotland. "What do you propose?"

"I assure you; I am not attempting to trap you in marriage. In fact, if it were up to me, I would much prefer not to have you accompany me on this journey at all. But since I am to be saddled with you, please refrain from offering empty platitudes or attempting to sway my favor with your relentless efforts to be charming."

He opened his mouth and shut it, then repeated the process three more times before gathering enough of his thoughts to form a coherent response.

"You actually despise me." He blinked as a feeling he hadn't felt since his father was alive slithered over his skin. Disapproval. Rejection.

"Clearly," she answered and focused on the view out the window as they made their way to the edge of the city. He still had time to abort this mission and run home, away from her judgement and the pain of being found lacking.

But he was no longer a child who ran away from things that troubled him. Especially not irksome women whose opinions didn't count for anything.

He would not allow her to chase him away from something he truly wanted.

And what he wanted was to go to Egypt.

He needed an adventure before he was leg-shackled to some proper society chit who would bore him into an early grave with discussions of the weather and high fashion.

This expedition would be the highlight of his life. The thing he would look back on and say, "I did something amazing, before I sacrificed my love of adventure to take care of the people who depended on me."

He leaned closer, resting his hands on his knees so he could look into her eyes with the utmost seriousness.

"Did I personally do something to earn your contempt, or do you hate all men?"

"You truly do not remember me, do you?" Her eyes went wide.

"Should I?"

He realized immediately that his retort wounded her. He should have been pleased. He'd scored a hit after taking a barrage from her. But he was anything but pleased to see the pain cut across her face.

Her eyes glistened and for a moment he worried she might actually cry, but he should have known Miss Bantham wouldn't succumb to something as mundane as human emotions.

"No. I guess you shouldn't remember me."

She pulled the walls up as one would shrug a cloak closer on a cold day.

He allowed her to retreat and tend to the wound he'd unknowingly inflicted. He needed a moment as well. Had they met before? They must have for this was personal for her. He had hurt her in some way and not even realized it.

He was sure enough in his honor to know anything she might have considered an insult could not be so serious. He'd never forced a woman for so much as a kiss, he'd never spread mistruths, he'd never lured an innocent to wickedness.

He was not guilty of any of the horrid sins that happened in the shadows of a ballroom when the *ton* was otherwise distracted.

He felt sure he had done nothing to injure her, yet he reached out and took her hand, glad he still wore his gloves since she did not. He was sure touching her skin to skin wouldn't help the situation at all.

"I am truly sorry for whatever I might have done to cause you distress, Miss Bantham."

She pressed her lips together and looked everywhere but at him for a moment. She put her other hand out on the wall of the carriage as if to steady herself.

Finally, she pulled her hand from his and nodded once.

"Perhaps we should focus on our excavation of the ruins in Scotland." The smile she offered was strained to the point of breaking, but she held strong and he did something he so rarely did. He offered her a smile as well.

The smile itself wasn't a rarity for he was hardly without it while in the company of other people. But this pull of his lips was offered with sincerity.

Somehow, she seemed to detect the difference when so many others—even perhaps his best friends—did not.

"I would be happy to do so," he easily agreed.

With a stiff nod and a look that held no hint of her former scowl, she began telling him what he should expect when they arrived at the site.

He was absolutely enthralled with her knowledge. When she shared the names of the tools he'd purchased and what each of them were used for, he nearly wanted to kiss her.

No nearly about it.

She was lovely when she was discussing something she was passionate about. Her understanding of archaeology was vast and probably more than he needed to know, but he listened and asked what he hoped were informed questions.

She didn't belittle his inquiries, rather she seemed to appreciate his interest.

"When was the last time you were home?" she asked quietly when their conversation had dwindled to silence.

Home. She meant Scotland.

He smiled. "Just a few months ago. My friend Hale and his wife just had a child, and I came to welcome her properly as her Uncle Julian."

She looked confused as if he'd broken the mold she'd fit him into.

Instead of asking more personal questions, she went back to speaking of digging in the dirt. Twice they'd even shared a joke.

By the time they stopped that evening, he felt they were well on their way to friendship.

He couldn't remember the last time he'd engaged in such exhilarating conversation with a woman. Since he'd been old enough to learn of the more intimate allure of women, most of his interactions had been with a singular goal in mind.

But with Miss Bantham he made sure not to do anything that would be considered flirting. He didn't want her to think he was attempting to sway her with seduction. And, in truth, his original plan to charm her had transformed into a determination to befriend her.

He genuinely *liked* her.

And wasn't that sure to be a horrible mistake?

CHAPTER SIX

E LAINA STOOD IN her room at the Lucky Goose Inn deciding whether she should go down to meet the earl for dinner or take her meal in her room to avoid him.

After spending the entire day with him in the carriage, she shouldn't want to see him again. She shouldn't have anything left to say.

But she apparently hadn't gotten her fill as was evident by the way she was already halfway down the stairs before consciously deciding to do so.

He had apologized. It was clear he had no recollection of what he'd done so his apology was empty and worthless. Scotland had plenty of bugs and worms that could find their way into the earl's bed. Except it meant she would have to collect them herself and the idea was less than pleasant.

Guilt pricked at her conscience.

This was not good. This was her chance for vengeance—though she had not as of yet come up with a proper plan—she couldn't allow guilt to plague her moment of revenge.

She would have been better off staying in her room and gathering what was left of her defenses around her. Preparing for the next battle. Considering her options for making him pay for the pain he'd caused all those years ago. For the earl had clearly won today.

She'd promised herself she wouldn't speak to him but found

herself sharing stories of The Orient and South America for hours. All the while he asked her questions as if he was genuinely interested in her answers.

She'd been sure she wouldn't fall victim to his charms, but she'd laughed at his tales of mischief with his friends when they attended Heriot's in Edinburgh. She loved the way he said certain words, enthralled by his accent.

She'd never in a million years thought she was in danger of becoming friends with the man who had ruined her debut and broken her heart, yet she'd laughed with him as if they'd known each other all their lives.

He'd broken through her every defense and she could barely remember the pain he'd inflicted or the anger she'd held for him.

"Miss, Lord Melville has secured a private dining room, this way," the innkeeper said while gesturing to the door opposite the taproom.

She was pleased not to have to deal with the loud, boisterous men in the other room or have to navigate inappropriate conversation as unchecked men were likely to engage in.

While she was no demure girl, she also didn't want to spend the evening with a group of ribald miscreants. And if she was also pleased to have Lord Melville to herself, it wasn't worth mentioning.

And when had she started thinking of him as Lord Melville rather than Lord Mel-villain? This was not good at all.

She stood on the battlefield with nothing with which to defend herself, spare the smile that came to her lips when she entered the room. He stood to greet her, his own smile pulling up.

"Miss Bantham, I hoped you would join me for dinner though I didn't want you to feel obligated."

He'd hoped? For her? Of course, he hadn't meant it the way she'd rearranged his words in her mind.

"Sharing a meal is better for digestion is it not?" she said, sensibly.

"I whole-heartedly agree. Would you care for some wine?"

"Yes, please," she said as he assisted her into her seat across from his as any fine gentleman would.

In her darkest days, she'd envisioned the man as a monster. Seeing him with his elegant manners on display was surprising, though she couldn't remember a time over the last few weeks when he hadn't been the very thing of gentlemanly behavior.

The scents of beeswax candles, roasted meat, and whatever fragrance clung to Melville provided additional comfort to the cozy room. The exposed beams and the stone hearth gave it a homey feel.

After he had poured her wine, he raised his own glass.

"A toast to new friends and old treasures."

She hesitated just a moment before smiling and tapping her glass to his. He'd made it clear he was only interested in friendship, and she hadn't expected more. She wished she hadn't thought of more. How had she gone from hating him to wondering what it might feel like to kiss him in the space of one day?

Was she so fickle? So desperate for a man's attention? So weak?

She didn't think herself so, but the smile that pulled up on her lips in answer to his was proof she wasn't as formidable as she'd thought herself to be.

Familiar disappointment and irritation flared as he put her soundly in her place. Friends.

The first bricks of her wall came up. She was in danger of wanting the very man who made it quite clear he would never want her. Another brick and another went up as she ate the meal that now tasted of ash and listened to him weave his web of betrayal. With every laugh and every glimpse of that dimple that only came out when he smiled in earnest, she repaired the wall he'd so easily brought down.

She would have to keep a better watch. He had declared them friends. It would be difficult to extricate herself now.

If nothing else, acting the part of his friend would allow her access to mete out her plan of retaliation, though she had yet to settle on a proper retribution. She shouldn't have lost sight of what she'd wanted because he'd been kind to her during their travels.

He was still the Villain Melville she'd first encountered many years ago. She was a fool to expect anything else.

⇶⇷

IT SEEMED AS if Julian was starting from the beginning with Miss Bantham. She'd offered a smile for his toast, but he certainly felt a chill coming from her.

He didn't know what he'd said to offend her again, perhaps she was just of a constitution to sway from one emotion to the next at random.

He'd called them friends to ensure she didn't think he had entertained any lewd thoughts of her, even if he had more than a few the entire time he'd changed for dinner.

As they'd traveled, he'd worked hard for every laugh and smile and been rewarded more easily as they moved north. He'd shared things with her he hadn't told another soul and now he wondered why.

Miss Bantham was a sorceress with powers his mortal mind could not grasp.

It was not as he'd thought originally, that his interest in her was simply the mystery she presented by her unjustified anger. Perhaps it had started out that way, but he found he simply liked spending time with her.

"I see you managed to dress without your valet," she noted as the serving maid left the room after bringing them another bottle of wine.

"It might be the first time since I became the earl. I nearly forgot how it was done," he joked and earned an indulgent smile from her.

He wanted to get them back to where they'd been in the carriage. Sharing and laughing.

"I can only imagine what he'll have to say about my cravats when I arrive in Scotland."

She blinked. "Your valet is meeting us in Scotland?"

"I sent him ahead with my trunks so he can set up before I arrive."

She set down her glass and pressed her lips together. In the short time he'd spent with her, he understood the expression. She had something she wished to say.

"What is it?" he prodded.

"It's surely not my business, but generally we are much more relaxed when on an expedition. We don't dress formally when our clothing will become soiled or damaged. There's no point in it."

She shrugged and went back to her meal.

"I recall you referred to me as a dandy at the ball…" He paused and took in the slight wince and blush from his reminder. "But in truth, it isn't the assistance with my wardrobe, or any concerns with fashion that had me bring my valet."

"Oh?"

"You may find it strange, but I feel I can share things of a personal nature with you." He waited to see her response, hoping this confession would bring down whatever obstacle had wedged its way between them in this short time.

She offered a small shrug as she finished chewing her roast.

"If you're concerned I will gossip about it at a ball, you have nothing to worry about."

"It's nothing so odd to merit gossip I wouldn't think. It's just that Bentley, my valet, is a dear friend."

"You are friends with your servant?" she said in surprise but did not seem put off by it.

"Yes. I think of him as the father I never had."

She took a sip of her wine and sat it down as if pondering.

"You became the earl at four and twenty. So, you did have a father all of your youth."

He couldn't help the grin that exploded across his face.

"And how did you happen to remember that?" he teased when he probably shouldn't have.

She was only mildly flustered before collecting herself.

"I checked into you when my uncle informed me we would be going on this journey together. I didn't wish to travel with someone unsafe."

"Of course," he agreed, but wasn't so sure. Rather than let it go as he should have, he pressed another matter. "You knew I was left-handed." He held up his fork in his left hand.

"Excuse me?"

"At the shop when you were helping me purchase my set of tools. You presented them to me for a left-handed person. Did whomever you hired to look into me share that fact?"

"No. Over the years you have attended several of my uncle's Expedition Balls. I have had the misfortune of sitting next to you on three occasions. Each time on your left side where you proceeded to bump into my arm with every bite."

"Is that so? I don't remember being seated beside you."

She let out a sigh he could easily translate as annoyance.

"That is because on every occasion, a beautiful woman sat on your *right* side to capture every second of your attention. I am better suited for intelligent conversation than physical appeal, so it is not such a surprise you chose as you did."

He set his glass down and stared at his plate a moment.

"I can't help but feel I've been insulted."

"You are permitted to feel any way you wish, as am I."

His attempts to have her warm to him were clearly going in the opposite direction. He needed to do something to rectify the situation.

He thought of a hundred things he could say to charm his way out of his awkward situation.

I obviously didn't know what true beauty was back then. This had some truth to it, but not enough to win her over.

I knew you were too good for the likes of me. Even more truth, but she wouldn't believe he was sincere.

When I was a child I spoke as a child and was distracted by breasts. No. He couldn't win her respect with blasphemy. Besides, that was a lie. He was still distracted by breasts. Currently hers. Blast it all.

What was wrong with him? He could come up with a cheeky quip that would have worked on any other woman of the *ton.* Except this one, apparently.

Rather than address the reason he had ignored her on multiple occasions—because he truly had no answer—he shared something he hadn't shared with anyone.

"My father didn't allow me to be left-handed."

She blinked, no doubt as surprised by what he'd said as he was.

"Did he believe you to be evil? I thought that thinking had been done away with long ago."

Julian shook his head and set down the fork on the left side of his plate so he could flex his fingers. The pain from being cracked on the knuckles was long gone, but he remembered the ache.

"No. He didn't think I was evil. He thought it *unfitting of his heir.*"

Her brows creased as she stared at her plate. If she was attempting to find reason in his father's rationale, she would be disappointed. There was nothing rational about his father.

"There were actually many, many things about me he found unacceptable. I was never smart enough, brave enough, fast enough. I was too tall, too unruly, too… *left-handed.*"

He offered a strained laugh but continued. In for a penny, as it were.

"I was reminded daily that I was a disgrace. Being Scottish made it more difficult to be taken seriously in London, and he could only be glad he would be dead when I took over the title so he wouldn't have to see such an abomination."

She reached across the small table and rested her hand on top of his, shattering whatever distance had settled between them earlier.

He hadn't felt such comfort since he'd been a lad and his mother had been alive. Though the way his body responded to her touch made it clear he didn't think of her in a motherly way. At all.

He needed to stop this before it went too far and he did something she would truly have a reason to hate him for.

Slipping his hand out from under hers was one of the most difficult things he'd ever done, but he did so and offered a smile.

"After he died, I went back to using my left hand. My penmanship is now legible if not a bit smudged, and I don't spill nearly as much of my dinner on my lap."

She smiled and he could see the kindness in her eyes. That she would allow him to brush off the uncomfortable situation with a jest was greatly appreciated.

Strangely it wasn't as uncomfortable as he expected. Being with her felt freeing in a way he'd never experienced with another person.

He puzzled over it as they fell in companionable silence while finishing their meals.

One theory was that he had nothing to gain in winning over the irksome miss. But he knew immediately that didn't fit. He cared. He cared a great deal what she thought of him.

Perhaps it was that her expectations of him were already low or non-existent that the pressure to dazzle her was just as low. But again, that didn't feel right. He wanted to dazzle her, he just wanted to do so by being himself instead of the jester he normally played to win the affection of the *ton*.

He choked on a bite of parsnip.

He'd known he liked her. He had wanted her to like him. He hadn't realized he *needed* her to like the real Julian.

Dear God, what a disappointment he'd set for himself.

CHAPTER SEVEN

L AINEY CLOSED THE door to her room and slumped against the wall, her mind warring with confusion and irritation. Say nothing of her heart which was beating madly for a man who had once again wiggled his way past her defenses.

How was she to manage stealing all of his smallclothes after he'd shared his feelings so?

She'd attempted to put distance between her and the earl, but instead, she found herself touching him at one point during the meal. It had been only to offer comfort, but he was the enemy.

One did not offer comfort to their enemies.

Yet, she hadn't wanted to stop with a mere pat of the hand. She'd wanted to pull him into her arms and offer him a safe place. To ease the pain of the boy he'd been when told repeatedly he wasn't good enough.

She feared she was in danger of liking him. She needed to do a better job of hating him. If she couldn't manage hatred, she could possibly muster up disgust. Dislike? Something she could use to shield herself from the danger he was to her heart.

She'd never have guessed it would be so difficult. Not with the way she'd felt in regard to the earl over the years. But one day with him and she felt as exposed and vulnerable as she had the night he'd…

She closed her eyes and pushed the memory away. It didn't matter anymore. He didn't matter.

Except when he'd escorted her to her room and hesitated for a moment while staring at her lips, she'd felt hot all over and a bit out of breath. She didn't know how he'd managed to stir up such a response, but she needed to make sure it didn't happen again.

He was incredibly attractive. She'd known that since she'd first seen him across the ballroom during her come out. He had a beautiful smile. This was not news either. She should have been better prepared to deal with him. Or better yet, prepared to deal with her reactions to him.

But from across the ballroom, long ago, she'd not noticed how very dark his hair was. The way it nearly shined blue in the dim light of the dining room. Upon closer examination, she'd seen how his eyes had bursts of gold in the center giving depth to the blue.

Blast and damn. She shouldn't be intrigued. It didn't matter that the outer package was so appealing. Not when his insides were rotten.

Except he'd brought his valet because he thought of the man as a friend rather than a servant. How rotten could he be?

She changed for bed and slipped under the blankets, exhausted but nowhere close to sleep with her mind whirling the way it was.

She found herself holding her breath so she could listen to the sounds coming from the room next to hers. Was he in bed looking up at the ceiling the way she was? Was he thinking of her? Of her eyes?

She laughed and rolled to her side facing the wall that separated them. It was possible he wasn't even in his room. He might have returned to the tavern below and found company with one of the women.

That thought caused a sharp tug in her chest. She wasn't jealous. She couldn't be.

She *wouldn't* be.

Tomorrow she would raise an invincible wall between them where she would be safe from spending another night like this one.

⇶⟫⟪⇷

AFTER EATING BREAKFAST alone, Julian met up with Miss Bantham at the carriage. He helped her in and she thanked him coolly. Before the carriage had left the village, she pulled a book from her bag and began reading.

From his seat across from her he couldn't make out the title on the spine. When he squinted, he noticed there was no title in sight. He entertained himself by trying to guess what she was reading.

A tome on archaeology? Perhaps she could read it aloud to help him prepare for the excavation. Or maybe it was a gothic novel complete with a grisly murder. Was she contemplating acting out such a thing and researching ways to dispose of his body?

Perhaps a tale of romance. Did she imagine herself as the fair maiden and he the dashing knight? Maybe she thought to offer her virtue in gratitude for him saving her from the barbarians?

That would not happen. Not only because there were no barbarians to be saved from. But there would be no surrendering of virtues for any reason. Not hers. Not to him.

Though he was a man, and the thought roused a recently neglected part of his anatomy causing him to shift uncomfortably in his seat. He noticed she also shifted uneasily. He continued to watch as she flipped page after page.

She was lovely. In the morning light coming through the window, she had a glow about her. Actually, as he examined more closely it wasn't a glow.

She seemed to be glistening with a sheen of sweat on her brow. Then her skin began to take on a sickly greenish hue and she swallowed often.

He was about to ask if she was unwell, when she rapped on

the roof to stop the carriage and tumbled out the door to be sick on the side of the road.

He jumped down to offer assistance, but she waved him away as she retched once more. Having spent more than one night drinking with his friends, he was accustomed to standing by as someone cast up their accounts on the street. Though he'd never been in such a situation with a lady.

He held out his handkerchief and she snatched it from him as if he were responsible for her condition.

"Was something off with your breakfast?"

"No," she snapped, her voice rough. "I feel better. Let's just be on our way."

"Are you sure you don't wish to take a bit of air?"

"I don't need air," she assured him.

He thought to make a joke about how she did need air, but at her glare, he kept it to himself and helped her back inside the carriage. She placed her hand over her stomach as she settled and Julian recalled seeing Hale's wife do the same thing when she'd been carrying their daughter.

"Oh," Julian said out loud without meaning to.

Her eyes narrowed.

"What?"

"I'm sorry. I didn't realize you were… Not that it's any of my business." Except that he was traveling alone with an unmarried, pregnant woman. Was this a trap?

He looked toward the door considering jumping out himself.

"What didn't you realize?" she asked.

"That you were in a family way." He nodded toward her lap where her hand still rested on her stomach.

"A family—?" she all but screeched. "Why ever would you assume such a thing?" She put her hand up to stay his answer and shook her head. "Never mind. It is morning and I am ill."

"And you placed your hand on your stomach," he added, but regretted it instantly.

"Do you not put your hand on your stomach after you've

been ill? If for no other reason than to simply reassure yourself, it is still with you?"

He chuckled and nodded. "Very well. I'm sorry for jumping to conclusions."

"I can assure you I am not sick for that reason. It would be quite impossible. Not that it is any of your business, as you already said."

He tilted his head to the side.

"If it's not that, and it wasn't a bad breakfast, do you have an illness? Perhaps we should find another inn so you can rest. Or a doctor."

"No. It isn't an illness. It's…"

She took a breath and closed her eyes as if she would rather do anything else but continue this conversation. He simply waited for her to explain.

"I get sick when I read in a moving carriage." She spoke rather quickly. He barely caught the words, and then thought perhaps that was her intention. But hear them he did, which only left more questions to be asked.

"Then why would you attempt to read in a moving carriage."

She huffed another breath and rubbed her forehead.

"Because I didn't want to have to carry on a conversation with you today."

Every bit of information he managed to drag out of her just led him to more questions that required more information.

"Let me see if I understand. You actually prefer to make yourself sick rather than speak to me?" He felt the gnawing feeling of unease in his chest. Just as he had all the times his father listed out the many reasons Julian was hopeless.

Anger flared.

Had he not spent a restless night in his bed, staring up at the ceiling while thinking of her? The fullness of her lips pulled up in a smile. He wondered if the curves of her body would match up to his since she was taller than most women.

Her openness and humor. Her intelligent conversation and

flirty quips.

To find out she despised him to this level made him want to lash out so she wouldn't know how badly it hurt him.

"I don't want to like you," she admitted without looking at him. "And I fear spending another day talking with you will put me that much closer to doing so."

For whatever reason, her twisted explanation made him feel better, though repeating it in his head didn't help him find a particular compliment in her words.

"Perhaps if you could tell me why you don't want to like me, we could come up with a solution," he suggested.

"Perhaps we could just travel in silence today."

"Very well." He pressed his lips together but watched her as she squirmed on the opposite bench. After stealing glances at him a few times she let out a sigh and spoke.

"Do you have to keep looking at me like that?"

"How am I looking at you?"

"Just…" She waved her hand in the direction of his face. "Looking. With your eyes."

He couldn't help but chuckle at her disgruntled pout.

"Pardon me, for looking with my eyes. Do you want me to sit here in silence with my eyes closed? Maybe that would solve the problem—not that I know what the problem is exactly because you haven't really said."

"Nor will I, because I'm beginning to understand how ridiculous it sounds."

She rubbed her forehead in what he could tell was utter embarrassment.

He realized then he was standing at a crossroad with this woman.

He could either push her and risk her retreating completely, or he could let it go and never know why she disliked him so much.

Neither option felt appealing. As with most things, he leaned on his charm to guide him.

"I have a proposition for you," he said and watched as she peeked from behind her hand. She was a curious one, which would work in his favor. Or at least he hoped.

"Since I do not suffer the same affliction as you when reading in a moving carriage, perhaps I could read your book aloud. It would serve to entertain us both and I daresay won't do anything to change your feelings toward liking me or not."

And yes, his offer might have had something to do with his curiosity in discovering what she was reading.

"You would grant me such a kindness, after I was so horribly rude to you?"

"Of course."

"You see, this is the exact thing I feared. How can I not like you when you are being so generous?"

"I feel as though I should apologize, but I'm not quite sure what I'd be apologizing for. So sorry to not be a boar, maybe? Apologies for being utterly magnificent?"

She scowled, but unlike before, this gesture was utterly playful in nature.

"Yes, perhaps magnificent is rather grand," he allowed.

"I don't understand you," she said with a frustrated wave of her hand. "That is, I thought I did, but perhaps I've been wrong all this time." She seemed utterly perplexed, but he had no idea how to assist.

All this time? How long ago had it been that he'd been charged and found guilty of whatever crime she'd assigned to him?

"I am quite pleased to hear that," he answered before planning to speak. "Not so much that you were wrong. It would be ill-mannered of me to mention that. But to hear you are befuddled by me. Because I surely don't understand you in the least."

To his surprise she laughed and handed over the volume with only the slightest hesitation.

He was holding a gothic novel by Ann Radcliffe. Another surprise.

"We should start at the beginning, so you don't miss any-thing," she suggested.

"Very well."

He smiled as he opened it to the first page of the book and shook his head as another thread of her enigmatic behavior was revealed.

He definitely did not understand her, but he was so very interested in learning more.

CHAPTER EIGHT

A S THEY BOUNCED down the road, Lainey's stomach finally settled as the earl's low, even voice relaxed her as he read. His voice rumbled over the words and he accented different words than she would have. The more she listened to him speak the more she enjoyed his brogue.

Many people of the *ton* thought it a savage dialect, but she found it fascinating. Mesmerizing.

She'd had no idea such a service as reading a book would seem so intimate until the carriage was filled with his melodic rumble and she closed her eyes to soak it in.

Then he removed a flask from his coat and took a sip to wet his throat before he offered it to her.

She'd tasted a wide selection of spirits on her travels. But none tasted sweeter than the whisky she drank from the flask where his lips had touched before hers. It was warm from being tucked in close to his body.

She thought of what that might feel like. Not being a flask, but touching his chest. She imagined it would be hard with muscle, for the earl was lean even with the bulk of his shirt, waistcoat, and overcoat.

She'd heard he fancied visiting Gentleman Jack's and caught a vision of him in the ring, sweaty with exertion as he swung his fists at his opponent. Did he smile even in the heat of a match? His smile seemed to be affixed to his face.

She thought of the smiles he'd given her a few times yesterday that brought out that devilish dimple and lit up his blue eyes. That was his real smile.

She took another fortifying sip and handed his flask back. He reached for it without interrupting his reading and tucked it away in that place she wanted to place her hand.

"I must say." Though he'd been speaking all this time, the change in his voice to conversation startled her from her thoughts. "I wouldn't have put you for someone who read gothic novels," he said as he positioned his bag to one side of the squab and leaned back upon it to stretch out across his seat. He was much too long, so he bent his knees so he would fit. Tucking the novel against his thighs.

He looked rather comfortable there, so she mirrored his pose, propping herself in the opposite corner so they could look at one another as they conversed. Or so she could continue to watch him as he read to her.

Rather than bend her knees, she settled one foot over the other ankle.

"Are you not enjoying *The Mysteries of Udolpho?*" she asked when she was comfortable.

"I'm seeing a striking resemblance of *Signor Montoni* to my sire."

He'd mentioned his father a few times and had yet to say a kind word about the man. In truth, the late earl did sound like a monster in Lord Melville's life. She thought herself to be similar to Emily in the novel because she'd been orphaned, but in truth, after that trauma there had really been nothing horrible to note.

Except what had happened at her come out.

Her anger was stirred but didn't gain the usual heat. How could she be angry at the man who'd offered to read such a scandalous novel to her because she couldn't read it herself?

With a sigh of resignation, she cast off her plans to fill his fine boots with horse dung.

And even worse, he seemed to be enjoying himself. Perhaps

anything would be better than having to converse with an irritable shrew such as herself.

"I'm sorry your father was so horrid. Do you wish to talk about it?" she offered.

"God, no. That blighter doesn't deserve to be discussed. He should be forgotten. Allowed to drift into nothingness. That is a true punishment is it not? To not be remembered by anyone?"

"I suppose it is. While I can't speak on what you have gone through, I do know that I remember my parents often with fondness and I feel that is an honor to them. By default, I have to think you have something with your plan to let him drift off into nothingness.

He nodded, seemingly happy with her assessment.

"Very well, I should get back to this. We don't want to leave our poor Emily in a lurch now do we?" He picked up the book to start reading again, but she wasn't ready to drift back into the story.

She wanted to talk with him some more.

"You have a lovely voice," she said before she'd thought to stop herself.

"Thank you," he shifted, and his cheeks darkened the slightest bit. "My accent doesn't put you off?"

"No. It is quite lovely."

He cleared his throat.

The earl, as outlandish as he sometimes seemed to be, was uncomfortable with true compliments. Interesting.

She imagined it had something to do with his father. If he was even a fraction as awful as *Signor Montoni*, he would have to be a monster indeed. How had Lord Melville survived living with such a man while still holding on to his pleasant disposition?

She might have asked more, but the sound of the carriage traveling over dirt, changed to the louder rumble of wheels on wooden planks.

A bridge.

She bolted back up to a sitting position and gasped while

reaching out for the side of the carriage.

The earl sat up as well, his face shifting from his relaxed expression to one of concern. Before she'd had the chance to completely come undone, the sound changed back again.

A small bridge. And they were over it already before fear could grip her too terribly. But not before the earl had noticed.

"Are you well?" he asked, his hand reached out as if to steady her, but it hovered just short of actually making contact. She found she would have welcomed his touch. But of course, that wouldn't have been proper. And he was a gentleman as he'd claimed.

She couldn't doubt that.

"Yes. Forgive me. It was nothing." She forced herself back to her earlier position of leisure even while her heart battled to escape her chest. "Please continue."

His gaze narrowed slightly, but he nodded and did as she asked without pressing for more information regarding her strange reaction.

She was more thankful than he would ever know.

⁕⁕⁕⁕⁕

THE PANIC HE'D seen in Miss Bantham's eyes concerned him, but satisfying his curiosity was not justification enough to force the woman into sharing her fears with a near stranger.

He wondered what had happened to bring forth this lasting fear in Miss Bantham. As they continued their travels north, he saw her respond in a similar way a few more times. Once while she was laughing, it caught her completely off guard.

He'd pieced together the cause, though he didn't pry to learn the reason.

Bridges.

The longer the bridge, the more severely the fear stole her breath and leeched her knuckles white as she grasped onto anything she could reach, including his knee on one occasion.

Each time, she seemed embarrassed and upset, so he took to reading louder, or filling the moment with chatter until the episode passed.

She had dozed off on the rear facing seat while he was reading. The sun, which had not shown itself all day, was giving up the fight with a hazy finish.

Unable to see to read, he set the book next to him and looked out the window. The road curved toward the left, and Julian saw the reason. They would be crossing a river up ahead and the only way to do so would be to travel over a bridge.

He reached out and woke Miss Bantham.

"Sit up," he instructed.

"What is it?" she asked.

"We're about to cross a stream," he warned.

Her eyes widened and she slid to the side of the carriage where she could grasp the door loop.

"Deep breath," he said when he heard the first hoof hit the timbers of the structure.

When they were across, she calmed more easily than before.

"Thank you," she said.

"It helps to be prepared."

She offered a small nod and fixed her skirts.

"You must think me silly."

"Not at all. And I hope you wouldn't think me silly if ever you see me encounter a spider. Fears are often irrational, but does it matter if I'm large enough to fend off an insect?" He tapped his temple. "If our minds think otherwise, it is as good as truth, is it not?"

She stared at him for a moment before letting out a breath and shaking her head. "You're doing it again."

He didn't need to ask what she meant. He simply offered her his brightest smile.

"I daresay, by the time we arrive, you will be my biggest admirer."

"I doubt that whole-heartedly." She flicked a bit of imaginary lint from her skirts.

"I can dream, Miss Bantham. I can dream," he teased.

Rather than taking offense, she simply rolled her eyes. After a few moments of silence, she cleared her throat.

"If you are ever overcome by a spider, you have only to call for me. I shall come to your aid and protect you."

She wasn't mocking him. Rather she seemed completely serious. As if she wanted to reassure him as he had done for her.

Whether she'd wanted it or not, they had certainly become friends.

They arrived at Dalkeith Castle in the Highlands the following afternoon.

Julian explained that the grand, stone house was only a short distance from the castle ruins they would be exploring.

"It will be nice to spend our evenings in such comfort after spending our days digging about in the dirt like savages."

This would be their home for the next two months. And until the Leightons arrived, they would be living there alone but for his staff.

"I imagine this is far different than our accommodations in Egypt?" he asked.

"Yes. Quite." Her answer was short, as it often was on the occasions they spoke of the trip to Africa. As if she were unwilling to confirm he would be going.

It didn't stop him from testing her resolve. He hoped to catch her off guard and get her to admit she planned to include him. He was much too impatient for such things as surprises or waiting to hear news on something.

This was torture.

"Mr. and Mrs. Leighton should already be here." She seemed so happy to see the other couple. As if desperate to have a reason to get away from him.

He assisted her from the carriage when it stopped. It was a pleasant day though the skies to the east threatened to bring foul weather.

A few servants emerged from the house and Julian smiled when he noticed one of them as his valet.

"Ben, I hope your journey was without trouble."

"Nothing to note, my lord."

The wheels could have fallen off the carriage and Bentley himself could have been made to carry the conveyance the rest of the way on his back, and the man would have reported *nothing of note*.

That was just how he was. Never a complaint, even if one was warranted.

Julian noticed Miss Bantham standing close by, watching the exchange. He turned to introduce them.

"Miss Bantham, please let me introduce my good friend and valet, Mr. Bentley. Ben, this is Miss Bantham, our guest, and my instructor for the next few months."

"Very good to meet you, Miss Bantham."

"Lord Melville has told me many things about you. I feel we are already acquainted."

"I hope he hasn't shared the embarrassing stories."

Elaina slipped her arm through Ben's and leaned closer to whisper.

"You've known the earl much too long to think he wouldn't have told those stories first."

Ben chuckled and patted her hand.

"You have the right of it, my dear."

And like that, the woman had utterly charmed his valet. And they hadn't even made it through the doors of the house.

Julian was equally charmed that Miss Bantham treated Bentley like a treasured guest rather than a servant, as many women of her class would have done. But, of course, after spending the last few days with her, he knew her better than to expect such a thing from her.

They all ascended the stairs as the other servants carried in Miss Bantham's trunks.

A sturdy older woman came forward. Julian remembered the housekeeper and noticed the small smile she aimed toward Ben.

Good for you, old boy, Julian thought and wrestled his grin into submission.

Miss Bantham looked toward the stairs and turned to the housekeeper.

"Where will I find the Leightons?" she asked.

The housekeeper shook her head.

"Afraid they haven't arrived yet, miss. They sent a message for ye. I put it in your room. I'll show you there."

Julian nearly put out his hand to steady Miss Bantham for she looked as if she might fall over.

"This won't do. We can't stay here alone," she whispered the last part.

He couldn't help but chuckle at her scandalized reaction.

"We're hardly alone. We are under more supervision here than we have been all the nights we stopped at inns during our travels."

"I suppose, but here there are people who know you. If they found out…"

"Do you want me to leave?" He almost hugged her when she shook her head.

"No. That won't do. I would never run you from your own home. Besides, there is nowhere close enough for you to stay that wouldn't be a bother getting to the site in the mornings. We'll just have to make do with our present accommodations."

"You are quite safe with me, Miss Bantham. I swear it." He hoped he could keep that promise. If she so much as fluttered an eyelash in his direction he feared he might relent.

What was it about her he found so intriguing? He still worried it was simply that she didn't fall into a giggling pile of awe in his presence. Was he really so shallow?

Possibly.

Probably.

"I'll have baths brought up to each of your rooms," the

housekeeper went on. "Nettie will be tending to ye, miss, during your visit at Dalkeith."

"Thank you, Mrs. McGregor," Julian said.

The tiny Nettie came forward and dipped a nervous curtsey before saying, "This way, miss."

The entourage moved up to the next floor and Julian took note that Elaina was shown to a room just two doors down from his own on the same side of the corridor.

Not that it mattered. It wasn't as if he had plans to sneak down the hall to her room in the night.

Except, he *was* thinking of that very thing and how convenient such an endeavor would be having her so close.

Shaking his head, he went into his own room. He must push away all thoughts of such things. Elaina was not to be trifled with. And he needed to stop thinking of her as Elaina. It was Miss Bantham.

Attempting to seduce *Miss Bantham* would only ruin his chances at being invited to attend the expedition in Egypt.

He would need to be careful not to offend her in the slightest.

His fate was in her hands.

$$\text{\small\textbf{◆}}$$

CHAPTER NINE

AFTER HER BATH, Elaina had a tray brought up so she could dine in her room. Mrs. Leighton's letter held an apology for their delay, but it was clear from the way she spoke of her new grandson she was completely smitten and unable to tear herself away so soon after meeting the baby.

Elaina couldn't begrudge the woman more time with her new grandchild. But it meant she was here alone with Lord Melville. In his home. Alone.

As he'd said, they'd been alone the entire journey, but it was different. Sharing a home together was somehow more intimate and she didn't know if she was equipped to keep him at a distance under such circumstances.

She realized as she'd sat in the tub of warm water and thought of how the earl was just down the hall, she was in danger of forgetting what he'd done to make her dislike him.

Disliking him had become impossible when he'd been so kind to her. She'd hoped when they arrived at his home, she could put some space between them until she was able to assemble her irritation with the man once again.

And he *was* a man now, even more handsome than he'd been at two and twenty. More confident. More enticing.

She'd spent so much time with him during their journey she'd gotten to know him. To like him.

But she couldn't forgive him. Not that he would ever ask for forgiveness. Not that he would feel remorse for what he'd done.

The familiar rush of anger came unbidden as it did most times she thought of him. She welcomed the anger and the power it had to steady her. She'd allowed him to get too close. She'd been weakened by his charm.

Seeing him with his elderly butler, the way he clearly cared about the man. A servant. Someone many lords wouldn't even address let alone call a friend.

It confused her.

Perhaps the earl had changed over the years. She surely had.

She remembered her silly hopes and dreams when she'd been a blushing debutante. And how Melville—then known as Lord Huntly because his father still lived—had dashed them all away, leaving the angry woman she was today.

It didn't matter if he had changed and was now an honorable man who cared for his elderly servants and read to her for hours on end in the carriage.

He needed to pay for what he'd done.

She would make sure he did.

⋙⋘

IT WAS STILL dark when the pounding on his door startled him awake. Julian groaned and stumbled to the door to answer it, forgetting he was naked until Miss Bantham gasped and averted her eyes.

"Pardon," he mumbled as he donned his banyan and rubbed his eyes. "What is amiss?"

"Nothing is amiss, it is time to go," she answered sharply, still looking away from him.

"Go? Where are we going exactly? It is the dead of night."

"It is five in the morning."

As he'd just said, the dead of night. At least for one who only went to bed at two.

After eating dinner alone last night, he'd made his way to the study and partook of too much whisky. He'd stared into the fire and tried to fathom what he could have done to earn Miss Bantham's ire. And more importantly how he might charm her into friendship once more.

It seemed each time he made some bit of headway with the woman, she pushed him away and turned cold. He hated how long he'd spent trying to puzzle the woman out to no avail.

He hadn't thought her the flighty sort, but she was all over the place with regard to how she interacted with him.

One moment she was angry, another she was laughing at his antics. One moment she was ignoring him, the next she was sharing intimate details of her life. One moment they were so close their knees bumped and then she didn't come to dinner, leaving him alone in his huge house until he finally went to bed much too late.

She was an enigma. An infuriating one. He shouldn't care that she didn't seem to like him at all. What did her opinion count anyway? Other than allowing him to go to Egypt, and he didn't have to be her friend to prove his competence.

He just needed to focus on impressing her with his skill. However, focus was not something easy to come by so early in the morning.

"It is still dark," he said when the issue of the time didn't result in her leaving so he could go back to sleep.

"By the time you have dressed, eaten, and gathered your supplies, it will be first light and time to leave for the dig."

He took a deep breath and nodded. The fog of exhaustion had lifted somewhat, and he was better able to process her demands.

He couldn't very well refuse to go with her the first day of his test. It would surely seal her decision to reject his request to join the larger expedition.

"I will be down in a quarter hour," he promised, hoping to appease her.

"Ten minutes," she countered and walked away.

"Very well." He closed the door while grumbling how whatever was to be found by them in the dirt had already been there waiting to be unearthed for many years so another hour wouldn't have hurt.

A bleary-eyed Bentley scurried in to assist.

"You can go back to bed, Ben. I am wearing simple work clothes today and don't need assistance to dress." In truth he only really needed Ben to get into his tighter-fitting evening coats. "Best one of us get a full night's rest."

"I will prepare your shave."

Julian waved him off. "Don't bother. It is just myself and the harpy digging in the dirt today."

"Harpy? I found Miss Bantham to be a lovely young lady."

"She is lovely, and then when you least suspect it, she transforms before your eyes into a bitter shrew of a woman that drags you from your sleep to go out in the dark to dig in the earth. She's a witch."

"You've always given to fits of dramatics when awakened too early," Ben muttered.

"It's true. You should be careful, old chap," Julian said without the least bit of dramatics.

"I see." Ben looked skeptical. "Consider me warned, my lord." The valet busied himself in helping Julian get ready in the ten minutes he'd been allotted.

Still a bit disoriented, he arrived in the breakfast room as the woman who looked much too lovely for this hour had finished and set her napkin beside her plate. More proof she was a witch. When she stood to leave, all he could do was stare.

His mind was still a bit groggy from sleep, but he would have had difficulty with the scene before him even at midday.

"You... You're wearing breeches." He pointed at them as if the woman wasn't aware she stood in the formal breakfast room wearing men's clothing. Her shirt was similar to his own. Including the way it gaped open at the neck, revealing her delicate collarbone. Her golden red hair was tied back in a thick braid that fell over her shoulder.

"Please don't tell me you are scandalized by my attire. I wouldn't think you of all people would be a stickler for propriety."

"I'm not a *stickler*, I'm just… surprised." He was mostly surprised by how seeing her dressed in men's clothing made his body react. He never would have thought such a thing would be so alluring. "And what do you mean by me of all people? Because I'm a barbaric Scot?"

She frowned at him.

"No. Because you are flush with scandal."

He nodded, though that was no better a reason. He couldn't think. Looking at her muddled his already befuddled brain.

The breeches clung snugly to her womanly curves in a way breeches had no business doing. The shirt was thin enough that he could just see a hint of whatever she wore under it. And what looked like lace edging. Feminine colliding with masculine in the most sensual way.

By the time his gaze landed on her feet, he was already envisioning her in his bed wearing nothing but those knee-high boots.

"You're so… That is…" What was he to say? He couldn't think of words. Any words. At least not English ones. He settled on *"Buaireadh aingidh."* For she *was* a wicked temptress.

She rolled her eyes and muttered something about why anyone found him charming.

"We leave in ten minutes," she announced and left the room.

He caught himself from arguing or speaking at all. He was certain whatever came out of his mouth at that minute wouldn't be acceptable. Besides, he only had mere minutes to put something *in* his mouth. It was best to focus on that.

He had no doubt she would leave without him if given the opportunity.

He slurped down a cup of coffee and fisted three pieces of toast and a rasher of bacon to carry with him as he hurried toward the mews in the back of the house.

She was driving a cart, serviced by two gray mules, out of the building as he arrived. He tossed his knapsack filled with tools in the back beside hers and climbed up in the seat next to her.

Without the fullness of her skirts, he managed to sit close enough that he could feel the heat of her body as her leg bumped against his. He moved away quickly and cleared his throat as she snapped the reins to get the mules moving.

Part of him wanted to be a gentleman and ask if she wanted him to drive, but the other part warned that such a gesture might get him tossed off the conveyance and left behind.

Besides, he needed both hands to finish eating.

It was a fortunate thing that Julian knew the way to his mouth well as the rutted lane they took to the castle ruins made the act of eating rather difficult.

He looked up and gasped, which didn't work well when his mouth was full. He began to choke and cough, but Miss Bantham drove on as if she hadn't noticed. Or perhaps hadn't cared. Still without addressing him she bent then passed him a small jug he hoped held water.

He removed the cork and took a swig. After a few more barking coughs he was restored. Or was certain he wouldn't die, at least.

He pointed at what had caused his surprise in the first place. The sun was shooting pink and gold rays across the sky.

"I've forgotten how beautiful the sunrise was from here," he croaked.

"Do you not see the sunrise often, my lord?"

"Nay. 'Tis difficult to see in town. Though I'm often awake at that hour."

"I assume you mean on your return home rather than rising at that hour?" She lifted her brows in a saucy smirk and he felt the tug in his breeches again.

He shrugged rather than answer. Though Hale had settled down, Kit, Graham, and Julian still went out most nights. They mostly kept to drinking at their clubs rather than gambling or carousing. But still he had arrived home many times after dawn had broken. And soon that would all be at an end because he would need to marry.

Rather than ruin the breathtaking view with thoughts of his father's plans, he smiled at the woman next to him.

She darted a glance in his direction before staring straight ahead once more.

"Every time I think we have turned a corner to being friends, you put me back in my place as the lowest creature you've ever encountered. It's quite maddening."

"I find you quite maddening as well, Lord Melville."

He smiled, as she glanced at him again.

"Why are you smiling? It wasn't a compliment," she said, clearly irritated.

He affected her. So far, it wasn't in a good way, but he would try to win her over by being his pleasant self.

He was often praised for his optimistic attitude. And why wouldn't he be happy? His father, the man who constantly judged him during his youth was long gone. And he was free to enjoy life. Or had been anyway.

"We are going to be friends, Miss Bantham. You wait and see."

"I fear neither of us have the kind of time needed to wait that long." Despite her words, she was smiling. If he'd thought the sunrise impressive, it was dim compared to seeing Miss Bantham impressed with her clever quip.

"We shall see. I don't give up so easily." Not when it was something he wanted as much as he wanted to win her over. What he would do if—no when—he did so, he wasn't quite sure.

CHAPTER TEN

ELAINA DIDN'T NEED to wait and see to know she and Lord Melville would not be friends. She would allow him to bumble about the site in order to evaluate his abilities as she promised to do. But when the time was up, she would gladly write home to Uncle Henry to inform him she couldn't recommend the earl for their trip to the pyramids.

She was certain the earl would contest her decision, but Uncle Henry would stand by his promise and it would be over. She only had to get through the next sixty-three days—yes, she had counted—and she would be free of the meddling man.

When they arrived at the site, he seemed to be more alert.

She only felt the slightest bit guilty for how she'd woken him and rushed him through his morning rituals. Obviously, he'd not had time for a shave. His jaw was covered in dark stubble that gave him the look of a pirate.

Why did her stomach flutter so from seeing the man unkempt? She'd seen plenty of men in a casual state during her travels. Some countries didn't bother with appearances the way the English did. But seeing Lord Melville this way felt too intimate.

She glanced away, unhappy with her reaction.

He unloaded their tools and laid everything out per her instructions.

Occasionally, she caught him staring at her and part of her

wished she'd worn something other than her ratty work clothes. He was used to being with beautiful women who wore lovely gowns without fear of getting them dirty. After all, how dirty could one get while embroidering or playing the pianoforte?

Well, she wasn't there to look pretty, and she knew better than to think a pretty dress would make a difference.

He might charm and flirt with her, but she knew it was all a ruse to win her favor so he could get what he wanted.

He would be disappointed when he realized it wouldn't work. And even more so when he discovered he wouldn't be joining them on the voyage to Egypt.

She almost wished she could see the look on his face when Uncle Henry made the announcement at the ball in October. It would go a long way to getting the vengeance she sought.

"According to William Cunnington's book *Ancient Historie of Wilshire* we are to do a site report before we start?" he said.

"You read a book on antiquary?"

He nodded. "Of course. How else would I prepare myself for an expedition? I will say, I was a bit discouraged when I engaged the bookseller on acquiring books on the topic and he suggested a book by Johan Joachim Winckelmann. I was sure the man was making a joke. I mean, who would think such a name was real?" He shook his head. "Something to note, booksellers generally take their work quite seriously. Best not to laugh."

She made sure her mouth didn't hang open and betray her surprise. He had read a book to prepare himself for this expedition.

Though, of course, she knew the man could read. He'd been educated and wouldn't have gotten out of Heriot's without learning something of value. And he'd graced her with his reading on their journey to entertain them.

But he'd read a book on antiquary. Such books are far from entertaining to most people. And not only had he read it, but he had retained enough to know they needed to do a site survey before starting.

She'd thought him a bored dandy who'd thrust himself upon her for his enjoyment.

She swallowed at the odd warmth when she'd thought the words "thrust himself." Strange.

Shaking her head to clear it, she squared her shoulders as Lord Melville rocked back and forth on his heels before holding out his hands.

"What would you like me to do? I will cede to your expertise."

Cede to her expertise? What the devil? Was this part of his game?

Cocking her head to the side, to study him for a moment, she found she could no longer stay quiet.

"I thought, like most men, you would expect to be in charge after reading a book on the matter." Even Uncle Henry occasionally got caught in the trap of explaining something to Aunt Rose that needn't be explained by someone who didn't know it any better than she did.

But Lord Melville was shaking his head with that bright, friendly smile on his face.

"I should hope you find I'm not like most men. I don't pretend to be better than the men who would be so bold as to think you needed a man to run things for you, but perhaps you would agree I'm at the least, not as bad?" He winked and the odd warmth returned.

"Very well." She closed her eyes briefly trying not to think about the winking. "We need to take some measurements. Please get the measure from the box of supplies."

She pulled her blank journal from another box and took out a pencil to take notes. She started with writing down the date and the members of the team on site.

Miss Elaina Bantham and Lord Melville

Surely, she shouldn't feel such a thrill at seeing their names written out together like that.

"If you'd rather, you can use my given name, Julian Huntly." He gave a nod to the page and smiled.

Julian.

"I think everyone is familiar with who you are," she said, while clenching the pencil to keep from writing out his name.

Julian.

"You may call me Julian, if you wish."

Her eyes went wide. "I can't do that. It wouldn't be proper."

"Do you call everyone on expedition by their full names?"

"No. But we don't usually have titled gentleman on our digs."

"We are the only people here. I don't think anyone would care." He waved his arms around at the barren plot where they would be working.

Damn her reluctance to have a chaperone. It seemed completely unnecessary since she knew without a doubt, she would never allow a man to compromise her. And the inconvenience of dealing with a meddling woman on a site was not worth the sense of propriety no one cared about.

So, she wore men's clothing. It was easier to work without the hindrance of a full skirt catching at her legs as she tried to move. A chaperone would never allow such a sneer at fashion. In fact, the one time she'd had one, the woman had expected her to sit in the shade and watch the work rather than be part of it herself. A lively argument had ensued and the woman may have fallen in a large puddle of mud.

To this day Uncle Henry still accused Lainey of pushing Mrs. Kirkpatrick rather than woman stepping back into the mud by her own power. It was possible that Elaina's threatening step closer had forced the woman to make a hasty retreat that resulted in her ending up in a puddle. But Elaina hadn't actually touched the woman.

Still, a chaperone would be too restricting. And for what reason did she have to protect her virtue at this point?

She was a spinster and as such was ignored in most things, including scandals involving handsome men. After all, if she had the skills needed to lure a man like Lord Melville—Julian—in that way, she would already be married, would she not?

"It might be amusing to you that I wish to keep things professional including our proper names. This is not a randy party, my lord. It's business."

"I see. I'm sorry if I offended you. Or if you thought I wasn't taking this seriously. I assure you, I am."

Yes. So far, he had proven as much. And in doing so had once again impressed her. But she didn't want to like him. It was too dangerous.

She'd liked him five years ago, and that had been a horrible mistake. Even if he didn't seem much like the same person who had acted so callously with her tender feelings, she wouldn't let down her guard. Or let go of her pain.

She took charge of planning the site, fully expecting Julian— Lord Melville, rather—to try to take over or complain, especially when she'd tasked him with a few duties that were less than pleasant.

But he went about his assigned tasks without a hint of irritation. Even checking to make sure she was pleased with what he'd done.

"You truly do not mind moving the dirt about?" she asked.

"No. I assumed there would be a great amount of dirt moving actually."

"But wouldn't you rather be the one digging? So you might find some vast treasure?"

His brows pulled together as he looked around the area.

"My understanding was that we were here to unearth something of interest. I don't think we Scots were left with anything to be called vast treasure after the English stripped everything at the end of the Jacobite rising."

"Yes. You are right. I assumed—"

"I think it's safe to say you have assumed a great deal about me, and while I'm not usually so pleased to tell a beautiful woman she is wrong, well..." He sighed dramatically, letting his shoulders fall as if in utter disappointment. His wicked smile, however, proved otherwise. "You should know, I don't want to go to Egypt to find vast treasure either."

"You don't?"

"No. Not that I would shove it back in the sand if I were to find some."

She couldn't help but laugh at the very idea.

"Then why do you want to do this so badly?" It was clear by now that he had no intention of giving up because the work was difficult. He was not a bored dandy, but rather a conscientious student.

"I have my reasons." He frowned and she thought perhaps she'd found a weakness. "But they are my reasons. You only need to know that I understand this is hard work, with possibly no reward. But it is something I have always been interested in. And I want the opportunity to see the process up close while I still can."

While he still could? Did that mean… Was the earl sick? Was this his dying wish?

She swallowed down her shame at how she'd treated him. He looked the picture of health, strong and virile. Surely, she didn't need to consider that last thing, but couldn't help herself.

Though not all illnesses left the person stricken to their beds until they were more advanced.

She would watch him more closely, not that she'd had any difficulty with that thus far. If he grew weak and needed to rest, she would accommodate his needs. He seemed the type that wouldn't stop until he had no choice.

"It is certainly not my business, but I will be sure to keep from making assumptions in the future. We all know that assumptions often get one into trouble. Please accept my apologies."

He smiled that devilish smile, the one with the dimple that proved it was sincere and not a mask he put on for the masses. She almost felt as if it was just for her. How ridiculous.

"Come on, then. Leave that dirt for now and come with me so I can show you how to dig for nonexistent treasures."

They spent the rest of the day with their heads bent close together, sifting through dirt and finding nothing. But a smile remained on Julian's face throughout the day. There was no hint of disappointment to be seen.

And before she realized it, she was having fun and smiling back.

Revenge set aside yet again, and she couldn't bother to care.

"How was the first day?" Ben asked as he put everything in place for Julian's bath. And Julian surely needed a bath more than he probably ever had. Not just because of the dirt—which seemed to find its way into every crevice of his body, including the very uncomfortable bits—but from the sweat of physical exertion the likes he'd never known in his pampered life.

It was incredibly fulfilling.

His father always frowned on physical activities and didn't approve of anything that remotely resembled labor. It wasn't done by *their kind*.

But it was invigorating. Especially when Miss Bantham was right there beside him.

He was impressed not only with her knowledge, but by her entire lack of decorum while on a dig. She was every bit as dirty and sweaty as he had been and from the smile on her face, she had enjoyed it just as much.

He had seen her at the ball last month and knew she was able to transform into ballgowns, curls, and feathers when needed. Somehow knowing both women were wrapped up inside such a delectable package made her even more alluring.

At one point during the day, he'd said something witty and she'd tossed a clump of dirt at him which exploded all over his shirt. His response was, of course, to throw one back and for the next several minutes, a war of dirt throwing ensued until they were both laughing and covered in the substance.

He'd even gotten some in his mouth.

"I enjoyed it immensely, Ben. Who would have known toying around in the dirt could be so exciting? I'm sure it would be even more so if we'd found something, but still, I'm already looking forward to going back tomorrow."

To spending the day with Miss Bantham again. To making her smile and laugh with his antics.

His own smile dimmed slightly. Would he be starting over anew the next day? It seemed any time she was given more than two minutes alone, she came back to him with that sour look of displeasure on her face and icy dislike of him.

"And Miss Bantham?" Ben asked.

"What of her?" Julian stalled and cleared the smile from his face. It wouldn't do for Ben to know he favored the woman. Julian recalled the time he'd had a crush on the coachman's daughter. He'd only been twelve and Ben had deviled him terribly.

"Did you win her over? While she was clearly enchanted by me, she didn't seem to care for you overmuch. What did you do during your travels?"

"You know very well I didn't do anything of that sort."

"I do know you only dally with consenting, experienced women. But that doesn't absolve you from doing something else she may not have found amusing."

"You mean to say I am not as charming as I think I am?" Julian splashed water at the man.

"I'm saying sometimes people of substance are not so easily charmed. They need more than just a flashy smile and bit of wit."

"You know damned well, it's more than just a *bit*." Julian smirked at his valet who rolled his eyes, proving his earlier comment to have some merit.

Ben saw the real man behind Julian's façade. Perhaps Miss

Bantham did as well?

When he was clean once again, Ben helped him into his clothes and he paused only a moment before heading down to dinner.

Would he be dining alone? Or would Miss Bantham forgo eating in her room to join him?

After spending many evenings locked in his room as a boy because he'd dissatisfied his father, Julian preferred to eat anywhere but in his room. And he preferred to have people around him.

But as he descended the stairs toward the foyer, he realized he wouldn't suffer from a lack of people.

The Leightons had arrived.

While he was not unhappy to see them, he was disappointed that he would have to share Miss Bantham. No more intimate dirt battles and laughter. He couldn't imagine the older couple would appreciate such a thing.

A wave of irritation came over him as he took in the happy greetings below.

He wanted Miss Bantham to himself.

He wanted her to be his alone.

The thought was utterly ridiculous.

CHAPTER ELEVEN

WHEN MISS BANTHAM hugged the older couple in greeting, Julian wondered what it might feel like to be embraced by her. She was rather tall and sturdy. He imagined she would give a proper hug when given the opportunity with a partner she cared for.

"Gregory, Minerva, please allow me to introduce Lord Melville. He is trying his hand at archeology."

"Yes, we met at the Expedition Ball. It is a pleasure to see you again, my lord."

"The pleasure is mine. And I welcome you to Dalkeith Castle. I hope I will not hinder your enjoyment of the dig. I am new at it, but I have hope this smaller expedition allows me the opportunity to join the larger journey to Egypt when they leave in December," he added and saw Miss Bantham frown. The woman gave away nothing. It was maddening.

"It is all just a bunch of mucking around in the dirt. I daresay, there isn't a wrong way to do it," Mr. Leighton said with a hearty clap to Julian's shoulder.

Julian exchanged a quick look with Miss Bantham and saw her clear disagreement with the man's assumption. Even after only one day in the field he knew there was a proper way to muck about in the dirt as it were.

Thinking of mucking had him recall their battle earlier and he smiled. To his great surprise he saw her smile back, her cheeks tinged a light pink.

Ravishing.

"We are so sorry to have left London without you. As I said in my letter, we needed to stop at our son's home to visit our newest grandchild."

"It cannot be," Julian said. "You don't look old enough to be a grandmother." Julian used the tone that won over all manner of women. Except, of course, the one he truly needed to endear to him.

"Oh, you," Mrs. Leighton said with her cheeks pulled up into a wide smile.

"I'm sure I don't know how I got so lucky as to choose a wife who refuses to age," Mr. Leighton doted on his wife, making her blush deepen in a delightful way. It was nice to see a couple who appreciated one another.

"Elaina, I daresay, when you choose a husband, make sure he is completely besotted."

Elaina.

He swallowed the urge to speak her name almost more than he could manage.

Elaina frowned at Mrs. Leighton's comment.

"I will be certain to do that." Even the little Julian knew of her he could tell it was a lie. She pressed a smile back on her face and turned to him.

"Lord Melville, the Leightons will be joining us in our quest for relics tomorrow."

"I am delighted and look forward to digging about in the dirt next to you for the foreseeable future. But tomorrow? Don't you wish to rest after your journey?"

Why had he said that? Had he sounded as obvious to the others in the foyer as he sounded to himself? Did they all know he wished to be alone with Miss Bant—*Elaina*?

"I assure you we will be quite restored after a good night's sleep and will be ready at first light," Mr. Leighton said with a bow.

Apparently, it was normal to head out at an ungodly time of night. He'd almost thought she'd done that on purpose to dissuade him from coming.

"We have time before dinner if you wish to freshen up from your journey. Are you hungry?" Elaina asked like the perfect hostess. He rather liked seeing her playing the role of hostess in his home.

"I might have eaten my shoe already if I didn't know I would be needing it," Mr. Leighton joked, making all of them laugh, including Elaina.

Why did she laugh at this man's jokes, yet Julian had to work extra hard to get so much as a smile or a chuckle?

Mrs. Leighton looked around the foyer.

"Dinner sounds lovely. Will we see Henry and Rose then?"

Elaina shook her head.

"I'm afraid they were unable to accompany us on this trip. Uncle Henry had things to see to in London."

Mrs. Leighton frowned and looked about the foyer once more as if Lord and Lady Darlington would pop out from behind the potted palm and surprise her.

With her voice dropping to a whisper the woman asked, "Who else accompanied you on the trip?"

Elaina straightened her shoulders. It was just a subtle shift, but he noticed because he was watching her so closely. The question made her uncomfortable.

After all her bluster that she didn't need a chaperone to spend days upon days in a carriage with him, she was now embarrassed to confirm the arrangement with the other woman.

"It is just Lord Melville and myself this time. And now the two of you, of course."

"Oh, dear." Mrs. Leighton rested a hand over her lips in dismay. "This is all our fault. You were counting on me to serve as chaperone and I let you down."

"Of course not. You know I don't require a chaperone at my age."

"You are still unmarried." The woman's words seemed to cut Elaina for she flinched just the slightest bit. Again, he only noticed because he was studying her every breath.

"Very unmarried. But still, my age puts me well beyond any silly rules of propriety."

When the woman's frown deepened it seemed as if Elaina had met her tipping point.

"If I were so alluring as to attract a man such as Lord Melville, wouldn't I have received an offer of marriage already and have a husband? I can assure you, he was the epitome of gentlemanliness. As one would expect when someone like him is forced to travel with someone like me."

"Of course. How silly of me," Mrs. Leighton said quietly, having finally realized she had tread heavily upon a sensitive nerve.

Julian frowned at Elaina's explanation of the situation as well as Mrs. Leighton's easy agreement. He opened his mouth to explain how he had been enticed by Elaina on many occasions during their travels north.

But thankfully, he caught himself before he'd admitted something so foolish. However true it might be.

He would go along with the idea he was unaffected by the woman, but the truth was, she intrigued him like no other woman he'd met. Perhaps it was simply the fact that he hadn't won her over yet as he'd originally thought, but he didn't think so.

He did appreciate a challenge when one was presented. But beyond that, he actually liked her. Despite the fact she didn't seem to like him very much at times.

He wasn't even close to giving up.

WHEN LAINEY LED Mrs. Leighton to the drawing room after

dinner, she expected the woman to continue the conversation about her traveling with a man alone.

Lainey understood, it *wasn't done*. But truly, riding in the carriage with Lord Melville was no different than riding with her aunt and uncle, or even the Leightons.

Or so she tried to convince herself.

"Was Rose aware you would be traveling alone with the earl?" Mrs. Leighton asked as soon as they were alone.

"No. When I received your note, I knew she would offer to come, and I couldn't be the reason she left Uncle Henry for months. They hate being parted from each other."

"I understand, but coming alone. Surely there was someone you could have brought with you. A maid…"

"I have no maid. And we didn't have time to find someone so last minute." That wasn't exactly true. There was really no reason they couldn't have delayed their departure for another day or two. In fact, Julian probably would have preferred it. "As I said, it was fine. Nothing untoward happened on the way."

Nothing at all. Even if she imagined different scenarios in which he might kiss her or even hold her hand.

"We spent most of the trip reading. Very uneventful." Even if his voice alone had made her insides feel rather singed.

She shook her head and planted a smile on her face, ready to change the subject. But Mrs. Leighton didn't cooperate.

"He is most handsome, is he not?" she asked. "There is nothing quite so striking as a large Scot."

"I hadn't noticed," Lainey lied. What could she say? That when he smiled in earnest and that dimple peeked out, she wanted to kiss it? No, that would not convince the women that their travels were nothing of concern.

Mrs. Leighton made a sound that could only be disbelief before she waved her hand.

"And so charming too. If I were a few decades younger and single, I can tell you I would have seen that I had a reason to require a chaperone."

The woman's eyes widened and she leaned in closer.

"If you wanted to snag him, you have more than enough cause. If word of this got out your reputation would be ruined and he'd have no choice but to offer for you."

Lainey choked and shook her head.

"No. Definitely not. I beg for your discretion. Nothing happened. We were simply two explorers traveling in the same carriage. Nothing more. I don't want to… snag him. Please!"

"Very well. But I fear you're missing out on a wonderful opportunity, dear. If you don't want to marry him, you could have at least taken advantage of the nights in his bed."

"Mrs. Leighton," Lainey nearly shouted in shock before a laugh escaped from the woman's lips. Lainey knew Mrs. Leighton was not a prude. She was always a lot of fun on expeditions. But to say something so scandalous.

"Are you telling me you do not find the man handsome at all?" Mrs. Leighton's chin rose as if challenging Lainey. There was really no way to get through this without the woman seeing the truth. Best to just get on with it then.

Lainey sighed. There was no sense trying to convince anyone she didn't find him attractive. It would be like arguing the sky wasn't blue.

"Fine. He is not unpleasant to look at." It was the best she could do. "But it doesn't matter. Looking is all I would ever do."

When Mrs. Leighton rejoined the men, Lainey continued on to her room.

She felt out of sorts and couldn't quite figure out why.

She disliked the earl and had for many years. Yet, she couldn't help but like him as well. He was… charming. Worse, he was most charming when he wasn't even trying. Lord help every female on the planet if he were to learn that fact.

She attempted to distract her unsettled thoughts by reading, but at some point the characters in the story she was reading transformed from the shy vicar's daughter and the investigator to Lord Melville and herself.

She had been a vicar's daughter once, but she wouldn't consider herself shy. She had no qualms telling Lord Melville—

Julian—how things should be, or more importantly how they never would be between them.

For that reason, the book didn't fit with reality. However, the investigator in the story was said to be handsome and strong, as all heroes were expected to be.

She read the hero's dialog with a soft, rumbling brogue, and modified the character's description to include inky, black hair that did what it wanted, and eyes so blue they warmed a person to their very soul. And that mischievous grin that put his dimple on display. Those lips were surely for more than jests and laughter. He would know how to kiss a woman properly.

Would his mouth taste of the port he'd enjoyed after dinner?

Would he touch his tongue to hers? She'd heard that tongues were often used in sensual kissing. Not that she had personal knowledge of kissing at all.

It was rare for her to regret never being kissed. It was the way things were, and wishing for something different never did any good.

But at that moment, she did wish she had some experience to pull from so the fantasy she was weaving could be somewhat realistic.

Instead, she was left to guess such details as what he would taste like and what it would feel like to have him so close. His lips touching hers. Breathing the same air in the small space between them.

Where would he put his hands? At first, she envisioned them as one would during a dance, but no, that wasn't how a man held a woman when he kissed her.

She remembered seeing Mr. McCabe—one of her uncle's hired men—embracing a woman in Alexandria. He'd not known Lainey was there as he'd greeted his lover enthusiastically.

His hands seemed to be in constant motion as if he couldn't wait to touch the next part of her and the next. Her hips, her waist, her bottom—he'd stopped there for a moment and gave that particular body part a squeeze as if it was a favorite—he'd also squeezed her breast which drew a pleasant gasp from the woman.

As Lainey remembered the encounter, she once again substituted Julian and herself in the roles of the couple.

Kissing, touching, breathing, moaning. Somehow, they were naked as her hands trailed over smooth, bare skin. She had seen a man without a shirt so she felt she did an adequate job imagining that, but she'd never seen a naked man below the waist so that part of her fantasy was a bit muddled.

It didn't matter because the parts she had been able to visualize were pulling her into warm, blissful need. Her body burned and ached for him.

She heard his deep rolling voice telling her how much he wanted her. How much he needed her.

And she needed him as well. She didn't know why or for what, but she had never needed anything more.

"Yes," she whispered, the word sounding like a plea.

"Do you want me to touch you?" he asked.

"Yes." She may have repeated the word more than a few times.

She felt his lips pull up in a smile against hers.

"Good," he said. "Then wake up."

She started awake, causing the book she'd been reading to slide from the bed to the floor.

She was out of breath as if she'd been running up hill, and even as she shook away the remnants of the dream, she felt the heat fading. She slumped against the pillows; her unsated, restless body writhed unconsciously as instincts she didn't know she possessed took control.

Tossing off the covers, she went to the wash stand and splashed cool water on her face to gain control.

Restraint was hard won, but eventually she settled back in bed and closed her eyes.

Earlier when she'd told Mrs. Leighton she would only ever *look* at Lord Melville, it had been a lie.

She would apparently *dream* of him as well.

Even if she didn't want to.

CHAPTER TWELVE

J ULIAN MADE SURE he was up with plenty of time to get ready to leave for the dig the next morning. He didn't want to give Elaina any reason to leave him behind. Nor did he want to hold up the expedition now that they had additional members to their team.

He was the first to the breakfast room and made haste in getting his food in case he was wrong and Elaina was already out pulling the wagon around.

When the Leightons appeared, he relaxed knowing Elaina wouldn't leave everyone behind.

He accepted a second cup of coffee and chatted with the couple over the fluffiest eggs he'd ever consumed. He tried to hide his distraction the third time he looked toward the door expectantly.

Where was she?

Perhaps she *had* left all of them behind?

When the dishes were taken away, he was about to suggest they find their own way to the site when Elaina rushed into the room bringing her lemon and sunshine scent with her.

He breathed out a sigh of relief, unsure why he should feel that way in her presence. If anything, he should feel the opposite. For when she was around, she frequently found something to disagree over.

But he found he rather enjoyed it. Maybe even encouraged it.

She was real.

And at that moment she seemed a bit muddled as she poured tea in her coffee instead of cream and was buttering her bacon.

"Miss Bantham? Are you well?" Mr. Leighton was the one to ask the question Julian needed an answer to.

Her hair was already coming loose from its pins and the buttons on her dress were not fastened properly.

"Me? Yes. Of course. It's only that I overslept. My apologies. I never oversleep."

As she mumbled her response, he noticed she hadn't looked at him. Not even the smallest glance in his direction.

Had he done something? He usually knew when he had. Perhaps even did things on purpose to vex her. But he hadn't remembered doing anything the night before to put her off.

"We have plenty of time," Julian said. "The artifacts waiting in the ground have been there for some time and won't mind waiting another hour to be discovered while you break your fast." He gave a pointed look to the mess on her plate. "Allow me to help you."

Without a word of consent, he went to the sideboard and arranged her breakfast in the correct way. Once the butter was on the *biscuit* and the coffee contained the perfect dash of *cream*, he returned to set down the offerings in front of her.

"I believe you will find this more to your liking, Miss Bantham."

"How generous of you, my lord," Mrs. Leighton gushed, but it wasn't Mrs. Leighton he had hoped to impress.

Miss Bantham pressed her lips together as if deciding whether to cast aside his offerings and continue on with her mutilated breakfast. He guessed hunger won out over her stubbornness.

"Thank you, Lord Melville."

"Julian, please. We will be working together side by side again today. It is easier to keep things simple."

It was an overt hint that she give him permission to use her name. Elaina, or Lainey, as her aunt and uncle referred to her.

But instead, she turned to her meal and ignored him.

He conversed with the Leightons as she ate her breakfast and gulped down her coffee hastily.

"I am ready. I will bring the wagon around."

"I can bring the wagon. Why don't you take a moment to visit with our guests?" he suggested.

"How kind of you, my lord." If he was attempting to charm Mrs. Leighton, he could call it a huge success. But Miss Bantham was another thing. She was not so easily won. He knew because he'd been trying for some time.

But in this, she simply offered a tight smile and a single nod.

"Thank you, Lord Melville." Not Julian. He chose to take her reluctant agreement as a symbol of goodwill.

"I'll meet everyone out front in a few minutes."

He headed to the mews and met up with the groom who had the wagon ready and waiting. Taking the team in hand, he led the wagon around to the front of the house noticing how much more difficult it was to drive a rickety wagon than to maneuver his fancy curricle. How had the woman handled it so efficiently?

But of course, he knew. She was unlike any woman he'd ever met. He doubted there was much she could not do. Except perhaps give him a chance.

When he reached the front of the manor everyone was waiting. He jumped down to assist, but Miss Bantham managed on her own and Mr. Leighton assisted his wife.

Following the same path Lainey had used the day before, he set the team on their way as the Leightons chatted easily. He found it interesting that the Leightons—Mrs. Leighton, particularly—spoke to him and Elaina as if they were a couple.

He pulled up to the site and saw to the mules as Mr. Leighton set up a chair and table in the shade for his wife. Apparently, Mrs. Leighton didn't mind being on expedition, but drew the line at getting dirty herself. It was nice to see how easily she sacrificed her time for her husband. Though Julian doubted she would see it as a sacrifice at all.

Lainey was already setting up her tools and supplies where she'd been working the day before. Julian followed suit, moving to his corner of the recessed area.

"I will work over here unless you have another suggestion," Mr. Leighton offered.

Lainey gave the man a smile Julian wished had been directed at himself.

"Wherever you would like to work is fine with us. Please select the area you feel will uncover the greatest treasure."

Julian thought his greatest treasure would forever be seeing that smile. If only he could be the one to earn it.

He wasn't ready to give up. He would win her smile eventually.

But then what? He wouldn't be content with a smile. He would want more. He would want all the things he thought of late at night in his lonely bed.

And he couldn't have them. He couldn't have her. She would certainly never pass his father's strict criteria for Julian's wife.

And why was he even considering such a thing?

Elaina as his wife?

He would never be bored, that was for sure. Or so he would have thought.

For the next few days, they fell into a routine that was almost boring in its lack of deviation.

They rose and ate every morning to ensure they left promptly at half past five. They arrived and started working without so much as a misguided lump of dirt aimed in his direction the entire day. Luncheon was brought around midday and they paused to eat in near silence. The Leightons occasionally spoke about their new grandson or about other digs they'd been on, but Lainey hardly shared anything of herself.

Even when he asked direct questions, she often responded without any elaboration.

What made it worse was she didn't seem to be angry with him anymore. Rather she was resolved to be only pleasant.

Had he thought he wanted her to be pleasant? Now he wished for a stinging lash of her tongue so he could volley back something equally witty. He missed sparring with her.

And that is something he never thought he would say.

LORD MELVILLE—SHE'D GONE back to thinking of him as such, rather than Julian—seemed intent on charming her despite Lainey's decision to ignore him. Since the Leightons had joined them at Dalkeith, he'd been ready and waiting in the breakfast room every morning when she arrived.

After that day of arriving late herself, she made sure not to fall prey to thoughts of him before bed. She couldn't spend each night tossing and turning restlessly, wondering what he could do to alleviate the ache in her body.

Surely, he would find it amusing to know she didn't know all the ways her body worked. And she would die before admitting that apparently her body wanted his very much despite not understanding the details.

She blamed Mrs. Leighton for putting the thought of his bed in her mind at all. It was entirely too distracting. She'd taken to being simply pleasant rather than risk their usual banter.

In truth, he'd done nothing to earn her disapproval anyway.

He was beyond helpful when it came to working on the site. Always offering to drive the wagon and do whatever needed done without a hint of complaint.

She was left with no choice but to take back her initial accusation that he was a dandy looking to be entertained. He was more than that. Much, much more.

She wanted to blame her realization of how handsome and kind he was on Mrs. Leighton as well, but Lainey's notice had started even before they'd arrived.

A week later, they returned from the dig in the afternoon to a few letters.

Lainey had received a letter from her aunt wishing her well.

"Oh, dear," Mrs. Leighton let out a gasp and clenched the correspondence she'd received tightly.

"What is it, love?" Mr. Leighton rushed to read over his shoulder.

Lainey watched as his eyes darted back and forth as he read. Each line seemed to make his eyes grow wider.

"I'll make the arrangements. We'll leave first thing in the morning."

"But we could get a few hours closer tonight. I don't think we should wait."

"Of course, you're right." Mr. Leighton turned to Elaina. "My apologies, but we need to leave right away. Our daughter-in-law has taken ill."

"Oh, no. The daughter-in-law who just gave birth recently?"

"Yes. Though our son didn't say her illness was related to the birth. He only asked that we make our way to his home to assist. He sounded distressed in his letter." Mrs. Leighton wrung her hands anxiously.

"But that could be the worries of a new father left to care for an infant on his own for the first time, rather than anything truly serious. We won't know for sure until we get there," Mr. Leighton attempted to offer another reason for the desperate plea they had received.

"Then you should go to them. I shall help you pack," Lainey offered and put an arm around Mrs. Leighton's shoulders as they maneuvered the stairs.

"What can I do?" She heard Julian ask with fierce sincerity.

Calling for Mrs. McGregor, the three women began loading trunks as fast as the footman and Julian could carry them down to be loaded onto the waiting carriage.

"Forgive me," Mrs. Leighton said with tears in her eyes. "I'm sure I shouldn't be leaving you alone in the house with a man and no proper chaperone."

Lainey frowned but shook her head. There was no time for this again.

"Don't worry about me. Just go see to your family. I'll be fine. As I said before, I'm not concerned. Any damage to my reputation is already done anyway. Please give your daughter-in-law my wishes for a speedy recovery."

"Of course." She pressed her lips together as the final trunk was loaded. "Perhaps it won't take long and we'll be able to return."

"Don't think of it right now. You must think of the ones who truly need you. Nothing else matters."

Julian turned from the carriage. "I asked Cook to gather some cheese and meat. I've packed it in the carriage so you'll have something to eat on the way. I know you might not be hungry, but you need to keep up your strength. You can't help someone if you are too weak to help yourself."

"Thank you, my lord, we'll put it to good use."

A few minutes later, Lainey was standing next to Julian, waiving at the carriage as it rambled down the lane at a brisk clip.

When they could no longer see the carriage, they turned to face one another and exchanged a rather uncertain look.

"I believe I will take my dinner in my room. I'm rather tired," she said when he opened his mouth to speak. It was clear by his reaction, he had not been ready to suggest the same thing.

"Very well then. I shall see you in the morning?" He bowed formally.

"Yes. The same time."

He looked relieved. "Good. I was concerned we would have to call our expedition short."

She understood his concern.

"Do you want to return to London?" she asked.

"Nay. Definitely not. But I would, of course, defer to you if you wanted to go. You hadn't planned for it to be only the two of us, and if you felt I wasn't suited to help you as you needed, I would understand."

That was very considerate of him. She shouldn't have needed to be reminded he wasn't a selfish nobleman who didn't care about anything but the adventure he was promised.

"I believe you have proven yourself since we have arrived. I have no concerns that you'll not be able to assist me on this expedition."

His smile was brilliant and tugged at something tender in her chest.

"Thank you for saying so, Miss Bantham. I won't let you down. I promise."

For whatever reason, she found she believed him. Even though he'd let her down before. Many years ago, before they'd even been introduced, she'd expected something from him and he'd disappointed her. Broken her faith in people in general, but particularly in young men.

As she continued up the stairs to her room, he bid her a good night with that wide grin that brought out the dimple on his left cheek.

She almost wished she hadn't made plans to eat in her room. It might have been nice to share a meal and talk with him. She'd missed him while the Leightons had been there.

She shook her head. It wouldn't do to admit to such a thing as missing him. She would be smart not to count on him. He would only disappoint her again.

CHAPTER THIRTEEN

WHILE JULIAN NEVER would have wished for anything to happen to the Leightons' daughter-in-law, he'd be lying if he didn't admit, at least to himself, that he was happy to have Elaina to himself again.

Even their morning ritual felt different as he teased her about taking all the bacon and leaving him only a few pieces.

"A gentleman would never accuse a lady of stealing food," she said primly with a small twitch to her lips.

"Ah ha! A lady only points out what a gentleman shouldn't do when they are guilty."

"Perhaps a little." Her nose scrunched up in the most adorable fashion before she let out an indignant huff and reached into her shirt to pull out three pieces of bacon she'd wrapped in a napkin. "Very well. Here…"

She held it out to him and he couldn't help but laugh.

"Are you offering me… *bosom* bacon?"

She was also laughing.

"As if you are so picky. Just two days ago I saw you drop a biscuit on the ground and then eat it without so much as brushing off the grass."

"Damn. I didn't think you were looking." He was guilty as charged. A little grass was of no matter when he had been starving. He wouldn't point out that Mrs. Leighton laid waste to the luncheon before any of them even got there. That would indeed be considered ungentlemanly.

"Let that serve as a warning. I am quite skilled at watching you without your knowing."

"Is that so?" He raised a brow, intrigued by her admission.

"I am supposed to be evaluating your skills on the site, am I not? It seems the best time to get a true glimpse of your efforts is when you do not know I'm watching."

Very well, that was an extremely viable reason to be observing him. He hid his disappointment. Why he would want her to be watching him because she was interested in him made no sense. For he could not be interested in her.

Not in that way, at least. Not as a man who was interested in a woman he had come to care for.

He'd only wanted her to stop hating him. Or if he was being greedy, for her to consider him a friend. But only so their work here would not be so boring and maybe she would include him in the larger expedition to Egypt.

That was all he wanted from Miss Elaina Bantham.

He didn't want to kiss her or become more acquainted with the places she hid her bacon. Except…

Oh, dear, but he did.

He snatched up a piece of the offered breakfast meat she had squirreled away in her shirt.

"Mmm… Lemony," he teased her.

As she blinked, he realized he'd revealed he knew her scent. Another thing a gentleman did not comment on.

"Perhaps we should get going. I'll get the wagon and meet you in the front," he offered as a way to escape.

"It's just the two of us now. I can accompany you to the stable to get the wagon."

"Very well." But he wouldn't have a moment to himself to get his head on straight and prepare himself for spending the day with her alone.

Rather than say anything that would further incriminate himself, he drove the wagon to the site in silence. She was equally silent on their journey. Perhaps she had other food items hidden in covert places and didn't want him to puzzle it out. Regardless, they arrived just as the sun was coming up.

Or rather the dim glow on the horizon in the east. It didn't appear they'd get a full day of work in before it began to rain.

In silent agreement, they went to their areas of the dig and began working. Moving small sections of dirt from where it had been to a new pile.

For whatever reason, he began to sing a song his stablemaster used to sing when he'd been younger.

Our boots and clothes are all in pawn
Go down, you blood red roses, Go down
It's flamin' drafty 'round Cape Horn
Go down, you blood red roses, Go down
Oh, you pinks and posies

She was watching him with a smirk on her lips.

"Go on then. This is where you would sing—"

Before he could tell her, she belted out the next bit of lyrics.

"Go down, you blood red roses, Go down"

They sang it through a few more times for good measure before he started singing something he realized wasn't suitable in a lady's presence.

But, of course, Miss Elaina Bantham knew the words to that ditty as well and didn't blink an eye as she sang about a bailer's arse.

When the sky turned gray before their lunch was expected, she frowned up at the clouds.

"I believe we should head back before we get caught in the rain. It's not warm enough to spend the day drenched," she said.

They gathered their tools and stowed everything in the wagon. They had just pulled up to the stables and unhitched the mules, when the rain dumped. With a squeal, she ran for the building and he followed after her.

There was only a boy of fifteen from the village who was tending the horses and mules while they were in residence. He'd taken the mules to the far end of the stable to brush them, leaving Julian alone with Elaina.

It was peculiar. They were alone all day at the site, but here with the sweet scents of hay and rain, it was more intimate.

"I'm sorry to say, it appears we are stuck out here for the time being," she said.

He shrugged.

"I don't know I wouldn't use the word *stuck*. It sounds like a place one wouldn't want to be."

"And you don't mind? Being here?" She swallowed and he could almost hear the words *with me* at the end of her question.

"No. Though I am a bit peckish after missing our lunch. You wouldn't have anything else down your shirt, would you?"

She smiled and shook her head.

"I'm afraid not."

"I'm not so sure I should trust you. Perhaps I should check for myself."

He'd meant it as a joke, but only realized what he had really said when her eyes grew wide.

"Of course, I would never," he said quickly.

"Of course," she repeated in a tone that almost sounded put out. "I'm going to make a run for the house. I don't need to worry about catching a chill when I can take a warm bath inside."

With that she rushed out into the rain leaving him there to wonder what he'd done to irritate her this time.

THE MAN WAS irksome. Elaina had known it for some time, but each day she spent with him it became more and more obvious.

The worst part was she wasn't exactly sure why she was put out with him at the moment. Because he'd quickly retreated on his comment about checking down her shirt for bacon?

How ridiculous. She would never allow such a thing. But for whatever reason she was a bit ruffled that he'd said that he would never do such a thing.

Never?

Because he had no interest in her in that way. A noted rake and flirt had no interest in her as a woman. She well knew where she stood with the earl. He'd made his preference known years ago.

But in that moment in the stables, she thought she saw something else in his gaze. She had allowed him to make a fool of her yet again with his silly songs and witty jokes.

In her room she rang for Nettie and asked her to have a bath readied. When she was warm and dry, she settled in by the window to read. The constant tapping of rain against the glass distracted her from the words on the page.

Or perhaps it was her thoughts.

She was a coward. Just as she had been five years ago. He'd hurt her feelings and she'd run away so the pain would go away.

But it hadn't gone away. Instead, it had transformed into ugly anger, turning her into a hateful shrew who hid away from the possibility of further rejection.

Yet it was so easy to let down her guard with Julian as he teased out her smiles and made her laugh.

She wanted something he couldn't offer. Was that his fault?

She thought perhaps it was no one's fault.

But where did that leave her? She couldn't be angry with herself for not being the type of person he was attracted to. And she could no longer be angry with him either.

He had never led her to believe differently. Maybe the way he'd communicated his lack of interest could have been handled in a less hurtful way, but he hadn't lied.

When it was time for dinner, Lainey dressed and rested her hand on the door. Taking a deep breath, she opened it and went down the stairs toward the dining room where Julian most likely would be waiting for her to dine.

She'd planned to stay in her room and request a tray be brought up with her dinner. But she wasn't going to hide anymore.

It was time to move on. To let go of the past. And that was what she planned to do.

CHAPTER FOURTEEN

WHEN ELAINA STEPPED into the dining room it took Julian two whole seconds to jump to his feet and nod a bow. Even as he waved off the footman to help her in her seat himself, he was a bit baffled.

She'd come down to dinner.

After whatever he'd done that made her flee his company in the stable earlier, he expected her to be hidden away in her room all night. But here she was, with a smile even.

It might not be the smile that made his heart race, but for whatever reason she was attempting to be friendly.

"I'm so glad you decided to join me this evening," he said.

He nodded that the food should be served and thanked the footman who presented his plate. While things were less formal here in the Highlands, his staff was able to show up any London home.

The food was always plentiful and tasty.

"I am impressed that your cook here at Dalkeith doesn't grow bored when you are away and run off to another household," she said after taking a bite.

He smiled.

"Mrs. Carn quite enjoys the quiet but doesn't mind cooking on the rare occasions we come to stay. *We* being myself and my friends," he explained. "We've even been known to host an occasional party."

Julian loved parties and entertainments. Being with people meant more people to charm and prove his father wrong. It was rather embarrassing which is why he never planned to tell a soul.

She nodded and seemed to relax as she cut her meat into tiny pieces. The very picture of proper etiquette. This woman who ripped bread with her teeth during their luncheon and held meat in her shirt was so dainty at the dinner table. What an enigma she was.

"If you would prefer to have a less formal dinner, I would be happy to oblige."

She cast a look at him.

"I am rather surprised to see you turned out for a meal in the country."

"Ah. That is because of Ben. Had I not packed an appropriate dinner jacket I am certain Ben would weave an evening coat from horsehair and grass, such are his talents."

Elaina laughed. A real laugh with a real smile that lit her warm brown eyes.

It was not a game, but if it were, he would be awarded another point.

He shared stories until their meals grew cold. Then they meandered to the drawing room and sat by the fire where she read to him until they were both overcome by yawning.

"I must say goodnight, before you are forced to carry me upstairs to my bed," he said, earning a chuckle. "The wretch who runs this expedition beats me out of bed each morning before dawn."

"*The wretch* wishes you pleasant dreams but reminds you that if you are not ready to go by first light, she will leave you behind."

"Hopefully the wretch won't snatch up all the bacon tomorrow."

"Perhaps if you arrived earlier, you would have first crack at it."

"Or maybe I will just hold her up by her ankles and shake out whatever she has stashed away."

They laughed as they slowly made their way upstairs. They paused in the empty space between their rooms. Her closer to her room, he closer to his.

"Goodnight," she whispered before turning and darting through her door. He hadn't had a chance to say anything in return.

As he closed the door to his bedchamber, he wondered if he would have said anything or would have *done* something instead.

Something, like kiss her.

And damn if he wouldn't be thinking about that all night.

WHEN JULIAN ENTERED the breakfast room the next morning with his bright smile, Elaina felt something akin to butterflies in her stomach and excitement in the vicinity of her chest.

How had this happened? How had she gone from irritated and angry at him to... well whatever she was now. She didn't quite have a word for it. All she knew was it was unwanted and distracting.

She didn't want to go back to hating him, she didn't feel it was deserved and her quest for vengeance never became much of a plan in the first place. But this... attraction that had taken over was disturbing.

What was she going to do? She couldn't act on this unfettered interest in him. She knew well how that would be received. She'd lived through that already and didn't want to feel that type of rejection ever again.

She needed to find a place in the middle. A place that was safe from both extremes. For now, that place would be the far corner of the site away from the man who tempted her to distraction.

Elaina sifted through a pile of dirt while thinking over how she could get rid of Lord Melville. Not in a permanent way, though there was plenty of dirt and tools with which to dig a fitting grave if it came to that.

At one point, weeks ago, she may have briefly considered it. Briefly being about an hour, but surely not a minute more.

She'd been infuriated with him and might have thought things would be easier if he no longer walked the earth. She wasn't proud of it, but it had been a thought.

Now, she didn't want him to go to Egypt for an entirely different reason than she had before.

She had completely given in to his charms. Worse, she didn't think they were charms as much as he was simply an inherently good person. She didn't understand it. This version of him didn't fit with the man she'd met years ago.

She spent most of the day as they worked thinking of how she might handle the situation. It was nearly time to pack up and return home.

"Ho there! I think I've found something," he called and pointed to the dirt in front of him.

They had yet to find anything on this dig and she didn't really expect to, so she assumed he had come across an interestingly shaped rock. But when she came closer, she could make out a handle. Like one would find on a pitcher or a jug.

"Very good," she said excitedly. Her earlier quandary put aside for the moment, she kneeled in the dirt next to him.

She loved this part of excavation. It made the hours of combing through dirt worthwhile.

"You'll want to use the small probe and the brush to loosen the dirt in small sections and brush it away until the entirety of the artifact is revealed and can be moved whole."

"Don't you want to do it?" He gestured to the piece of pottery sticking out of the earth.

She would have loved to take over and exhume the piece herself, but he'd found it and it was his right to see it through. He'd yet to have the chance and it wouldn't be fair to take it from him. Enemy or not.

"You found it. You get to remove it from the earth."

"But if I break it…"

"You won't. Do it just like we talked about. I'll help you."

He stood and stepped away. Then came back. She realized he was pacing in a small circle, staying well away from the artifact and her. His fingers squeezed and released as he breathed as if he'd just run for an hour or so.

She didn't know what was wrong with him, but he was clearly in distress. His breathing had become shallow and quick.

She cut off his next lap and gripped his wrist to make him stop.

"Julian?"

Hearing his given name made him look at her in surprise.

"Why don't you want to unearth the piece yourself? What's wrong?"

She could feel the tension coming off him and when she took his hand it seemed to soothe him.

"Tell me. What is the matter?"

He rubbed his forehead, leaving a smudge of dirt there. She reached up and wiped it away.

He blew out a breath and shook his head.

"I'm sorry. I'm being utterly ridiculous. I just think…" He looked up at the sky and everywhere but at her for a moment. "I just think it would be better if you did it so… So, I don't ruin it. It's too important for me to do something wrong. I do everything wrong and I will wreck this." He said a bit more but had shifted to Gaelic. He repeated the words, *gun luach* under his breath as he paced again.

He came to her and held out his brush with a shaking hand, his blue eyes begging her to take it. As if it would release him from this intense pressure he'd placed on himself.

For a second or two she just stood there, trying to determine how she should proceed.

She was in a perfect position to take over and use this situation as a reason why he couldn't accompany them to Egypt. After all, what good is another person to help look for treasure when the person couldn't actually do the job?

But seeing the way his hand trembled as he held out the brush to her again, she only wanted to help him.

She couldn't very well accuse him of being reckless, when he was worried into a panic over doing something incorrectly.

"I think you were right," he said, his voice barely a whisper. "I have no business here."

He was all but offering up his surrender on a silver platter and she… couldn't accept it.

She shook her head.

"I was *not* right. I said you wouldn't care, but you obviously care a great deal. And because you care, I know you will do a smashing good job of it. Come on. Let's work at it together. Back in the pit you go."

She gestured to the spot where the artifact waited for them.

She tugged on his hand and he took a step forward and another. Once they were crouched by the artifact, she moved the lantern so they could see better.

"You remember the books you read?"

He nodded.

"Tell me what you read," she encouraged as she held out a small metal pick. He took it and let out a deep breath.

"I should use the probe to feel about and loosen the dirt. Then brush it away. Just a little at a time. And go very slow."

"That is just it. You can do this."

He nodded and cleared away a bit of the dirt. Over the next few minutes, he revealed more of the pottery and had taken over completely while she only watched and gave a bit of instruction and more encouragement.

He stopped a few times to take a breath before continuing and she felt him relax as he felt more comfortable with the procedure. His hands had steadied.

When all of the dirt was completely cleared away, she went to find a crate to secure the artifact.

"Before you put it inside, you'll want to mark the crate so it can be identified. The name of the dig, and the grid location. Then, date it and add your name because you were the one who found it."

As he documented the find on the wooden crate, he smiled and then when it was secured the smile grew wider.

"I did it," he said more to himself than to her.

"You did," she answered anyway. "Just like I knew you would."

He laughed and she joined him. She had not thought he could do any of this when he'd first asked to join the expedition. She'd been wrong and didn't mind one bit.

"I'm sorry for my…"

She shook her head. "You're not the first person to be overcome by the gravity of unearthing something of value. It is a great responsibility."

He nodded. "It is."

She recalled the first artifact she'd been charged with uncovering. She'd been only thirteen and it had been a tattered scroll. It seemed to take forever and she worried the whole thing would blow away in the breeze, but eventually it was freed and she'd felt relieved and not a little triumphant.

Julian's experience seemed to be more than just nerves.

Once the crate was packed in the wagon they rode home quietly. He seemed exhausted, but she didn't say anything.

He dropped her off as he took the team back to the stable.

Inside she sought out the housekeeper.

"Mrs. MacGregor, might I bother you?"

"You're no bother, miss. What can I do for you?"

"Do you speak Gaelic?"

The woman nodded, her lips pulled together as if expecting this to be a bad thing.

"I wonder, can you tell me what *gun luach* means?"

The woman's eyes went wide and Lainey worried she'd said a curse. But the woman nodded and spoke.

"It means worthless."

"Worthless?" Lainey repeated and frowned.

"Aye."

Lainey thanked the woman and headed for the back of the house, heading off Julian as he came inside.

"You were not just nervous about the artifact, were you?" she asked when what she wanted to ask him was why he would ever think himself worthless.

He shrugged.

"I might as well tell you all of it. I can't make a bigger fool of myself in front of you at this point."

She waited as he blew out a breath.

"Often when I feel pressure to do something difficult, I remember the things my father used to say. How I bungled up everything I touched. How I couldn't do anything right."

"Worthless?"

His eyes went wide. "Ye know Gaelic?"

"No." She shook her head and looked away.

"Ah. Mrs. MacGregor. Did she—"

"She told me nothing else. Forgive me for saying so, my lord, but your father was a right arse."

He chuckled, which then turned into a laugh before evolving into full on hilarity.

When he managed to speak, he nodded.

"You have the right of it, Miss Bantham. I know he was indeed an arse. What I don't know is why I still care. Why can't I just let it go? He's gone, has been for some time, but he haunts me still. I never feel like I'm good enough because of him."

His head fell and his shoulders slumped. She'd never seen him look so defeated.

"I manage to hide this constant... worry, that I'm incompetent from everyone. But for whatever reason, I haven't managed to hide it from you. You've known all along I couldn't do this. I wish I had listened."

He was embarrassed. She could tell by the way he wouldn't

meet her eyes. Anyone would be in that situation.

She was ashamed that she hesitated a few additional moments to ponder how she might use his plight as a mechanism for her revenge, but she knew she couldn't do that. She was no longer angry at him.

It was time to be honest.

✦

CHAPTER FIFTEEN

"**I** WAS WRONG."

Julian's head shot up at Elaina's words. Not only were they not true, he never imagined he would hear her say the words if they had been.

She disliked him or had originally. She'd listed all the ways he was unfit for this task. But now she had said she'd been wrong.

He shook his head and opened his mouth to correct her, but she placed her hand on his arm. He hid a gasp of surprise at the pleasure he felt in that simple touch.

In the midst of his fit, he'd only vaguely noticed the way she'd taken his hand. It had been a point to focus on in order to catch his breath and steady his churning thoughts. A light in a turbulent storm helping to guide him back.

The heat of shame washed over him again.

She'd seen everything. The way he'd broken when tasked with more than he could handle.

Except... he'd handled it.

She'd helped him through it. She hadn't allowed him to shy away as she took over. She'd stayed by his side and offered encouragement.

Why?

She'd made no secret of how much he irritated her. Not from the moment her uncle had told her of Julian's plans to join them at the Expedition ball.

Why would she want to help him?

A braver man might have asked as they walked into the house. But he needed to escape.

"Nay, you were not wrong. I may have managed not to muck things up too badly today, but you were not wrong about me." When she opened her mouth, most likely to refute his argument, he shook his head and held up his hand. "I thank you for your assistance and understanding, but if you'll excuse me, it's been a trying day."

In his room, he just stood there, unsure of what to do next. He was physically exhausted after his episode, and his mind couldn't grasp onto just one thing to think about.

"Are you well?" Ben said quietly as he found him standing there with shaking hands. Julian wasn't sure how long the man had been standing next to him before he'd spoken.

"No," Julian answered. Then changed his response to, "I'm not sure."

"Did something happen?" Ben asked.

"I had an episode. In front of Miss Bantham." He rubbed his temples and hung his head.

"I see." The man had seen such attacks before. He'd always been patient and kind as Julian found his way out of them. It was bad enough for his friend to see that, but for Elaina to be put in that position.

"As you know she's not endeared to me, I can't imagine this will help. And I can't blame her—now that she's seen my deficiencies up close—to pass me over for the trip to Egypt. I wouldn't want someone on such a voyage who wasn't able to dig a piece of pottery out of the dirt without breaking down. She didn't want me to come, and now I've given her a valid reason to restrict my passage."

"Did she say something in that regard?"

"Well, no. She was most pleasant and patient, and really good about the whole matter. But still…"

"Perhaps you are making more of it than it requires? After all, there is nothing to be done for it one way or the other. If she decides to hold this against you, she will. And if not..." Ben shrugged.

Shrugged.

As if this were no big deal. As if this were not Julian's only chance to do something meaningful with his life before ceding to his father's demands.

"Since when does having a valid reason to worry come into it?" Julian asked. For years he'd known his attacks were unfounded and outrageous. But once he'd latched onto something he couldn't just let it go. It was beyond him.

Ben sighed in what could only be defeat. Telling someone there is nothing to worry about rarely ever stopped them from worrying. People didn't work that way.

"I can't think of even one time," Ben relented.

"Right. Telling me I have no reason to worry only makes me worry more."

"Then by all means, please continue in your worry. I shall go ready a bath so you are suitable for dinner."

"*Dinner?* I can't go down to dinner." Had the man not been listening? He was getting on in years, but Julian had never seen him anything but lucid.

Ben tilted his head.

"Do you plan to leave this room again? Ever?"

Julian glared at the older man. He was being ludicrous now, and well he knew it.

"Of course, I will need to leave the room. I'll just need to do so when Miss Bantham is otherwise involved so I don't ever have to speak to her again."

"Very well."

Julian knew that *very well* was spoken with layer upon layer of sarcasm.

He swallowed and hoped Ben would accept his next recommendation.

"Perhaps we should just go back to London."

"You are saying you wish to run away on the off chance the woman refuses to allow you to attend the larger expedition. But if she has no intention of doing so, your cowardice will most likely ensure that she will forbid you from coming. Therefore, you are creating your own fate rather than waiting for the actual outcome. I see. How direct and efficient you are."

"When you put it like that, it sounds utterly ridiculous."

"Oh, good. You also think you're being ridiculous. I enjoy when we reach an understanding."

Julian rubbed his temples and paced about the room.

"I know it might not make sense, but I don't want her to welcome me to the expedition out of pity. I'd rather she reject my offer if she truly feels that way than make special provisions because I made an arse of myself in her presence."

"And mine," Ben said but hid his insolence behind a cough.

"You're supposed to cough while you say it to disguise your rudeness."

"But how will you know I'm being rude if I hide it behind a cough?"

"I'm quite capable of dressing myself. I don't know why I keep you around."

"Because I tell you the truth whether you wish to hear it or not. As any good friend should do." The man had him there. He was a good friend.

"What do you suggest I do?" Julian asked. Ben was right. It was better to hear the truth from a trusted source when one was behaving irrationally, rather than have it known to all the *ton*.

The best thing about Ben was, he didn't point out how he had offered up numerous suggestions already and Julian had ignored each one. Instead, he considered seriously for a moment while tapping his chin before speaking.

"I think I shall get you a glass of whisky while you're in the bath. So you might relax before going down to dinner."

Julian stared at the man who generally spoke of the foolishness of overindulging. And who was now suggesting he drink his problems away.

Giving in, he simply nodded and went to change.

If the whisky didn't work, he could always leave for London in the morning.

⤜⟫⟩⟨⟨⤛

LAINEY WAS WAITING outside the dining room when Bentley came downstairs, heading for the study at the end of the hall.

"Good evening, Miss Bantham," he greeted her with a bow and a smile.

"Good evening, Mr. Bentley." She swallowed and decided to ask for the man's help. "Could I bother you for a moment of your time?"

"It is no bother at all. You may have as much of my time as you require."

She didn't miss the way his gray eyes darted toward the stairs as he answered. As if he didn't want to be away from Julian for very long.

"I am worried I may have made a grave error in regard to Lord Melville."

"There is a fair amount of worrying going around. What has you concerned?"

"You see, at the site earlier today, Lord Melville became distraught over removing an artifact from its current location in the ground."

"It is my understanding this is the whole purpose of archaeology, is it not?" the man mentioned casually.

"It is. But you see, Jul—Lord Melville found the artifact and was then reluctant to continue the extraction for fear he might ruin the piece in some way."

"And what has you worrying over his worrying?"

"I fear I may have pushed him to do something that truly made him uncomfortable. I wanted to be encouraging, but according to my uncle, my version of encouragement occasionally borders slightly into... well... bossiness. I assure you I had every intention of helping the earl when I practically forced him to continue unearthing the pitcher. But now, after some time to think, I realize I may have pushed too far and maybe caused real damage. Not to mention, ruined this experience for him."

Mr. Bentley smiled in that kind, knowing way of his.

"Shall I pass on an invitation to join you for dinner where the two of you may discuss the situation and work it out before moving on?"

"Oh." She blinked. When the man said it like that, it seemed like the easiest thing in the world to do. "Yes. Please."

"I'll do it straight away. I'm fetching him a restorative."

"Do you mean whiskey?"

"Quite."

They shared a smile and Mr. Bentley leaned a bit closer.

"For what it's worth, I think you handled the matter perfectly. Julian needs more people telling him he is capable and not at all what his father told him he was. Not everything he touches is destined to fail because he had a hand in it. I think he often believes that to be the truth."

"*Gun luach,*" she whispered. What a horrible word whether in English or Gaelic.

"Aye." The man suddenly looked heartbroken.

"We must convince him otherwise." Lainey was always happy to find an easy solution to a problem.

"Aye, lass." He winked. "I'll see that he is down to meet you momentarily."

Lainey went into the dining room to wait for the earl. Usually when they'd dined, she'd taken the seat at the far end of the table across from him.

But this evening she needed to speak with him about more personal things, so she allowed the footman to seat her to the left of the head of the table where Julian would be sitting.

As the clock on the mantle ticked, she began wondering

about her request to have him join her.

She understood he might be embarrassed by his upset earlier in the day, but she wanted to reassure him there was nothing to be ashamed about. In fact, she wished to make sure he didn't spend the evening thinking about the incident at all. She well knew how welcome a distraction could be when one was set on overthinking something.

When he entered the dining room, he was dressed in formal dinner attire. He paused only a moment at the door, while obviously taking in her position at his side of the table.

She could tell what he was thinking because he looked pointedly to the opposite end of the table as if surprised to find she was not sitting there.

"Miss Bantham, good evening." He offered a bow.

"And good evening to you, my lord." Since she was already seated, she returned a genuine smile.

"My valet insisted I join you. He said you wished to speak to me."

"Yes. After the evenings I spent in my room, I wanted to make sure you knew I hoped to share a meal this evening."

"Of course."

He sat and the footmen came forward to serve the first course.

They sat in silence as they finished their soup. She stole a glance at him and could feel the heat of his stare when he looked at her.

As the footmen took their dishes away and served the next course, Lainey recalled all the times Aunt Rose noted Lainey's lack of patience. It seemed tonight was going to be another one of those times she gave into her impulsiveness.

"Thank you," she said to the servants. "If you'll just put all the food on the table, we will manage from here. Please give us the room."

"Of course, Miss Bantham." The footman nodded to the others standing about the room and they filed out in a line as if they'd practiced it to perfection.

Thinking of perfection made her turn her attention to Julian and the nervous look in his eye.

She let out a breath and began cutting into her roasted duck.

It seemed she was not the only person at the table who struggled with patience, for Lord Melville set down his cutlery and let out a breath.

"Will you be dismissing me from the expedition, Miss Bantham? I understand you are well within your rights to do so. I agreed that you would make the decision regarding Egypt based on my performance here, and I've been less than successful during this trial period. I want to thank you for the opportunity and assure you I wish you no ill will for making such a decision."

She stared at him in surprise. He had been thinking about this in great detail. She felt relieved she'd suggested they share a meal to clear the air. It was evident there was a great deal to clear.

"When you say you've been less than successful, I feel the need to point out that you were actually *quite* successful today. The goal is to preserve the artifact as best as possible as it is removed from the ground. You did that carefully and correctly, following my every instruction to ensure the pitcher was handled with the utmost care. You were, in fact, perfect."

She should have said he'd behaved perfectly rather than admit to his perfection in general, but it was out now and taking it back would only call more attention to her misstep than ignoring it. Or so she hoped. Ignoring it was surely the easiest route.

Julian smiled. That devilish smile that started with the left side of his mouth, engaging his dimple before his lips lifted on the other side to match.

"You think I'm perfect?"

She rolled her eyes. "Of course, you would focus on those words rather than the rest of what I said."

"It's not every day a beautiful woman declares me perfect. Allow a man to bask in a compliment for a moment."

"I wouldn't say I *declared* anything." She rolled her eyes.

"I couldn't help but notice you didn't argue that you are a beautiful woman."

"You are being ridiculous." Her words were true, but ridiculous or not, it had given her a thrill to hear his comment.

"Will you give me another chance?" he asked.

"You do not need another chance. Nothing that happened today was so egregious as to end your trial arrangement prematurely. We still have another two weeks before we leave for London. I can only recommend that we continue on as we were."

"Thank you, Miss Bantham."

"You are quite welcome, my lord. For the record, I would much prefer someone who cares maybe too much over an extraction than to deal with someone reckless. Once something is broken it can be repaired but it can never be made whole again."

She may have been speaking a little of herself rather than an artifact.

She had been broken five years ago and had not been whole since. She'd gone into her come out an eager, naïve girl and a few hours later she'd faced a harsh dose of reality.

Silence fell over them again, not as uncomfortable as before, but she found she didn't want to go back to how they'd been. For whatever reason the young man who had hurt her years ago was not the same man that was here with her now.

Or at least she'd seen no evidence of the cruel person who'd caused her to give up on her plans for a husband and family of her own.

"My parents died when I was eleven," she blurted out, feeling the need to share something intimate to maintain the closeness they'd managed to build in the last few minutes.

Julian's eyes went wide as he waited for her to continue.

"They drowned in a carriage accident. I was in the carriage with them when it ran off a bridge and landed on its side in the river. My mother was killed instantly, but my father was alive and fairly unharmed. As the water rushed into the carriage, he tried to open the door but he couldn't get it open. I was small enough to fit through the window. So, he boosted me through the opening and told me to swim for the shore."

She felt the chill as if she was soaked to the skin standing on the riverbank on that dreary October evening.

"I stood there crying and shivering. I didn't run for help. I did nothing except exactly what he told me to do." She took a steadying breath. "Not a day goes by that I don't wonder what might have happened if I'd found someone to help rescue him. I might have saved him. But I didn't."

"That is why you tensed when we went over a bridge during our journey."

"Yes. That's why. My point is, that I am haunted as well. My father was a wonderful man who loved me, so I don't understand that element of what you suffer with. But I still grow anxious when I go over a bridge after all these years."

He nodded and placed a hand over hers. Offering comfort as she had done for him.

"When I remember how useless I was that night, I feel that same sense of panic as if it were just happening in that moment. They say time heals all wounds, but some are so deep they remain. We all have demons. Maybe sharing what brings them about with a friend means we have someone to help us when they try to pull us down."

"But—"

"If you are about to tell me you are a formidable man and shouldn't be stricken by memories the same as a woman, I will thump you in the nose, Julian Huntly."

He chuckled.

"I would never say such a thing." He tilted his head to the side. "I was going to ask... *Are* we friends? For I was certain you hated me for some unknown and unjustified reason."

"Unjustified?"

"Yes. I used that word specifically so you would prove me wrong and therefore justify your dislike for me."

He was smiling as he said it, and she decided they had spoken enough about emotional demons and baggage. Including the past she'd shared with him.

"Let's just say, I thought you were someone else. And now I think I know the real you."

He blinked in surprise.

"Is that a good thing? That would mean you disliked the person you thought I was? But how would you have known me?"

"It is not important now," she said and found it was true. Whatever his crimes back then, he hadn't even had the title yet. He was still struggling to come into himself and find out who he was.

She was certain the man before her now had paid his punishment tenfold at the hands of his worthless sire. The vengeance Lainey had originally sought was unnecessary.

Aunt Rose often accused Lainey of wanting to help every downtrodden soul she came across, and it was possible this was the reason she was willing to forgive Lord Melville so easily. Whatever the reason, Julian was no longer a villain, but a damaged soul that needed her assistance.

Or perhaps her willingness to forgive him had more to do with the way his smile made her stomach flutter.

Chapter Sixteen

T HINGS WENT ON as normal between Julian and Elaina over the next week. Or rather better than normal, if normal had been her constant wariness of him. Now he thought them friends.

For whatever reason, his episode seemed to create a bond between them. He'd been vulnerable and she, in turn, made herself vulnerable as well. Sharing the very personal story of the night her parents had died.

And now they were joking and laughing as if they were old friends. And unlike the other times he'd thought he'd won her over, there was no regression as there had been before. Where it seemed she'd let her guard down with him only to regret it later and put the wall back up between them.

He enjoyed their banter and the way she laughed freely at all of his jokes. Or if not *all* his jokes, then at least his better ones.

He still wondered why she'd disliked him at first, but he was happy enough to have her as a friend that he didn't mention it. She no longer found him unacceptable and that was all that mattered.

He was also grateful that she never once brought up his episode. Which meant he was left with no alternative but to believe that it hadn't been as serious as he'd initially thought. Just as Ben had predicted.

"It's almost as if seeing my weakness made me more likeable to her. But it makes no sense. She is so unlike the women I'm

"

accustomed to. They would have been whispering behind my back to one another before I'd had the opportunity to catch my breath."

"Of course, Miss Bantham is not like the ladies of the *ton*. She is lovely. Anyone can see it," Ben said.

"Are you considering her for yourself?" Julian asked the older man who scoffed.

"Of course not. I have my hands full seeing to you. She is much too active for a man of my age."

Julian rolled his eyes. Ben was all of fifty and in fine health. If the housekeeper's smiles were anything to go on, Ben had his hands full with other things as well.

He might have inquired if he thought Ben would ever admit to anything.

"Besides, I was considering her for *you*," Ben said as he brushed the shoulders of Julian's dinner jacket.

"Me?" Julian chuckled. "I will say, I've managed to shift her hatred to something more like comradery or dare I say friendship, but to think she would consider me for more than that…" Julian thought of the tempting freckle that hovered just above the curve of her upper lip. The way it moved when she smiled. The sparkle of gold in her brown eyes that took them from warm to sizzling when she laughed. The way she filled out a pair of breeches.

Julian cleared his throat and the inappropriate thoughts away. It didn't matter if he found the woman intriguing, or even pleased that she no longer despised him as she had initially. She wouldn't pass his father's strict criteria.

Julian felt the smile on his face fade away.

"It doesn't matter who I might want, does it, Ben? My father has tied things up quite thoroughly. I must find a *proper* wife."

Ben frowned and let out a sigh.

"Yes. I don't imagine Miss Bantham is what the late earl had in mind when he thought of the next Countess of Melville."

"Could you imagine what he would say about her? Breeches? Digging in the dirt." Julian smiled at the thought. "I don't know if there would be a name for the color of his face."

The usually stoic Ben even laughed at that.

"All the things that make her unsuitable to be countess, make her more charming, do they not?"

"Indeed, they do," Ben agreed. Julian noted the shadow of sadness on both their faces in the mirror's reflection.

Julian felt the loss of a life he would never have with a wife of his choosing. A woman that brought him joy, not because she was the best countess, but because she was his friend and partner.

In that moment, he realized the disappointment of not being allowed something he hadn't known he'd wanted, and the pain of wanting it deeply.

Julian had never hated his father more than he did at that moment.

HAVING CHOSEN TO forgive Julian Huntly for the actions of his past, created a new problem for Lainey. Without her constant disapproval to grasp hold of, it was much too easy to notice how beautiful he was. How funny. How intelligent, and yes… eventually she even conceded to admitting the man was charming.

Before long she found herself slipping into daydreams of what it might be like if he decided to kiss her, or even more.

She was the granddaughter of a duke, and the daughter of a vicar. But she was also adventurous and curious about the relations between men and women in the bedroom. Propriety was often sacrificed for desire.

For the first time she contemplated such a sacrifice for herself and found it wouldn't feel like a sacrifice at all.

Who would care if she took a lover? She needn't even worry about a possible scandal. At her age, no one cared what she did. If she needed more proof of that, she need only look at their current living arrangements.

She was living alone with an unmarried man she wasn't related to.

Yet neither her aunt nor uncle even considered she might do something untoward with the man. Despite him being a known rake. It was as if she was excluded from such consideration because she was a spinster.

Their letters encouraged her to be polite to the earl. They didn't once mention the problem with the Leightons leaving them alone once more.

And while the Leightons' daughter-in-law was much improved, according to Mrs. Leighton's letter, it was clear they would not be returning before this expedition was over.

And what did it matter anyway?

Surely Lord Melville wouldn't spare a thought to seducing the likes of her. He was pleasant and laughed with her, but clearly the attraction she felt was one-sided.

Letting out a stiff sigh, she had worked herself up to irritation once more.

She knew she had no right to aim her displeasure in Julian's direction, but the fact that he was known to seduce more than a smile from any eligible female in England yet hadn't attempted anything with her spoke to his disinterest, while she was...

Well... interested.

Damn.

"Are you well? You look quite put out," Julian said as he entered the room for dinner.

"I'm fine." The words fairly snapped from her lips.

"But angry if your terse reply is any indication."

"You think you know me well enough to know whether or not my reply is terse or if I look put out?"

He came closer and ducked his head so as to look her in the eye. Not that he had to stoop very low to do so. He smiled, showing off the dimple that intrigued her.

"I think I have come to know you quite well since we left

London. We spend most of our time in each other's company, so it goes that we would have learned things."

She tilted her head to the side curiously.

"And have you only noticed when I am being unpleasant?"

He laughed and shook his head.

"No. Though when we first set off, you gave me plenty to study in that regard."

She tried to hide a smile and failed.

"I know you don't want to encourage me or give me the gratification of knowing you find me charming even when you do and that is why you press your lips together to hide your mirth."

"To no success."

"Obviously. I'm likely the most charming gentleman you've ever met. You don't stand a chance against my powers."

"Is that so?"

"Aye, it is. But not to worry—and I know you are unhappy with me for pointing that out because your copper-gold brows have pulled together—for I fell victim to your powers before we were even outside of the city."

"My powers?" She had no powers over this man. Or any man. If she did, she would have used them on her uncle to get out of this situation entirely.

"You disliked me, and that is my weakness. Most people like me. I see to it, work to make it so. But you..." He shook his head. "You see through my act. Right to the heart of me. It's rather frightening, but also exciting. And it just makes me want to try harder rather than give up."

"But I have told you I no longer dislike you. Shouldn't you stop trying to impress me now? The challenge has been met. You have won."

She didn't look away from his intense gaze. He was right, they had come to know each other quite well. If she glanced away, even so much as to focus on his nose, he might know she hoped he wouldn't give up quite yet.

He winked at her in that way that sent a tingle down to her

toes.

"I don't think I shall ever grow weary of winning your smiles, Elaina."

Dear God, he'd used her given name. She hadn't given him permission, but there was no way she could pretend not to like it. Not when he was sure to notice the shiver of pleasure that came over her at his words.

She was completely affected by him.

This was a dangerous game they played. One she was going to lose.

AFTER ANOTHER UNEVENTFUL day in the trenches, Julian turned over the mules to the stable boy and walked with Elaina to the house.

"So that is it," he said.

"Yes. Are you disappointed with our results? Just the one pitcher and a few rusty tools."

He shook his head. "Not at all. It isn't really about what we find, but the excitement of what might have been found."

"True."

They climbed the stairs and paused in the hall by the doors to their room.

"Will I see you for dinner?"

"Yes. I'll be down after my valet spiffs me to a shine." He stopped before going into his room and called back to her. "Will you have treats down your dress tonight? I only ask in case I'm feeling peckish before the meal is served."

"You are on your own. I'm afraid lady's gowns and corsets leave little room for anything but a few crumbs."

"I will be sure to keep enough for both of us. You can count on me, Miss Bantham."

He gave a jaunty salute before shutting himself in his room.

Ben assisted with getting his bath ready and helping him dress appropriately for dinner with the same person he'd spent the day with.

Julian had regularly enjoyed the social scene in London. He was often found at whatever ball or musicale was popular that evening. Anything to avoid staying at home alone.

He would have thought he would have missed having somewhere exciting to go and would be chomping at the bit to leave Dalkeith Castle for a change of scenery.

However, he found himself eager to spend the evening in. It seemed he had grown quite fond of the scenery at home and was in no hurry to leave.

Not that it mattered.

Tomorrow morning, they would leave for the return trip to London. How the months had flown by.

Time in general was passing much too quickly. Before long he would be facing another birthday, and with it the addition of a wife. But not the one he wanted.

"What is amiss? I thought you would be eager to go home to Lord Stormont and Lord Penbrook," Ben said as he helped him into his dinner jacket.

"I was just thinking the same thing and wondering why I am less than excited. While I have missed Kit and Graham, I still find I would much rather stay here. What do you think that is about?"

"I believe it is more about *who* you would be staying here with than simply staying at Dalkeith."

"I'm sure I don't want to try to argue even though it feels as though I should."

He had no defense to use against his valet. The man was right. He was running out of time with Elaina.

He wanted more of her laughter and smiles.

"You're going to miss her," Ben said, plucking at Julian's shoulders.

"I imagine I am. Isn't it the strangest thing? When we arrived, she could barely stand to look at me, and now we are..." He swallowed when he realized that "friends" wasn't the word he wished to use.

"Close?" Ben supplied with a raised brow.

"Quite. But there is nothing to say we won't remain close if she allows me to go to Egypt."

"You sound as if you still have doubts." Ben shook his head as if the thought was preposterous.

"She hasn't come out and said either way. I don't want to pressure her. She should do what she feels is best."

But he hoped with all his heart she would invite him. Not just so he could visit Egypt and satisfy his need for a final adventure, but because allowing him to go with them was proof of her acceptance. Something he desired more than he should.

And, of course, if she allowed him to join the expedition to Egypt, it also meant months of time spent with her. And he couldn't get enough of that.

"I'm sure she will do what is fair," Ben said.

There had been a time when Julian would have argued the woman didn't have a fair bone in her body, but now he knew her better. And he was certain she would do what was best for everyone.

Including him.

CHAPTER SEVENTEEN

I T FELT ODD to be wearing a gown. Especially one so elaborate as the green confection Nettie assisted Elaina into for their final dinner at Dalkeith.

"You look lovely," Lord Melville said as she descended the stairs to meet him in the foyer.

"Thank you. You are very handsome," she said before thinking on her words. Should she have admitted to thinking him handsome? She was only speaking the truth.

"You are too kind." He offered a quick bow and held out his arm to escort her to the dining room. As usual, he assisted her into the seat next to him.

She expected it to feel different, but touching his arm now felt exactly the same as it did when he'd helped her down from the wagon at the dig. Or assisted her in maneuvering a pile of rock.

The familiar tingle and heat radiated from the point of contact, up her arm and throughout her body. Lately, that tingle had resonated in a lower part of her body that was indecent, but delightful.

She shook her head to rid herself of the thoughts before they turned her cheeks crimson. It wouldn't do to be thinking of such things when she would be bundled in a carriage with him for days on end as they returned to England.

She couldn't believe their time had already come to an end.

While she looked forward to seeing Aunt Rose and Uncle

Henry, she would miss this time with Julian. She wasn't ready to leave Scotland.

Here at Dalkeith Castle, they were in a bubble of contentment. No external forces pulling them apart. No distractions. Just she and Julian in the evening entertaining each other with comical tales of their youths.

"Are you looking forward to returning to London?"

She opened her mouth to tell him she was not, but instead settled on, "I suppose it is time." Which meant nothing. "At least the Season will be over."

"You don't enjoy the activities?"

She shouldn't have shrugged for it was unladylike, but there were no words to properly answer in the way a shrug did. When he didn't say anything else, she felt the need to speak.

"I'm sure it's not a surprise to you to know I do not fit in with the other ladies of the *ton*."

"Do you think it a bad thing?"

"I used to wonder what it might be like to be… normal. It is strange, I always see the other ladies as so perfectly ordinary. I guess I always wanted a life like theirs. A normal life. But I have loved all the adventures I've been a part of and the places I have seen."

"And now?" Julian asked. "Which life would you choose? A staid existence that fits society's dictates, or the chaos and adventure of a life in foreign lands?"

She didn't have to think about it.

"I would choose the life I have with Henry and Rose." She smiled remembering those first days with them. "When I was eleven, I rather viewed their affection for one another with disgust. But now, I know it comes from true adoration. While many society marriages offer one another respect, it is rare to see any hint of passion between them. I would guess it is because there is none rather than they've mastered the ability to hide it."

"And you want passion?" he asked.

What an odd conversation to be having. But it was not surprising. Over the last two months she and Julian had often delved into very personal topics of conversation. There was only so much banal chit chat to be had with a person.

"Who wouldn't want passion if it was an option?" she asked, knowing she had no such options.

He let out a breath and nodded. "Indeed." Some sadness clouded his brilliant blue eyes.

Without looking at her, he broke the short silence.

"Do you think one could be happy without passion? If there was no other option."

She paused to consider the question rather than respond immediately with something vague. It was clear he wanted an honest answer. Something was weighing on him and she found she wanted to help.

"I suppose one could be *content* in an arrangement with someone they respected. Likewise, a relationship without respect would surely bring misery. But happiness…? I fear true happiness is only to be found as a result of passion."

"Yes, I think you might be right."

Normally she would have enjoyed hearing him say she was right. But not in this instance, when he seemed haunted by something that would keep him from finding the happiness he wished for.

JULIAN WAS STILL contemplating his grim future as the dishes were taken away.

It was what he deserved for discussing such unpleasant topics with Elaina. Happiness and passion and the concern he would spend his life with neither because of his father's cruel mandate.

On top of his concerns for his future, he was also slightly anxious about tonight. He had wanted to speak to Elaina on another matter. He'd rather not have their good humor slip on their return trip. He would hate it if she slipped back into her previous dislike of him.

He hated the weakness of wanting to be accepted all these years after he was no longer berated daily for his lack of acceptability, but there it was.

One could hide the damage caused by a storm, but behind the plaster and artwork, the wood continued to rot.

"Are you all right, my lord?" Elaina asked, concern clear in her brown eyes.

He was taken off guard by her question. Had he let down his guard?

"I'm fine. Why do you ask?" he whispered.

"I—never mind."

That did pique his curiosity. "Please. What were you going to say?"

"I thought I felt you tense."

"We were not even touching."

"Which is why I said never mind. I can't explain it properly. I obviously didn't *feel* you tense in a physical manner, yet I...*felt* it." Her tone was snappish and he grinned.

She often got irritable when forced to admit she didn't dislike him as much as she pretended. He rather liked putting her in such a position as often as possible. After all, they were friends.

Once again, he felt the word didn't encompass the way he felt for her. He was friends with Hale and Kit and even Graham. He felt an almost familial bond with Ben. But this connection he felt with Elaina was something different entirely.

And he was pleased to know she must be feeling it as well.

"I think I understand."

"I'm certain, that is impossible."

"Nay. I can feel something from you as well. I feel that you wish to drag me into the study and ravish me."

Such a comment would have caused gasps and swoons among proper society, but Elaina simply rolled her eyes. He smiled his real smile. He often used humor to keep others from seeing what he didn't want them to see. But it didn't work with this woman.

And she hadn't been wrong. He was nervous about broaching the topic of her previous dislike of him.

Drat the woman. How did she see so much? Or feel it, for that matter. He was well-practiced at persuading other people to believe he was at ease in any situation.

Deciding it was best to get things underway, he pushed his chair away from the table and stood with his hand extended to her.

"Would you care to join me for a stroll in the gardens?"

He almost expected her to point out that the evenings were chilly and reject his offer, but instead she placed her hand in his and stood.

Rather than drag it out, he got right to the point.

"In an effort to continue our journey pleasantly, I wish to know why it is you disliked me so much. I know it's me and not your general countenance, for you are pleasant to everyone else. Do I not even deserve to know what I'd done to earn your ire?"

If she was shocked by his ambush, she didn't show it.

"Very well." She crossed her arms. "It was my very first ball, five years ago at my come out."

"You had a come out?" As soon as the words were out, he realized he'd made a grave error.

"Yes. The woman who plays in the dirt had a Season." Sarcasm oozed from every word.

"My apologies, please go on." He was suddenly reluctant to hear the rest of her story. If she had come out at seventeen or eighteen, he would have still been under the rule of his father. He hadn't been the best person back then. In fact, he'd been a complete bounder.

"You will not be surprised to know that most men do not prefer me," she announced, surprising him.

"Why not?" He honestly wanted to know the answer. Other than her antagonism, he found her intelligent and funny. And yes, she was pretty when she wasn't scowling at him. As she was now.

"Don't insult me."

"I mean no insult. I truly wish to know why you think men do not favor you."

"It is not something I *think*. It is true. I am taller than many men and they do not care for it. When I saw you at the ball, I fancied myself in—interested in you."

"Because of my height?"

"Yes. I thought perhaps a man of your stature might find a taller woman a convenience."

He thought he knew why, but it didn't stop him from making her explain, despite her squirming.

"A convenience?"

She blew out a resigned breath and gestured toward her lips.

"For kissing. You wouldn't need to bend down so far to reach. It was ridiculous and soon—"

He stepped closer, enthralled by her courage and awareness of herself, even if she got many things wrong. Even if he had not noticed until now.

"I find I am quite fascinated to test your theory."

"Excuse me?"

"I've never kissed a woman as tall as you, and I'd like to try it. I can speak to bending over to kiss women in the past and while it's not been a problem, I am not getting any younger and must take care with my back. Let's give this a go, so I might see if it is more convenient."

"You are mocking me."

"I promise you, I am not." He raised his brow and took a step closer. "You admitted to finding me interesting. There must have been something about me that made you think of kissing." He couldn't stop himself from thinking of kissing her now that she'd said it.

"It was a long time ago."

"And we are here together now." He traced the edge of her jaw with his finger and watched her tremble as her eyes flared with excitement.

She swallowed and closed her eyes to him.

"You should know, I've already sent off the letter to my uncle with my decision, so seducing me—or attempting to—won't change anything. It's too late."

He nodded in understanding. He'd known he didn't carry much of a chance, and the slim one he'd been afforded had surely been lost after his episode. He'd known that this trip to Scotland might be the extent of his adventure and this woman had indeed made it an adventure.

Despite his disappointment in the outcome, there was one thing he was grateful for.

"Good," he said with a grin. "If it is too late, then you have no choice but to know I am sincere in my desire to kiss you just for the sake of kissing you." His fingertip brushed her bottom lip and a slight moan escaped her throat.

"I-I've never kissed anyone before," she admitted in a breathy whisper.

He hid his surprise. How had she gone this long without being kissed? But he knew Miss Elaina Bantham could erect some impenetrable walls when she needed to.

"We can change that right now. If you wish."

As close as he was and as pliable as she was in this hazy state, he would have her permission before he proceeded. He wouldn't give her yet another reason to hate him.

"I don't understand." She stared at him while he waited for her answer. "I assumed your flirtation was simply due to a lack of options."

Did the woman not know the attraction she held?

Elaina was exciting and unexpected. He loved to watch her lips while waiting for her next words. Not knowing what they would be.

Except now, he was watching her lips for a completely different reason. And the excitement he felt was much lower and pressing earnestly against her hip.

"I would very much like to kiss *you*, Elaina," he said to clear up any doubts that may have lingered. Or if she hadn't yet noticed his erection which seemed unlikely.

"Truly?" she whispered with her head cocked to the side as if she were waiting for him to declare everything a jest.

"Do you want me to kiss you?" he asked quietly. During the course of their discussion, she had not moved away, nor pushed him back. Instead, her fingers were clenched in his coat and he would need to remove them to escape. Not that he desired escape. Quite the opposite.

She studied his face for a moment before nodding.

"Yes. Please."

He didn't give her even a second to reconsider. It felt as if he'd been waiting for this chance too long already.

His lips claimed hers softly at first as one arm wrapped securely at her waist in easy reach of his own. His other hand rested along her jaw and throat to guide her through her first kiss.

He didn't take for granted this gift she was giving him. Her first kiss. The rest of her life she would remember it was him she had given the honor. He wanted her to think back on it with fondness. He would make it pleasant.

When he touched his tongue to her lips she opened with a gasp of surprise, and he took the kiss deeper.

She was not wrong about her height being a convenience, but that was not the only thing that made this kiss exquisite. Her innocent exploration of his mouth was unexpected and exhilarating.

He'd dallied with experienced women. Widows, generally, who'd wanted only sexual release from him. Kissing was just a step in the dance. Not the entire dance as this moment was.

They feasted on each other's mouths as if this was all there was.

And it was enough. For the moment at least.

Chapter Eighteen

Lainey had never felt so pleasantly out of sorts. Despite the fog of desire clouding her thoughts, she was also clearly present.

Every press of his soft lips and slide of his warm tongue was captured with crystal clarity in her mind. She would forever recall the way he tasted of port and rum cake. Divine.

She was kissing Lord Melville. No, she was kissing *Julian*. And more importantly, he was kissing her. She'd told him kissing her would make no difference in the outcome of her decision regarding Egypt. And yet he'd wanted to kiss her anyway.

Some small part of her mind also noted she had been correct about the ease of access their heights granted, but that was not important now.

She realized with a shock that as good as his mouth felt against hers, she also enjoyed his touch. The firm grip of his hand on her hip, holding her close to him. So close, she could feel the hardness of him growing between them.

She tilted her hips to press closer to him, the action as natural as breathing. As if his touch alone bestowed some carnal knowledge.

Surely, she should be touching him as well. Not just standing there allowing the kiss but participating in it too.

She rested one of her hands on his upper arm, but feeling only the fabric of his coat, she decided to move up so she could touch his skin. At his neck she tunneled her fingers through his hair so she could hold him to her.

With her other hand she chose to mimic his pose and placed her arm around him, but when she did, her hand inadvertently slipped into the inside of his coat instead of the outside.

The inviting warmth kept her from retreating and the groan of pleasure against her lips told her he enjoyed her error.

Her touch seemed to ignite him. Soon his hands moved over her body. Up her back at first and then down, and farther down until they rested over her bottom. His hands squeezed her there and pressed her closer to the ridge in his trousers.

This was no longer just a kiss. It was a prelude to something more. And she wasn't sure if she wanted to back away or reach for it.

Since she'd been a young girl trailing behind her aunt and uncle on an expedition site, she had never turned away from a new experience.

As she was debating her decisions, the earl must have been equally alert to the precipice where they stood.

With a groan unlike the others so far, he slowed his kisses and lifted his hands to a more respectable place on her back. She could sense his reluctance and knew the strength it must have taken to end the kiss and rest his forehead against hers while they panted to catch their breath.

More strength than she possessed for sure.

"You were quite right," he said quietly, his warm breath touching the moisture on her lips. "It is quite pleasant kissing someone of your height."

When he shook his head, it moved her likewise.

"No," he corrected. "Not someone. *You*. It is quite pleasant to kiss you, Elaina."

She smiled, unable to help herself.

"But you've stopped." She tried to hide the disappointment in her voice and failed.

"I didn't want to. But we were getting too close to a place we could not recover from. And I had only asked for a kiss."

"Do you wish to amend your request?" What was she saying? She couldn't allow him to ruin her. Him. Lord Mel-villain.

Except she realized that was not him. It seemed it never had been. He obviously cared about her enough to stop before it was too late.

Still, she was three and twenty. A spinster with no other opportunities to have this experience.

"No. That is, yes. Most assuredly yes. But I won't because I respect you too much."

"I see." She frowned. She certainly shouldn't be upset to have a man respect her, but with her body humming from his touch, she couldn't seem to appreciate his integrity at the moment. Perhaps later, when she was alone in her room, she would feel fortunate he didn't push her into something she might have regretted.

But right now… she wanted.

He caressed her cheek and she softened once again from just that simple touch.

"Please don't be angry at me for doing the right thing. I can't even be certain you like me most of the time and I don't wish to do anything to make it worse."

She laughed and nodded.

"You're right. I'm sure I will thank you for this later. I just don't like missing out on an adventure. Specifically, what would have come after that kiss had we not stopped. Surely it would have been an exciting exploration."

He kissed her again, a quick, soft touch of his lips.

"Perhaps another time, when you've considered it thorough-ly. I would never pretend to know better than you what you want and don't want. But that decision needs to be made with a clear head and I'm afraid neither of us can claim one of those at the moment."

He was right. She took a steadying breath and nodded. Her cheeks went warm when she realized she'd practically begged this rogue to take her virtue and he had refused her.

What a fool.

"I should go," she said as she took a step away from him. But he put an arm around her, holding her close and kissing her again. Why did she turn to melted butter whenever his lips touched hers?

"You have no idea how much I want you right now. And how surprised I am that I am not taking you up on your offer. But you need to know before you begin analyzing the situation incorrectly that the only reason I stopped is because you are too important and too special for a dalliance. Tell me, you understand."

Her doubts from a moment ago floated away as if they'd never existed.

She looked him in the eye noticing how dark his blue eyes had gone.

"I understand."

He nodded and brushed a piece of her hair from her forehead before whispering, "Good lass. Shall we go back inside?"

Lainey touched her lips, plump from his kisses and smiled.

"Yes." She turned for the door. They'd only gone two steps before she stopped him again. "Thank you, Julian."

Whatever he was or had been, he had given her the most perfect first kiss. She would remember it all her life.

And hoped it would not be the only one.

JULIAN TOSSED AND turned in his bed for what felt like the hundredth time. If it was just restlessness from being unfulfilled by her kisses, he could have eased the tension with his hand. But that was not the issue.

Or not the entirety of the issue. His body did still want hers, but he was resolved to treat her the way she deserved. To respect her. Because he genuinely cared for her.

What vexed him as he tried to sleep was that their earlier conversation had been interrupted. She'd started to tell him the reason she didn't like him, something that had happened the night of her come out, but they'd gotten distracted by the kiss.

Most assuredly the best kiss of his life for both her innocent determination and eager sensuality.

But he still didn't know what he had done to cause her initial dislike of him. Something that had happened at her first ball.

He struggled with memories from so long ago. Mostly because he'd gladly pushed them as deep into the dark recesses of his mind as possible. It was not a time he liked to think of.

It had been a part of his life he hadn't been proud of.

After leaving Scotland and leaving Hale and Kit behind for London, he'd spent his evenings with the chaps his father had encouraged him to build a friendship with. Proper English lords, he'd claimed them rather than the Scottish brutes Julian had known at Heriot's. But Lord Dunnage and Lord Heath had been conniving monsters. Acting the perfect gentlemen when their fathers were about, but showing their true colors when they were alone with Julian.

Only Julian's size kept him from being injured physically, but they had been terrors. He'd nearly forgotten all the cruel pranks they'd played.

Just as Julian was finally drifting off to sleep, his subconscious provided him with the answer he'd been seeking. A snippet of a memory.

The night of the Marksley Ball—always the first of the Season— when Robert had stolen a decanter of brandy from his father's study and they'd proceeded to drink it in the gardens before going back inside as the dancing began.

The heat of the room in addition to the warmth from the brandy forced beads of sweat to form on Julian's brow, a heavy blanket of drunkenness muddled his thoughts to the point that he found everything incredibly funny. Everything. Even things that weren't funny at all.

He'd stood by the wall, or rather he'd used the wall to hold him up, while Robert had gone off to dance. Julian knew dancing was beyond him in his state, he'd be lucky if he could walk. Had he drunk more than the others, for they seemed fine? Perhaps Robert's stalky build aided in his tolerance.

It seemed Robert had only been gone a moment before he'd returned with a girl. A very tall debutante with golden-red hair and warm, though nervous, brown eyes.

Robert introduced them. But Julian hadn't caught her name. He thought Robert had called the poor girl Miss Stork, but that couldn't be right.

He laughed again at how strange it was that he couldn't think straight. He laughed a great bit, he realized. When he settled enough to ask for her real name, the girl was gone.

He lurched up in bed from the dream. But awareness only brought the rest of the memory.

He'd thought he'd paid for his stupidity later that evening as he was casting up his guts in the bushes, or the next morning when his head pounded as his father shrieked at him. But no.

His minor discomfort didn't make up for what he'd done to Elaina. Instead of taking up for her when a bully made a joke of her, he'd…laughed.

It was no wonder she despised him so. He'd ruined her first ball. Her come out. His insensitivity could quite possibly be the reason she'd fled London and never married.

He jumped from his bed and went to raise Bentley.

Of course, she hadn't wanted him to go to Egypt. He'd tried to force himself into the life she'd made for herself after his callousness and thought himself justified to do so. He'd thought her unreasonable for not welcoming him.

But he must have caused her so much pain. He knew well enough what it felt like to be mocked. His father had done it often to make sure Julian didn't think too highly of himself.

And Lainey surely thought Julian had laughed at Robert's cruel jest when in fact, he would have laughed at anything. Or nothing.

Still, he'd hurt her deeply, then he'd selfishly forced her to help him. He felt the chill of shame run down his spine as he urged his valet to help him pack so they could leave at once.

He couldn't do anything to rectify what he'd done, but he would do her the courtesy of getting out of her life as she'd wanted initially. And if part of his retreat was because he was too cowardly to face her and offer the impotent apology she deserved, so be it.

Thinking of their kiss now, sickened him. He hadn't earned that honor.

Bentley packed his things without a word, either because he didn't know what to say or was still partly asleep.

Dawn hinted at the horizon as they loaded his trunks.

In the silence of the carriage as they rolled out the lane, the older man finally spoke.

"What has happened?"

"I'm too embarrassed to speak of it," Julian said, unable to look the man in the eye.

"Did you dishonor the lady? Because servant or no, I will turn this carriage around this instant if you need to offer marriage as reparations. Those mines are not worth a lady's—"

Julian patted the man's shoulder to soothe his anger and smiled at his closest friend.

"I assure you it was not that dire. But I can't… I can't face her. I surely won't force the woman to travel with me all the way back to London. The fact she has spent this much time with me and remained civil is beyond what I deserve."

Bentley eyed him curiously and Julian found himself explaining.

"It was years ago. I only just remembered tonight. I laughed at her, Ben. On the night that should have been the happiest of her life, Robert called her Miss Stork and I laughed."

"Lord Dunnage," Bentley muttered while shaking his head. "A bigger waste of breath I've never known."

"I can only think he is somewhere paying for his sins as we speak."

The blighter had been shot by an angry father after he had forced himself on the man's daughter. The House of Lords didn't punish the man who shot him, feeling justice had been served, and the world made a better place for the lack of such a blackguard.

"Why your father thought him a good friend for you, I'll never know."

They fell into silence as the sun came up. Julian thought perhaps Ben had fallen asleep, but after some time, he spoke again.

"You have always had a kind soul. I'm certain it came from your mother, because your father... well. He didn't understand you and thought to break you. But your kindness was too strong for him. You know you will not rest easy until you have made this—whatever you've done—right."

Julian only nodded. There was no need to use words when they both knew the truth.

He needed to make amends. He wouldn't bother her again until he had a plan to fix this.

CHAPTER NINETEEN

THE MOMENT LAINEY woke she recalled the kiss and smiled at the sun coming through the windows. It seemed like a dream, but she knew her dreams wouldn't have been so gloriously detailed.

It was a new day. And she was no longer a woman who had never been kissed.

She knew of girls who had been kissed and described it as if it was the greatest thing ever. She had thought it to be an exaggeration, but now she knew the truth. It was even better than they'd described.

Lainey wondered if the longer a woman waited, the better the first kiss would be. If that were so, she was glad she waited all this time for Julian's kiss. It had certainly been worth the wait.

Julian.

So strange the way she had gone from hating him, to tolerating him, to… whatever it was she felt now. Longing? Attraction? Respect?

It was impossible to compare the man she knew now—the man who had kissed her and protected her virtue despite his obvious urges—to the arse she'd first met at the Marksley ball. The man who had laughed at his friend's insult so heartlessly.

She had to consider the role one's friends played in how one behaved. After all, it had been the few friends she'd made on the edges of the dance floor that encouraged her to smile in Julian's direction in the first place. While he hadn't noticed, the barbaric Lord Dunnage had mistaken her interest in him and come to ask her to dance.

When the dance was over and he'd offered to introduce her to his friends, she was grateful for the chance to be closer to the tall lord leaning against the wall.

But then Lord Dunnage had made a mockery of her, calling her Miss Stork.

And Julian, the man with the sweet smile who had captured her fancy, had laughed.

She remembered the way her face had burned in mortification. How Lord Heath had joined in by flapping his arms about like a large bird.

She'd been so stunned it had taken much too long for her to retreat. And in that moment her gaze had met Julian's beautiful blue eyes. And she'd felt his betrayal like a brand to her heart.

But that was a long time ago. He hadn't truly betrayed her since he hadn't known her. She'd created a personality for him in her mind and he had not lived up to her expectations.

Except it seemed now, he had exceeded them.

She called for Nettie and tried not to seem in a rush to dress and go downstairs for breakfast. Today they would start their journey back to London. She'd have hours alone with him as they traveled.

She couldn't wait.

Strange that she had been lamenting this trip and now wished it wouldn't end. She didn't want to leave the bubble they had created here and go back to London. Back to reality.

She entered the breakfast room to find it empty.

When one of the footmen moved to serve her, she shook her head.

"I'll wait for Lord Melville."

She should have expected trouble when she saw the footmen pass glances to one another. When the footman by the door stepped out of the room, she knew something was amiss.

The butler stepped into the room and offered a sympathetic frown.

"Lord Melville departed at dawn, my lady."

"He left?" He'd left? He'd kissed her so passionately she'd wanted him to do more, and then this morning he'd… left? That couldn't have been coincidence.

She cleared her throat and offered a shrug of nonchalance.

"Did he leave a message?"

"No, my lady."

She forced a smile to her lips—the very lips the earl had kissed the night before—and nodded toward the footmen.

"Then I suppose I don't need to wait for him."

They filled her plate with food, and she thought she might be sick.

After breakfast, with her trunks loaded, she left Dalkeith Castle with Nettie as a companion. It may have been considered scandalous to travel alone with the earl, but it would be dangerous to make the journey home on her own.

The young woman kept to her knitting or embroidery and Lainey envied her ability to concentrate on such tasks while the carriage swayed, without getting sick. Lainey spent the first day looking out the window and trying her best not to panic on the occasions they traveled over a bridge.

It was impossible to not think of Julian and wonder why he had left without so much as a note to explain why.

She'd told him she'd already sent her decision to Uncle Henry. Had Julian decided it was no longer worth it to attempt to change her mind now that the die was cast?

She didn't think so. She'd felt the way his body had responded to hers the night before. She didn't know much of men's bodies, but she didn't think they could fake such things.

No, his kindness had been real. His passion had been real as well. She would know.

At least she thought so.

She'd never been kissed before but something had sizzled

between them.

If nothing else she felt awakened by his kiss. Much like the tale her mother used to tell her of Sleeping Beauty. Only one man had been able to unlock her from her frozen state.

Lainey had been frozen in anger for years and Julian was the only one who could release her.

She'd forgiven him, and her forgiveness had been sealed with a kiss. But then he'd left without a word.

She didn't know what to think of it.

By the seventh day of riding in silence with Nettie, Lainey was nearly ready to try reading again to pass the time. Fortunately, they arrived home the next day.

It felt strange to be back at Darlington House. So much had happened since she'd been there last. When she'd entered her home previously, she'd been filled with anger and didn't know how amazing a kiss could be. Everything had changed.

Aunt Rose was the first to come out of the drawing room to greet her. The woman smiled and hugged her tightly.

"I've missed you so much. I received your letters, but they lacked details. You must tell me everything." She tilted her head to the side and pressed a hand to her chest. "Please tell me you and the earl got along."

"Yes, Auntie. We did."

"I was worried when Mrs. Leighton wrote to tell us they needed to stay to help their son and daughter-in-law with the new baby. I'm so glad the new mother is improved, but I was concerned that the two of you were alone all that time."

Lainey hid her surprise, but asked, "Why?"

"It was no secret you didn't care for the earl before you left. I worried you would have hidden in your room and not spoken to him."

"Of course not." At least not the *whole* time. "The earl and I became good friends." Friends whose tongues had been in each other's mouths, she thought to herself. A sense of longing came over her. She wondered when or if she might have the opportunity to do it again.

"Splendid!" her aunt said shaking her from her thoughts.

Yes. It had been splendid, indeed.

JULIAN RECEIVED A note from Lainey a few days after he arrived home from Scotland. He'd used his hasty escape to stop and visit Hale and his family. But now he was back in London and so was Lainey.

Lord Melville,

I'm sorry you were pulled away to London so abruptly. I wanted to let you know I arrived home yesterday evening. Your box of tools was left behind. If you have a need for them, please come by at your convenience.

All the best,
E. L. Bantham

If his guilt for running away literally in the middle of the night, wasn't bad enough, now he felt worse for not asking after her to make sure she'd arrived home safely. Had she traveled alone? He'd abandoned her without a word, and yet she was inviting him to come by to pick up his tools.

They both knew he had no need of tools anymore. He wouldn't be going to Egypt.

Ben hadn't said much since they arrived home. While Julian's father had been very vocal in his displeasure with his only son, Ben's silence weighed on him. It seemed disapproval dug deeper when expressed without words. Or possibly it mattered more because Ben mattered more to him than his father ever had.

"I know you're angry with me," Julian said as Ben helped him dress the next morning.

"Who am I to be angry with an earl?" he said with a tight smile.

"You know I am not one to be coddled because of a silly title. If you have something to say, you should just say it."

"Oh, I can assure ye, you'll not want me to speak."

Julian let out a breath and nodded.

"You're right. I probably don't want to hear what you have to say, but I'm guessing I need to because you plan to point out how ridiculous I was for leaving the way I did. And you probably think it was ungentlemanly of me not to check to make sure she arrived home safely. I can tell you, she did. She wrote to me to let me know, and to mention I'd left my tools behind. As if I would have a need for tools." He held up his hand before continuing.

"But, of course, you would say I don't know that for sure, and running away certainly didn't help my cause to win her approval. But really, Ben. How could she possibly want me to spend even another minute in her sight after what I've done?"

Julian's shoulders slumped.

"You probably think I should have stayed and begged for her forgiveness and I did think of that briefly, but I worried that she might think the two things related. My begging forgiveness while also wanting her to include me in the trip to Egypt. It would rather make any apology seem insincere. And isn't acting better than words? I must find a way to *make* this right not just apologize with words for what I've done to hurt her."

He rubbed his temple.

"I hurt her terribly. I didn't even know it. All this time, I'd hurt someone as lovely as Miss Bantham and just went about my life thinking I was a kind person whom everyone should like. But no. I'm a monster, Ben. A selfish cad who laughs cruelly at young women and then arrogantly expects them to do what I want. Go on, say it."

"I think you've covered it and then some. Is it possible you're being a bit dramatic?"

"When have I ever been dramatic?"

"Well…" Ben paused a minute, but then seemed to decide to go down a different path. "You won't feel better until you've fixed this. How do you intend to do so?"

"I haven't a clue."

"Apologize to the girl, Julian. Look the lass in the eye and tell her sincerely how terrible you feel and she will have no choice but to believe you. For it is quite clear to anyone who looks at you that you feel terrible, indeed."

Ben left the room and Julian went down to his study to start his work on the books. A stack of mail awaited him as well. He flipped through the invitations to dinner parties and balls. Most of Society was in the country as they headed into late September, but the few who remained enjoyed hosting events.

He doubted Elaina would be at any of these functions. But then he paused on the one invitation he was certain she'd accept.

The Aubrey Ball. Lord and Lady Aubrey were huge donors to Lord Darlington's expeditions. This ball would be where the official announcement of the journey to Egypt would be announced to entice attendees to contribute funds to the expedition. Julian knew the Darlington's could well afford their own expenses, but the team needed to launch such an undertaking year after year. The ship and crew and equipment were a great expense to find treasure in the desert.

And no doubt Elaina would be there to charm the men out of every shilling without realizing it.

Yes, this would be the perfect place for him to go through with his plan.

CHAPTER TWENTY

JULIAN HAD COUNTED down the days and hours until this night. Finally, Lainey would have her revenge and she wouldn't have to lift a finger to get it. He was pretty pleased with himself for coming up with the most perfect plan. She would have no choice but to forgive him after this.

"Wish me luck, Ben," Julian said as his valet and friend brushed out his evening coat.

"Luck, my lord?"

"Tonight is the night I will face Miss Bantham."

"Ah. You plan to apologize for your behavior?"

Bentley helped him into his coat and picked up the brush again to remove more non-existent lint. The man was the epitome of thoroughness.

"No. Even better. I plan to offer her vengeance." Julian smiled at his valet's somber reflection in the mirror.

The older man stopped brushing to cast a frown in his direction.

"Forgive me, my lord, but this sounds like something that will cause more damage. You made a mistake. In fact, one would say it was a misunderstanding because you were far too foxed to laugh at the girl intentionally. Rather you were just laughing in general. But no need to explain all of that. Just tell her how deeply sorry you are."

"Can't."

"Why not?" The man tapped the brush against his leg in what was clearly irritation.

"If I apologize, she might forgive me and it would be too easy. She never married. She left London after that night. I ruined her life, Ben. An apology is not enough."

"Proper young ladies do not generally seek vengeance, my lord."

"No. You're correct." He let out a breath. "Miss Bantham is not what the *ton* considers proper."

If she were, perhaps he could marry her to fulfill his father's wishes while also having a wife he could actually care for and enjoy spending his life with.

But whomever his father had tasked with approving Julian's choice certainly wouldn't give his blessing for a woman who wore men's clothes and spent much of her time digging in the dirt for treasure.

While Julian was fascinated that she'd traveled to the Orient rather than attend finishing school and could care less if she had the skills to be a proper countess, he couldn't jeopardize the mines and the people whose lives depended on them by marrying someone so unorthodox.

But he thought often of their kiss and the way it had heated his blood like no other's had. He'd thought it was because he'd known it was her first kiss and he'd worked hard to make sure it was as pleasant as possible. But that didn't explain why it had been so pleasant for him.

It surely wasn't *his* first kiss. Far from it.

Perhaps that's why he had the perspective to know that the kiss with Elaina had been truly remarkable.

Whatever it was didn't matter for he wouldn't be doing it again. Ever.

And even if he could offer for someone like her, she would never consider him.

He might have softened her with a kiss and charmed a few smiles from her, but that was far from wedded bliss. He had only barely earned the brief friendship she'd offered during their time in Scotland.

Besides, she would be leaving for Egypt soon enough and he… wouldn't.

He would have to count the expedition to Scotland as his grand adventure. The only thing he would be exploring now would be his options for a wife.

His heart clenched at the thought of marrying some stiff, society, debutante who would meet his father's requirement and leave Julian cold.

It didn't matter what he wanted. Not tonight.

Tonight, was all about Elaina and making things right.

He was nervous on the way to the ball. There would be dancing, but not all of society returned in October for the session, so it wouldn't be a crush. He was rather disappointed by that. It would have been better had there been a larger audience for what he had planned.

At the end of the night, Lord Darlington would make his announcement on who would be going with the team to Egypt. He knew he wouldn't hear his name mentioned, but it was fine, for after he gave Elaina the chance to take her revenge, he planned to slink out of the house and go home to lick his wounds.

As planned, he was one of the first to arrive, but rather than go inside, he waited as the other carriages arrived.

When Lord Darlington stepped down from his carriage and reached in to assist his wife and then his niece, Julian launched into action.

He bowed before the group.

"Lord Darlington, Lady Darlington, you look lovely tonight."

"Thank you, Lord Melville," the woman said cautiously.

Had Elaina told her about their kiss? He knew Lainey was close to her aunt, but if she had, even a stolen kiss could be used to force a marriage.

"I wasn't sure if we would see you this evening," she added and he realized she must be unhappy he'd left her niece in

Scotland without escort home.

Damn if he could do anything right when it came to Elaina. He planned to rectify the situation this evening.

Pressing on, he turned his gaze to Elaina and felt his stomach flutter excitedly. She was lovely in a moss green gown.

"Miss Bantham, would you allow me a moment?" He gestured toward the spot where he'd been waiting some feet away from the Darlingtons.

"Oh. Yes." She turned to her aunt and uncle. "I'll be along in a moment."

"We shall wait for you just over there," her aunt said sternly with her gaze sharply on Julian. "Don't be long."

Julian touched Elaina's arm and led her away from the couple, not wanting to keep her from the entertainments inside. The cold look of the viscountess, as much as the chilly night air, prompted him to get to the heart of the matter rather than dither.

"I need to explain why I left Scotland without speaking to you."

She winced, just slightly, but enough that he saw.

"I assure you, there is no need to discuss the matter. I understand." She had yet to meet his eyes and her cheeks had bloomed pink.

"You don't. You see, before we…" He glanced around before finishing quieter, "kissed. We were speaking of the reason you disliked me. You didn't get the chance to finish, but I remembered what happened that night. I recalled being so foxed I couldn't stop laughing and then Robert came up and called you a horrid name as a despicable joke and I laughed again. Or rather, I continued laughing. Of course, you couldn't have known the true reason why. You only know that I laughed and that was… deplorable."

"You were drunk?" She looked at him then, her eyes wide.

"Horribly so, but it's no excuse."

"It is some explanation. I've been drunk and can confirm the ease with which one finds everything unreasonably funny."

He smiled. "I would quite enjoy seeing you drunk." He imagined it briefly but moved on. "Anyway, I wanted to make amends. And I think I have found a way to make it up to you."

"You do not need to—"

"But I do. I wronged you and I think my actions have impacted you far more than I've realized. You deserve atonement."

"Atonement?"

"Yes. Tonight, when the dancing starts, I will come to ask for a dance, and you will give me the cut direct in front of everyone in attendance. I only wish it was the Season so there would be more people to see, but this was the best I could do. Try to be in the company of a group of people so they will witness my disgrace."

"This is completely unnecessary." She shook her head, her golden-fire hair was piled up on her head in a mess of curls. He wanted it down, filling his hands.

Shaking the thought away, he continued.

"It is what I deserve. Come now. Your aunt is glaring at me."

He escorted her to the door where the Darlingtons waited.

He offered Elaina a wink before ducking inside to face judgement for his crimes.

Finally, he would be free from this guilt.

Or so he hoped.

ELAINA FELT AS if she were made of wood as they entered the ballroom, and not just because she was cold from standing in the drive speaking with Julian. It had been a cool summer and autumn was taking the same path.

Was he mad? Julian wanted her to give him the cut direct in front of everyone. Leaving them to assume he had done something dishonorable. To be judged by everyone for something he did many years ago. Something he was too drunk to have done purposefully.

She hadn't even considered the reason he was laughing could have had nothing to do with her. She had already forgiven him and now it seemed she might even owe *him* an apology for judging him without knowing his true intentions.

She smiled and greeted their hosts. The Aubrey's were a lovely couple who supported their expeditions graciously.

Music was already playing and people were gathered around the small area that had been cleared for dancing.

Staying close to her aunt and uncle, she looked for an opportunity to pull Aunt Rose aside and ask her thoughts on how to proceed. But too many people wished to speak to them about their upcoming travels to Egypt.

Her uncle would be announcing where specifically they planned to dig on this journey. As well as the team that would accompany them.

True to his word, Lord Melville stepped up as soon as the dancing began. She was with her aunt and uncle and two other couples when he bowed and extended his hand.

"Miss Bantham, would you do me the honor of a dance?"

She paused and looked into his face, his kind blue eyes winced slightly as he waited for her to deliver her retribution and embarrass him in front of everyone. Even with only thirty or so people in attendance, the gossip would spread. Everyone would speculate as to what he had done to earn such a reaction.

Months ago, she would have been more than eager to claim her revenge and destroy him. But now she knew him better.

It didn't take but a second for her to know what she wanted to do.

She placed her hand lightly in his and said, "I would be delighted, my lord."

He blinked in surprise but didn't miss a beat as he led her to the dance floor.

"What was that? You were supposed to give me the cut. This was your chance," he whispered too loudly and called the attention of the couple next to them. Lainey smiled and waited until they had twirled away before speaking quieter than the earl.

"My chance to what? Shame you for something you did so long ago, while you were drunk? No. Besides, I am a wretched dancer, so you see, the steeper punishment is to take you up on your offer and subject you to dancing with me." She laughed at her joke, but he only watched her.

"Being allowed to touch you can never be considered a punishment, Elaina."

A shiver of excitement ran up her spine and she wanted so much to be able to find some quiet place to kiss him again.

"I forgive you, Julian."

"You can't. I haven't even offered an apology. That's not the way it's done."

"Do you think to tell me what I can and cannot do, my lord, because I should warn you, that would be foolish."

He chuckled and shook his head.

"I have been tormented over this since I realized. Do you know how deeply sorry I am for hurting you as I did?"

"I think I do. I'm glad I know what really happened. To know that you didn't laugh to be cruel. Letting go of this anger has been the best thing for me. I feel so light and free. I'm ready to live again without fear."

"You deserve nothing less. You are amazing. Though a horrid dancer—you weren't wrong about that."

She smacked him lightly in the shoulder as he turned her and she stepped on his foot yet again, making him laugh.

"While we're on the subject of my abominable behavior, I must also apologize for running off the way I did."

"Why did you leave?"

"After I realized what I'd done, I thought the kindest thing I could do was get out of your sight so you wouldn't have to so much as look at me."

She tilted her head and considered him.

"I don't think I mind looking at you." She scrunched up her

nose before adding, "Very much."

She'd been too honest and attempted to cover it with a joke. Fortunately, the dance came to a close and he released her to return to her aunt and uncle.

Unlike a proper ball, there were only a few dances, so she wasn't able to dance with Julian again. Or sit with him at the supper table.

She was surprised he hadn't said anything about Egypt. She'd initially thought he would attempt to get in her good graces in order to ensure he was allowed to go, but he hadn't mentioned it at all. Except to wish her pleasant travels when dinner was over.

When the time came to make the announcement, her uncle called out in his booming voice for everyone's attention. The smaller groups gathered into one mass around him so thick that Lainey couldn't even see her uncle.

But she could see Julian across the room where he leaned against a doorframe away from the fray.

She noticed the slight smile at his lips, most likely meant to disguise his disappointment.

He was not the man she'd thought him to be. He wasn't a villain set out to ruin her life. He had been a silly, drunken boy who'd made a mistake and thought he should be punished for it, even now.

She wondered why he expected such judgement for something he'd barely been guilty of. Watching him now, with the veil of anger gone, she saw him.

She saw the pain he tried to hide in humor, and the belief he wasn't worthy of forgiveness. No doubt this was more damage caused by his miserable father.

Bloody bastard, she ranted silently. She almost wished the bugger was still alive so she could tell him how awful he was.

Lainey wanted to go to Julian and tell him how amazing he was. How kind and intelligent and good. She wanted to do something to heal the pain she now saw.

"For our next expedition to Egypt we will set up our site in the royal necropolis of Dahshur at the Bent Pyramid."

The group gasped appreciatively and clapped, though most had no concept of what the announcement even meant. If they recognized the name, they would have only seen the pyramid in drawings. They might not even know why it was called *bent*.

She didn't judge them for it, and her uncle seemed to appreciate their approval, even if it held little merit.

"And we welcome the addition of Lord Melville to our team." Again, the group clapped, but she was watching the shock on Julian's face.

Once he suppressed his surprise, he turned to her with a tilt to his head, questioning her from across the room as to why she had allowed this.

Before he could take a step in her direction, he was mobbed by several men offering congratulations by way of clapping him heartily on the back and raising their glasses.

Rather than wait for him to have the chance to question her, she drifted away. Aunt Rose found her and asked if she was ready to go home.

She jumped at the opportunity to escape.

Julian would have questions and she wasn't sure yet how she might answer.

CHAPTER TWENTY-ONE

J ULIAN ACCEPTED CONGRATULATIONS from the group of people who had unfortunately blocked his view of Lainey. He felt like a fraud, but rather than call himself out in front of everyone, he waited until the crowd dispersed and he was alone with Lord Darlington.

"My lord, I must ask, did you override Miss Bantham's recommendation?" If the man had cast Lainey's opinion aside, Julian would have no choice but to decline the honor. He wouldn't challenge her wishes.

"Pardon?" the man cocked his head to the side. "Oh. No. Of course not. I told you she would be the one to decide whether you were suited to join us."

"And she stated that I was?" There must be some mistake. There was no way Elaina would have approved of him. She'd seen him at his worst. And he wasn't only referring to his drunken laughter.

"Yes." The man chuckled. "You seem surprised."

"It was clear your niece didn't want me to go when I first made the request." He rubbed the back of his neck trying to puzzle it out.

Lainey had said she'd already mailed off the letter with her decision before he'd kissed her. But perhaps she'd changed her mind after the kiss. Had Julian seduced her compliance after all?

"When did she tell you she approved of me?" he pushed.

He knew he should just stay quiet and be happy to be included. It was what he wanted after all. But not like this. Never like this.

"She wrote to me while you were in Scotland to tell me of your performance there. She stated you were hardworking and quick to ask questions so you could learn how to do things properly. She told me how thorough you were while excavating a piece of pottery you found. She even said she was impressed that you never once dismissed her authority over the site."

"Of course not. It was clear she was competent in handling a site."

"Surely you know how many men would think otherwise simply because they are men and she is a woman." He raised one of his fluffy gray eyebrows.

"I dare to hope I am not so ignorant as that."

Henry nodded in approval.

"May I ask why you expected a different outcome?" Both of the man's eyebrows had pulled up now, and Julian felt the question shift to something resembling a threat.

"As I said, your niece didn't care for me when I first asked to be included. I wasn't certain she would allow me to go even if I proved myself."

"My niece may be impulsive at times, but she is fair. I trust her judgement implicitly."

"As do I," Julian agreed truthfully. Except maybe in this. Why had she allowed him to join them? It made no sense. "Thank you for this once in a lifetime opportunity. I look forward to our journey. I'll be counting down the days until we can set sail."

"You will soon see there is much to be done before we leave and the time will go by quickly."

The man was not wrong. There was much to do before being away for four months. Normally he would be in the country over winter, but this year he would be in a warmer climate.

Still, he needed to make sure all of his estates were handled. He met with the steward and made sure enough funds were available for any unexpected expenses. It would take quite some time to get mail in Cairo.

With only a week left before it was time to leave, he visited his friend Hale at his home in Scotland.

"You're doing what?" his friend said, confusion clear on his face.

"I'm going to Egypt to explore the pyramids. We'll be working on the Bent Pyramid."

"You were just exploring in Scotland."

"As I told you at my last visit, my father is forcing me to marry before I turn thirty next May and I want to do something adventurous before I settle down."

"Some days I'm not sure which of us had the worst sire."

Julian didn't answer, but he was certain he had it worse than Hale had. Hale's parents left him alone on their estates. He only remembered seeing his father twice. Julian would have rather had an absent father than one who was involved in every aspect of his life and found fault in every breath he took.

But he hadn't walked in Hale's shoes, so he couldn't know what the duke felt.

"At least yours hasn't come back to haunt you from his grave with his ridiculous demands."

"If you pick the right woman for your wife, every day will be an adventure." He pointed to where Gia, the Duchess of Roxburghe led a giant stallion from the stables.

"I doubt my father would approve of an adventurous bride. I need to marry the perfect countess." Proper, chaste, boring.

"You need to make sure you are happy. It is your life. Marry for love and the rest will work out."

"*The rest* is my livelihood and that of the tenants and miners that depend on me. I am destined to be shackled to a staid, *proper* woman."

Julian thought briefly of the tall, red-headed hellion who wore men's breeches while she dug through the dirt. A smile came to his face when he thought of how it had felt to kiss her.

How she'd touched him back. She was innocent, but she wasn't staid or boring. Unfortunately, she wasn't proper either.

He hadn't seen Elaina since the night of the ball when her uncle announced that he would be joining the expedition. He hadn't had the chance to thank her in person, though he had sent a few bouquets of flowers to their home.

Each time he'd stopped in to visit, she and her aunt had been out gathering things for their journey.

In a week, it would be the new year, and they would be boarding a ship set for Africa and he would be with her again.

"I don't know what has brought that smile to your face, but whoever she is, you should pick her."

When he returned home, a number of parcels had arrived from Mr. Harper's shop.

"What is all this," Julian asked Spencer.

"There is a note, my lord." The butler held it out.

He recognized her writing immediately. He recalled the way her tongue had caressed her bottom lip as she focused on filling out the logs each afternoon. Now he knew what that lip felt like and how she tasted. A smile tugged at his lips as he eagerly opened the letter.

Lord Melville,

I've taken the liberty of commissioning some garments for you and Mr. Bentley for the expedition. As you are aware, the pyramids are in the desert, and it will be rather warm even in January. Therefore, loose-fitting, light-weight clothing is preferred as it allows the air to flow and keep one cooler.

Please reach out to Mr. Harper if you need any adjustments made.

—E

The smile on his face grew as he considered her gesture. He was most appreciative she had taken the time to see to his comfort as well as to Ben's. But this was more than that.

This was her way of showing her acceptance.

The smile faded slightly as he recalled her offer of forgiveness before he'd even made a proper apology.

He didn't deserve her acceptance. He didn't deserve to be welcomed on this journey. But knowing that wouldn't keep him from going.

It wasn't just about the adventure and his last chance to enjoy his freedom before being forced into a marriage he didn't want.

It was about Elaina. He wanted to see her again.

No. He wanted to kiss her again. And he knew he bloody well didn't deserve that either.

What a selfish bastard he was.

Hale's words floated around him.

I don't know what has brought that smile to your face, but whoever she is, you should pick her.

If only he could.

⇛⇚

"I DON'T HAVE to tell you, it isn't done to purchase clothing for a man," Aunt Rose mentioned as she and Lainey were sitting in the drawing room alone after dinner. "Especially *intimate* clothing."

"Is it a good thing then that I forwarded the bill to him as well? And confirmed that Melville paid it immediately." She smiled mischievously.

"You know what I mean," Rose said with a raised brow.

It wasn't done to *buy* a man undergarments suitable for the desert. It wasn't done to *wear* men's undergarments either. It wasn't done to spend weeks alone with a man or kiss him. Or want to kiss him again. Even still, knowing how very *not done* Lainey was in general, Aunt Rose's reaction puzzled her.

"Actually, I don't know what you are getting at. Before, you told me to be patient and friendly to the earl. Now you are accusing me of being too friendly? What am I to do?"

Rose let out a breath and put her book to the side.

"I didn't like seeing you unjustly angry at the man, but you must also protect yourself, Elaina. The man, while pleasant and an enthusiastic donor is still a rogue."

Lainey stared at her aunt in shock.

"You knew this and still sent me to Scotland with him un-chaperoned."

"That was Henry's idea. He thought it would get you past your anger, and he assured me, Lord Melville—despite his reputation—was not a debaucher of innocents. We knew you would be safe in his company. And it is you who refuses a chaperone."

The last was said with the raised eyebrow again.

"I wouldn't mind a chaperone if they didn't need to be with me at all times, hovering and watching over me."

"Perhaps you don't have a sound understanding of what a chaperone is, for you just described their every duty."

Lainey smiled tightly. "It is of no matter now, anyway. I will have you with me on this expedition, so I need no cranky, meddlesome, older woman ordering me about and pointing out all the ways I fail as a proper lady."

"Was he dishonorable?" Rose asked, nonchalantly with her eyes back on her book.

"Of course not. He was a perfect gentleman." Her cheeks heated when she thought of his kiss and his improper flirtation. When she looked toward her aunt she found the woman studying her. This was not good. Her aunt had the uncanny ability to see into Lainey's thoughts whether she spoke them aloud or not.

Had Lainey been smiling? She looked away, hoping to prevent the woman's powers of intuition.

"Anyway," Lainey paused, as Aunt Rose still scrutinized her. "It will not be the same. The expedition to Egypt will be much larger. I will rarely see Lord Melville on this excursion."

"I see."

Lainey refrained from asking her aunt exactly what she saw. Could her aunt see how eager Lainey was to see Julian again?

How often she thought about the kiss they'd shared, and the dance, his hand on her back, warming her. The things they'd shared in Scotland. How he'd thanked her for helping him through his attack of anxiety?

No. Aunt Rose couldn't see any of that. If she did, she'd probably not allow the man on the same continent as her spinster niece.

But he would be on the same continent. The same ship. The same expedition. Just a few tents from hers when they slept.

"The man needed the correct clothing for the warmer climate. That is all." Elaina noticed how snappish she sounded and tempered it with a nervous smile.

"Of course. Forgive me for suggesting anything untoward." A few pages later, she added, "You are a grown woman. It wouldn't be the worst thing to share a discreet kiss with a handsome gentleman."

"Aunt Rose!" Lainey could feel her eyes widen in shock as her cheeks warmed.

"What?" Rose rolled her eyes. "I was a young woman once. Do you think your uncle waited until after our vows to kiss me?"

"This conversation is unseemly."

"Why?" Rose barely held back her laughter. "It is the way of men and women when there is a shared attraction. Just be cautious, love. One cannot un-ring a bell."

"Dear God," Lainey whispered before saying more loudly, "I assure you there is no attraction, shared or otherwise, between myself and Lord Melville." Lainey spat the lie from her lips forcefully to help establish it as fact.

And perhaps there was more truth in her words than she thought. After all, Julian had gotten what he wanted from her. Unlike a rake preying on an innocent, it wasn't Lainey's virtue he'd wanted. It had been her acquiescence to allow him to come on this journey.

She wouldn't expect him to pay her any attention at all now that he'd gotten what he wanted.

And why did that thought bring a sting to her eyes?

Aunt Rose had warned her to be cautious and had most likely meant in the way all virgins were told to be cautious. But Lord Melville exposed a far greater danger to her heart. He had broken down her long-standing walls with his kindness and laughter.

She was defenseless against him now.

CHAPTER TWENTY-TWO

AFTER HE AND Ben were situated in their adjoining rooms below deck, Julian brought the older man up on deck. This would be Ben's first sea voyage and Julian wanted to make sure he had a sound familiarity with the side of the boat in case he was to need it.

They came across their hosts, and Julian expressed his thanks once again after introducing them to Bentley.

"No need to thank us," Lady Darlington said.

"Then I shall thank your niece."

"I'm glad she overcame her resistance to your joining us," Lord Darlington offered.

Julian felt a twinge of guilt knowing the man surely wouldn't be glad Julian was onboard if he'd known he'd taken liberties with the man's ward. It had only been a kiss, but Julian knew Lord Darlington would not be pleased.

"It is a good day to sail," the man said.

Julian agreed. The sun warmed him despite the January breeze. It seemed everyone wanted to stay up on deck for as long as possible.

Lord Darlington bowed as they went off to greet the other guests.

It was as Julian was greeting Mr. and Mrs. Leighton that he noticed Miss Bantham. *Elaina.* Standing near the front of the ship. He could practically feel the eagerness to set sail radiating from her.

She was wearing a gown and a shawl. He should have expected as much. But in his fantasies of her, she was always wearing snug breeches and a thin shirt. And there had been plenty of fantasies in the months since he'd seen her at the ball. The ball where he'd attempted to make things right, but instead had danced with her.

"There she is," he whispered to Bentley, though why he thought he needed to whisper was beyond him. She was still much too far away to hear him.

"Shall we move forward to greet her or run in the other direction? I'm never quite sure."

He'd told Ben what happened at the ball. How his plans had been turned on their nose thanks to Lainey. Ben, of course, didn't seem surprised that she had forgiven him so easily. If Julian understood his valet's mumblings correctly, he'd said something about *dramatics*.

Julian chuckled. "Neither am I, but I think for the moment I'd prefer to do neither."

"Stand here staring at the lass, then?"

"When you say it like that it sounds rather disturbing."

"Quite."

"Do you think women are like food, Ben?" He blurted without thinking.

He turned to see his valet obviously thinking. Surely, he was trying to puzzle out what Julian meant.

"What I mean to say is, any food seasoned with hunger tastes like the most wonderful meal one has ever had. Do you think the more deeply you know a woman, the more beautiful she becomes? I must admit when I first met her, I thought her pleasant enough, but seeing her now with the breeze blowing whisps of her hair about, she is the most beautiful creature I've ever encountered."

"You've missed her," Ben said.

"Yes." Julian was nearly shocked by the truth of it. "Yes, I have missed talking with her. Hearing all the things she finds interesting. Making her laugh."

She turned her head to brush her hair from her eyes and noticed them.

He warmed over when a smile pulled up on her lips and she waved.

"I'm not sure if she missed you, my lord. But I'm certain she has missed me."

Julian chuckled at the man's wit.

When Julian didn't move, he added, "Perhaps we should go speak with her."

"Yes. Right. We should."

Their gazes held as he closed the distance between them. He wanted nothing more than to kiss her. The way her eyes lowered made him think she had considered the same thing, but recovered rather quickly.

"Miss Bantham, you remember my friend and valet, Mister Bentley."

"Of course. It is a pleasure to have you aboard, Mister Bentley. I hope you will find travel by sea enjoyable."

"Thank you. It is so wonderful to see you again, Miss Bantham. Might I say how lovely you look? The morning air agrees with you." Ben was quite the charmer with the ladies. Elaina blushed prettily from his compliment.

"Please, allow me to show you around," she offered.

The three of them strolled the deck together, Elaina explaining the different parts of the ship and their uses. When it was time to set sail, they made their way to the side of the vessel so they could watch as the shores of England grew smaller and smaller.

It was not long until they arrived in Calais for additional cargo and a few more crew members before they were off yet again.

Fortunately, Ben took to sailing like a fish.

"I must admit to a great deal of excitement," he said as he dressed Julian for dinner at the captain's table that evening.

"Thank you for allowing me to join you."

"After putting up with me for so long, you deserve a vacation, old chap. I know I'm not the easiest person."

Ben tapped him on the shoulder so Julian would look at him in the mirror.

"Don't allow your father's harsh opinion of you to cloud the truth, my lord. You are a kind man. A true gentleman."

"Thank you, Ben."

"Miss Bantham is a gem. Lovely inside and out. Perhaps that is what you see when you look upon her now."

"She was very angry at me before, and for good reason. But now that she's not..." He remembered their kiss and wished for her taste on his lips even more than whatever would be served for dinner.

"Well, don't keep her and the others waiting." He brushed Julian's shoulder in more a pat.

In the captain's quarters, Julian had hoped to be seated next to Elaina, but his title placed him in the seat of honor next to Captain Cartwright.

"Is this your first voyage to Africa?" the man asked.

"Yes. I traveled the continent. But it was rather without imagination. This will be an adventure."

The man nodded in agreement as Julian looked down the table and spotted Elaina.

An adventure, indeed.

LAINEY ENJOYED THE meal and conversation with Mr. Randolph who had accompanied them on a number of expeditions. At three and forty, the man's weathered appearance did nothing to detract from his handsomeness.

Lainey had once considered him a viable partner. After all, they were often on the same digs and enjoyed each other's conversation. But there were no real emotions involved.

She'd thought it wasn't necessary. But that was before she'd gotten to know Julian. At times she felt there might be too many emotions between them.

She glanced in his direction again and found him watching her. She pressed her lips together to keep from smiling as Mr. Randolph was speaking about a guide who had lost a foot to a crocodile and therefore was not a cause for grinning with joy.

But joy was surely what she felt bubbling inside her stomach at Julian's attention.

If she'd thought for a moment he had only kissed her in order to make his way on this ship, it was clear that wasn't the case. For he was already on the ship. His attendance assured. Yet he still looked at her as if he wanted to be closer to her.

When dinner was over, she found him on deck, leaning on the rail with the wind blowing his dark hair. He looked perfectly comfortable in any situation, she envied him that since she was quite the opposite. Never truly fitting in anywhere.

When he saw her, he stood up straight and offered a smile and a bow.

"Good evening, Miss Bantham."

"My lord." She curtseyed thinking it odd to be so formal with someone she'd kissed. But surely it was the way it was done. She couldn't go about calling him by his given name where anyone might hear.

Except they were alone at the moment so perhaps the formality was meant to keep distance between them.

"It's a beautiful evening, is it not?" She nodded at the sun setting with a colorful display like fire across the horizon. She pulled her shawl closer to fend off the chilly air. Soon she wouldn't have need for such things.

"It is. I've never seen the sky seem quite so big."

"Yes. The ocean serves as a mirror. Reflecting back the beauty of the heavens."

They stood in comfortable silence for a few moments, taking

in the view even as the sun dipped below the horizon. When the colors on the water dimmed, he turned to her.

"Why am I here?" he asked.

"Do you mean in the broader scope of existence? Seeing such a powerful display often makes one feel small." She knew, of course, what he was asking but decided to have fun with him.

He laughed as she expected.

"Why did you give your approval? Why did you allow me to come on the expedition? I didn't sway you by kissing you, did I? I didn't mean to—"

"You didn't sway my decision. As I said, I had already decided."

"But you hated me."

"My uncle asked me to evaluate your abilities. While I might not have wanted you to join us initially, I had to consider your request fairly. You are worthy of this opportunity, Julian."

"Thank you. I will do my best to ensure you don't regret your decision." His smile seemed more relaxed. If she'd still doubted his intentions, his reaction would have put her at ease.

He was a good person. He never meant to hurt her and had gone well beyond what was necessary to redeem himself.

"I doubt I will come to regret anything when it comes to you, my lord." She cleared her throat when she realized what she'd said aloud. "I'm only glad I managed to see past my anger. I would have surely missed out on a wonderful friendship, had I not."

Friendship? Were they friends? They had kissed. Did friends kiss? Or was she supposed to pretend the kiss hadn't happened? How would she manage to ignore something like that?

After a few moments of silence, she decided it would be best to handle the situation straight on. They would be spending too much time together in limited space on their journey to Egypt.

"Please forgive me, I'm not certain how one interacts with someone they have kissed after the fact. It feels rather awkward and I don't wish it to be."

"Ah. Generally, one just ignores it and avoids the person so it never comes up again."

"Is that what you want to do?" She hoped not.

"Heavens, no. I'm much too lazy for such things. Avoiding someone on a ship—though large as it is—seems like too much work."

They shared a laugh and when it died down, he reached out to take her hand. His touch sent a tingle up her arm and directly to the pit of her stomach.

"Perhaps kissing you again would be the answer. No awkwardness. Just a man and a woman, sharing a moment during a dwindling sunset."

She gestured to the deck they were standing on. "As large as the ship may be there are not many unmarried women onboard," she pointed out. Like in Scotland, his options were limited.

He tilted his head and blinked at her.

"I wouldn't care if there were hundreds of women on the ship. I want to kiss you because you are beautiful and I enjoy kissing you. Immensely. Especially since, as you've pointed out, I will suffer no risk of neck strain."

His words were lovely. What woman wouldn't want to hear a man desired her? But it was those very words that made her frown for they were completely unbelievable.

He studied her for a moment as if she were an unidentified artifact just plucked from the ground.

"You don't believe me," he said quietly.

She shrugged and looked away. "I know I'm not… beautiful. You don't need to charm me. I would rather you be honest."

He chuckled and shook his head.

"I have never been more honest. And I know you are not being coy. You truly believe you are lacking in some way? Is it because of what happened at your come out?"

She shrugged but said nothing.

"I know well how hurtful things are more easily believed. I can't tell you how often I hear my father's voice in my ear listing all the ways I am lacking."

"It isn't true," she said forcefully.

"And neither is what Robert Bloody Dunnage said that evening. He is no one of consequence. Yet his words have burrowed deep inside your soul and even now cause you to doubt me—someone I would hope you could trust at least more than that bastard."

She considered his words and was rather embarrassed to admit he was right.

"I guess it is true. The insult apparently penetrated deeply—" Her explanation was cut off. "You're laughing."

Julian wasn't just laughing. He was bent over with his arm across his stomach, fully enraptured in mirth.

"Forgive me," he said when he had settled enough to speak. "It's just..." Another round of laughter erupted. "You said 'penetrated deeply.'"

She pressed her lips together to keep from being pulled into his nonsense.

"Lord Melville, I think you should wear short pants as a warning to all you meet that your humor is still that of an adolescent."

"Or perhaps you want to see my bare legs?" He winked as she rolled her eyes.

"You are a menace."

"Forgive me," he sobered somewhat. "You should know I use humor to distract people from noticing when I'm uncomfortable. Often with inappropriate jests."

"And why would you be uncomfortable now? With me?"

"Because the pain and doubt I saw in your eyes is my fault. Because of me, you don't know the truth about yourself. You can't see it. All you believe are the cruel words Lord Dunnage spoke and my laughter. You are lovely. And a man—especially one who has already had the pleasure of your kiss—doesn't need a reason to want to kiss you beyond the sheer pleasure of it."

She swallowed as she looked in his eyes, searching for any hint he was saying this to manipulate her. All she saw was... the truth. She had allowed that piggish Dunnage to shape her view of herself when he wasn't worthy of that importance.

But this man before her was significant. And he thought she was beautiful.

"Oh," she whispered.

He smiled. "Now, if you don't mind, you have the most enticing freckle at the edge of your lip that is beckoning me to lick it."

She took a step closer in silent approval of his plan.

Like the first time he'd kissed her, it started off as a soft, slow press of lips, but this time it was she who escalated from there.

Knowing better what to expect, she reached for his hair pulling him to her so she could open her mouth and receive him. Mingling her tongue with his as his arms banded around her waist and back, securing her to him completely.

With her eyes closed she could feel the sway of the ship under their feet making her slightly unsteady. She opened her eyes.

He pulled back enough for a smile and kept his blue gaze on hers as he dipped his head to kiss her again.

Kissing is intimate, but kissing while looking at the person was even more so. As if he were looking into her soul. And he was just as open to her. She stared into his eyes and saw all the happiness, excitement, and desire within.

For her.

Everything she'd thought was true burned away, and only Julian's words remained.

"You are beautiful."

She believed him.

$$\textasciitilde \bullet \textasciitilde$$

CHAPTER TWENTY-THREE

JULIAN FELT HER lips pull up in a smile against his and he pulled her closer.

Kissing had always been a prelude to something more fulfilling. But kissing Lainey was different. He could feel something growing between them and it wasn't just his erection.

It was trust.

And it was enough. No. It was everything.

She had forgiven him already, but now she believed him.

And he had no choice but to believe her. She'd told him he'd earned the right to come on this journey and he would have to accept that. No matter what doubts spun around in his head.

He pulled back only far enough to look at her. His hands still rested on her ribs, he could feel her sides move with her breathing which was quicker than normal.

He'd done that.

She took a deep breath and tilted her head back. He mirrored her and gasped.

"They look so close, don't they?" she said in an awed voice.

"I've never seen so many stars." As she'd said, they did look close enough to touch. The way they reflected off the water enhanced the effect. He'd never seen anything so beautiful, and sharing it with the woman next to him, made the moment even sweeter.

He could almost believe his life could always be like this. He knew better. He knew what kind of life waited for him, but he would always have this, and he would forever be grateful.

"Thank you, Lainey."

"For what?" she asked turning to look at him.

"For giving me this. A moment I will cherish for as long as I live."

She leaned up and kissed him, something no other woman had been able to do. Joy passed between them and soon they were smiling as if they couldn't help themselves.

When she shivered, he suggested they retire to their rooms so he could get her out of the chilly, night air.

Instead, she snuggled closer to him, wrapping her arms around his waist under his coat. Yes, this was better than returning to their rooms alone. They shared the stillness in silence for some time. But soon he was thinking of all the reasons he didn't deserve to be there with her.

"I must confess something," he said finally.

"All right." She gazed up at him as if she trusted him completely. He didn't want to give her any reason not to. But he needed to be honest with her.

"I told you I was drunk the night I laughed at Robert's horrid jest."

"Yes."

"As I said, I was just laughing in general, not at you specifically."

"Yes."

He wanted to stop speaking right then rather than say something that could ruin this moment, but the truth bubbled free.

"I do worry that had I not been drunk I might have laughed anyway," he said hating himself for it.

"Why do you think that?" she asked, not reacting in any way.

"Not because you were laughable at all, but because at that time in my life, I was desperate for friends. My true friends were still in Scotland. I was alone and I wanted those despicable lords to accept me. My father thought they were acceptable and after spending my life with my father who never was satisfied with me, I might have felt obligated to laugh at Robert's foolishness so I fit in with them."

"And this bothers you?" she asked.

"Of course, it does. You seem to have forgiven me because I was inebriated, but I feel that is unjust."

"You still want me to seek my revenge so your conscience will be clear?"

"You must admit, I got off rather easy. You should have given me a right thrashing."

She crossed her arms and was even more appealing for her stern look. He wanted to kiss her until she cracked into laughter again. But he refrained.

"Very well. I will think on it and determine a proper punishment so you can finally let this go."

"Hale and Kit didn't arrive in London until after my father was gone."

"They accepted you?"

"Without consideration. It was rather like it was with you. At least after you stopped hating me. But it is easy to speak to you. Actually, even easier than with them."

"Because we know each other's demons?"

"Perhaps." He shook his head. "Actually, I don't think it is because of what you already know, but because I feel like I want you to know everything."

They stared into each other's eyes, not speaking but sharing something that went beyond words and then she leaned forward and kissed him.

LAINEY KNEW WHERE this kiss was leading and she didn't shy away from it. She wanted this with him more than anything else. She's spent most of her life seeking adventure, but in her heart, she knew nothing she had seen or would ever see would touch her the way this man did when he looked at her the way he was then.

She wrapped her arms around his waist and whispered to him.

"Please, Julian. Show me everything." She was unsure what exactly to ask for but was certain he took her meaning. He didn't refuse or seem shocked by her request, but he did back away, a bit of sadness returning to his lovely eyes.

"Before this goes any further, I must tell you something. It is very important you understand."

"All right. What is it?" she asked, worried about his seriousness.

"I cannot marry you."

She stepped back and studied his reaction. She had not asked for marriage. Had not assumed or even hinted. But somehow hearing him make such a statement hurt.

She stood straighter, her common response when under attack. But she saw by the pain in his own eyes that he did not intend to wound her.

"It is not that I wouldn't want to. My dead father threatens my most profitable properties if I do not wed a proper lady by my thirtieth birthday. More important than the money, are the mines I currently own. They would be turned over to a man who will surely put them back to the way they had been when I took over the title. It wasn't safe. There were children working all day. Their homes were unfit and they barely had enough to eat. I can't allow that to happen. Those people are my responsibility. Their safety and wellbeing are important to me. Which means I have to concede to his wishes."

He let out a breath as if in defeat.

"I have until the end of May to find a wife. And not just any wife. My father has someone appointed to approve the woman I choose. I know my father's definition of *proper* will be someone who has been training to be a lord's wife her entire life."

He shook his head.

Lainey suddenly felt as if something she had always wanted had been stolen away from her. But until he had mentioned marriage, she had not even considered such a possibility. Now, though, knowing it couldn't be, she felt the absence immensely.

"I always planned to do my duty eventually," he went on. "But it is being thrust upon me and I despise the blighter even more, and I didn't realize that was possible." He laughed sadly and shook his head.

"This is why you wanted to come to Egypt?"

"Yes. One grand adventure of my own choosing before I'm forced into the life he has selected for me." He rubbed his forehead. "I have no choice. Which is exactly how he planned it, I'm sure."

He pulled away and walked in a circle, clearly agitated as he discussed his father.

"My bastard of a father who has been dead for years continues to control me from beyond the grave. I must marry a *proper* countess."

Proper. She honed in on that word.

He swallowed and looked her in the eye. Neither of them needed to say with words what they both knew.

She would never be a proper countess.

"I'm sorry," she offered because she could see the pain this caused him.

"*You're* sorry? *You* have nothing to apologize for. I should have told you sooner. Before I'd kissed you. Before I'd touched you. But I am at least honorable enough to bring a halt to this before it goes too far. I will not take your virtue knowing I cannot offer marriage."

She shook her head.

"I would never force you to marry me. Especially now that I know what you stand to lose if you did."

"But what I would gain..." He looked away and shook his head furiously. "The man never approved of anything I did. Never a kind word of praise. Not one murmur of encouragement. And now he will take this from me too. Take you from me."

Seeing his anguish and hearing his words of regret steeled her decision.

She leaned up to kiss him, the touch of her lips calmed him instantly. She pulled away to look into the blue depths of his gaze.

"Take me to your quarters, Julian."

He blinked and his brows pulled together.

Making sure he understood exactly what she planned, she swallowed before saying, "Make love to me."

"I cannot. I won't do that to you."

"You wanted to come to Egypt to gain an experience you will never have again. I granted it. I am asking only for the same thing. I am three and twenty with no future prospects. I am asking you to give me this experience that I will never have again, so I too can have my own memory to treasure."

He looked miserably torn as he studied her face, his eyes flickering back and forth as if he was looking for something to dispute her words. He wouldn't find anything because she was resolved to this course.

She wanted him. Even knowing it would not result in a future with him.

"We only have now, Julian. Let's not waste it."

Her words seemed to unlock something inside of him and when he pulled her against him and kissed her, she realized he had been restraining much of his passion until now.

He pulled back, his breathing already ragged.

"I want to do the honorable thing and refuse, but you are not an impressionable maid. I have to trust that you know what you want."

"I do know. I want this."

"Then what right do I have to think I know what is better for you? I would be as bad as my sire dictating my will on others."

She nodded.

"I will take precautions, Lainey, but are you sure this is what you want?"

"Yes. I understand."

"Then lead the way."

CHAPTER TWENTY-FOUR

THE AIR WAS warmer as they descended into the lower rooms of the ship. Julian's quarters were larger than hers and down a narrow corridor from the other passengers, including her aunt and uncle.

Once inside the room, she felt her first wave of nervousness. Lainey had been so sure of her decision up on the deck while Julian kissed her, but now, she realized how much she didn't know of what happened between a man and a woman.

"If you've changed your mind, you need only to say so and I will escort ye to your room," Julian said softly as he took her hand and kissed her palm. His accent heavier.

A shiver of excitement stole through her body at such a simple touch.

"I have not changed my mind. In fact, I am more certain I want to do this with you. I'm just afraid I don't know enough to do this well. I don't want you to be disappointed."

He shook his head.

"Never. Even if you changed your mind."

She kissed him and then offered what she hoped was a flirty smile.

"You can give up on that, Julian. I am set on this path. Now tell me what I should do."

Rather than tell her, he kissed her again. But unlike their other kisses, she knew he didn't hold back at all. There was no reason to worry they were being swept away, when being swept away was the welcome expectation.

"I need to see ye," he said, his brogue more distinct.

She took his hint and reached to remove her gown, but he stopped her. She gave him a confused look, but he only smiled and turned her so he could see to her his gown himself. As if he were a lady's maid.

She might have laughed at the thought, but his touch on the bare skin of her back was anything but humorous.

It felt as if he touched her with a flame. She didn't even notice her gown was gone until he turned her to him again. His gaze lowered and she looked down to see what had his blue eyes darken so with lust.

Her shift was quite thin and in the low light of the lantern, it appeared to be transparent. She saw her tightened nipples through the light fabric.

She might have been embarrassed, but nothing in Julian's gaze made her feel anything but desired.

He bent and pulled her nipple into his warm mouth. She gasped at both the surprise of something so naughty as well as so pleasurable.

He moved to the other breast and treated it to the same thorough inspection before kissing his way up her chest, throat and jaw to come back to her lips.

His fingers tickled her collarbone as he untied her shift and pushed the fabric over her shoulders to drop at her feet atop her discarded gown.

She felt the edge of his large bed against her thighs and he guided her to sit. She reached for him, wanting to kiss him again, but he bent to remove her half boots. She expected him to remove her stockings next, but to her surprise, he left those in place as he kissed his way up her leg.

When his lips passed the threshold of stocking to bare skin she expelled a slight moan that caused his lips to pull up before he continued his path up.

She was bare to him and couldn't care what she might look like. He was giving her this experience and she was determined not to ruin it with inhibition.

She felt his warm breath against her center only a moment before his hot tongue stroked her damp folds. As if by instinct she reached for him as her own breath picked up. She sounded as if she'd run up a hill when all she'd done so far was lie there and let him do as he wished.

His mouth continued to move over her as she shifted restlessly, wanting more. And then he slipped a finger inside her body, stroking her in the same way from the inside as his tongue caressed her outside.

When she adjusted to that, another finger entered her and the fullness was nothing other than sublime. She was now moaning with each small pant that left her lips. Until his tongue focused in on one small spot and her breathing seemed to stop as she was catapulted into utter bliss.

A delightful throbbing rolled through her as he continued until the waves became smaller pulses. She opened her eyes to see he was now standing over her with the most adorable smile on his face.

"So beautiful," he said.

She smiled in response to his words, but smiling seemed to be all she was capable of doing at the moment.

What had he done to her? And when could he do it again?

JULIAN WATCHED ELAINA come back to him as he removed his shirt and tugged off his boots. She was without a doubt the loveliest woman he'd ever seen.

She blinked up at him and smiled and his heart nearly seized in his chest.

She thought she was the one who wanted this new experience, but he found it was a new experience for him as well.

He was no virgin, and he'd seen to make sure his partners were well satisfied in the past, but this was the first time he'd ever felt so overwhelmed with a need to connect with another person.

With his breeches still on he leaned down and kissed her softly. He was still hard and aching, but if what he'd done was enough for her, he wouldn't press for more.

Of course, his brave lass wouldn't be happy with that.

"While that was quite the most wonderful thing I've ever experienced in my life, I do know, at least, there is more to it." She nodded toward the bulge in his breeches. "That will go where your fingers were?"

He nodded. "Aye. But it will not be as easy as my fingers. It will hurt."

"But just at first."

"Yes," he answered, though he had no way of knowing for sure. He'd never been with a virgin before. "I think so."

They shared a long look before she nodded and said, "I'm ready."

"Are you sure, Elaina? We can stop now if you wish."

"No. I want it all."

He laughed. "Ye are demanding, but I am your servant, my lady."

He undid his falls and dropped his breeches.

When he looked back to her, she was studying his cock which was practically preening in her attentions.

"It is an odd thing, is it not?" his adventuress said.

He laughed and lay beside her so he could kiss her again. His laughter was cut short when she reached between them to touch him. Her soft hand wrapped around his length, eliciting a groan of pleasure from him.

Her other hand caressed the skin along his back. He'd surely been touched there before, but not noticed until it was Elaina who touched him so intimately.

When he rolled over her, she opened her legs for him in

invitation. He settled against her in the place they were meant to join. But rather than push as he wanted to, he held and looked into her eyes, silently asking again if she wanted this.

Her leg came up along his hip and wrapped around his waist as if it were the arm of an octopus pulling its prey toward its demise. Julian didn't attempt escape, instead giving into his exquisite fate.

She tensed when he entered her and he waited once more until she relaxed around him. He leaned down to kiss her and began to move.

Her eyes opened and she smiled softly at him. He realized he was smiling too, such was his happiness in this moment. All his life he'd searched for acceptance, and he didn't think he'd ever feel it so strongly as he did in that moment with Elaina.

He kept things slow for as long as they both could stand. She clung to him, grasping tightly and lifting her hips to meet his. When her eyes closed and her breathing turned into little moans, he reached down to touch her.

A few thrusts more and she broke around him, grasping him in a much different way. He managed to hold out until her grip on his relaxed and he pulled from her body to spend on her stomach where he hoped it would cause no danger for either of them.

He pulled her close, feeling her heart beating quickly against his ribs. He placed kisses to her hair and her forehead and then her lips. Noticing how right she'd been about how they fit together.

She was perfect for him in every way. So many people went through life never finding such a match. But Julian had it in Elaina.

And despite the odds and his overwhelming happiness, Julian would have to give her up.

But not today.

And not for the next few months to come.

CHAPTER TWENTY-FIVE

LAINEY WAS NUDGED awake what felt like hours later. She'd enjoyed sleeping next to Julian almost as much as the sex, however she wouldn't want to be caught in his room in the morning.

"I wish you could stay with me," he whispered as he helped her dress. She smiled sleepily liking that he felt the same way she did. He insisted on seeing her to her room even though it was only down the corridor and around the corner.

She had wanted to have this experience and was grateful for Julian that he had given her what she wanted. But as she settled in her own lonely bed, she was already thinking of all the nights that lay before them and how much she hoped they would spend them together.

The next thing she knew it was morning and people were moving about the ship. She was a bit sore, but in the best way. She told Julian as much which caused him to pull her behind a pile of cargo to kiss her.

They spent their days above deck enjoying the warmer weather that had met them along their journey. They visited with others. Ben spent a good bit of time on deck. As did her aunt and uncle and the Leightons.

Lainey always looked forward to the evening meal knowing that afterward they would spend the rest of the evening and into the night alone together.

They were treated to pleasant weather and made good time according to the captain.

They rose early one morning to a beautiful sunrise over the Rock of Gibraltar.

She had seen it many times, but never with Julian who stood awestruck by the beauty before him.

"This is something that can never be taken from me. This memory of this perfect moment with you." He looked around to make sure they were alone before bending to kiss the side of her neck, his arms pulled her snug against him. "I will never be able to thank you enough for allowing me to come on this trip, Elaina."

She shrugged. "I'm not so sure about that. You have made the trip quite pleasant for me."

He growled against her skin.

"I am not sure how you came to think I am making some great sacrifice to make love to you every night, but I shall allow you to continue to think me a gallant gentleman for it."

A week later, they docked at the Port of Alexandria. They had dinner that night with the Visiting Consul of Egypt who had become a dear friend of Uncle Henry's.

"I do not like the way he looks at you," Julian complained that night when they were in bed together.

"How ever does he look at me?"

"As if he plans to have his way with you."

"I believe you have spent too much time in the sun and heat. Your brain is causing you to see things that are not so."

"I know what a man looks like when he is interested in a woman. If you doubt it, you have only to look at the way I look at you and compare it to the Consul and see as much for yourself."

Lainey laughed off his accusation but the next morning as they ate breakfast in the palace, she did notice the special attention the man gave her.

Perhaps this experience with Julian was more enlightening

than she'd first imagined. The man bent over her hand and kissed her knuckles as they made ready to leave for Cairo.

Watching Julian's face when the camels were led out was a great thrill. She helped instruct him on how to mount.

"It isn't like a horse," she told him.

"I'm aware, Elaina. I've never had a horse spit at me before."

She tried not to laugh at his disgusted expression, but some snickers escaped.

"I'm beginning to think you allowed me to come on this expedition to provide entertainment for you."

"Lainey, it isn't polite to laugh at Lord Melville," her aunt chastised her.

"I am all that is apologetic for my insensitivity," she said. It might have been received better if she wasn't laughing through her apology.

Eventually, Julian wrangled his surly camel into obedience and they were on their way. Though they lagged far behind the others.

Lainey didn't mind overmuch since it meant she was alone with Julian.

"I'm riding a camel in Egypt," he said as if in disbelief. "Do you see this, Elaina? I'm on a real adventure."

Having been to Egypt a few times before as well as many other faraway places, Lainey realized she'd come to take their adventures for granted. Here was a man who only wanted but one thing he could always claim as something he'd done.

She looked out across the desert as if seeing it through Julian's eyes and realized how amazing this opportunity was.

"While I sometimes wish I'd had a more orthodox upbringing, I must say I'm grateful I did not. This is truly a gift."

They made camp each night as they traveled and since they were up at first light to leave and only stopped long enough to eat and sleep, Lainey stayed in a tent with her aunt and uncle while Julian stayed with Ben.

They were not alone enough during their travels to even steal so much as a kiss, but she knew she was not the only one who suffered. She was reassured that once they made it to Dahshur and set up more permanent residences, they would have an opportunity to be alone again.

It was midday when the first pyramid came into view. They were still days away from the Bent Pyramid, but as they entered the Valley of the Gods, it was most impressive.

She looked over to Julian who was silent as he took them in.

"I knew they were immense. I'd seen paintings, but you can't imagine this. It can only be understood when seen with one's own eyes."

She nodded.

"I don't know if I've thanked you, Elaina."

"Only about a hundred times," she mused.

"I am forever grateful you allowed me to come," he said. "Whatever happens, my father cannot take this moment from me."

Lainey planned to do whatever she could to give Julian an experience he would never forget. And she hoped he wouldn't forget her either for she would never forget him.

IT HAD TAKEN nearly a month to get to their expedition sight near the Bent Pyramid. The tents were put up in a cluster, but Lainey managed to keep hers closer to Julian's and further away from her aunt and uncle.

It was an easy enough thing to sneak into his tent when the camp fell quiet that first night. His bed was larger than hers since he was a proper lord of some size.

Like hers, his skin smelled of exotic oils from his earlier bath as he removed his shirt and pulled her closer to him.

"We must be quiet," she warned. "We are on the edge of the other tents, but we are only separated by fabric."

He smiled and kissed her. "As I recall it isn't me who makes so much noise as to wake an entire ship."

She smacked him playfully and moaned softly as he kissed down her neck and pulled her shirt over her head. Perhaps he was right. She would need to be cautious of the noises she made.

It proved to be one of the most difficult things she'd ever done as he slipped inside her body and began rocking them together in earnest. She'd missed him horribly and worried what would happen when they returned to London and she would go back to her life as a spinster. How would she manage?

When her body reached the critical point when she lost complete control over herself, Julian set a scalding kiss on her lips which served to muffle her climax. He was better suited for such a tryst as he made the smallest sound during his release and then held her close until he calmed.

She would need to learn how he managed such a thing so they wouldn't be caught. She lived in fear of such a thing, but wasn't willing to miss the chance to be with him. It was a reckless game she played. For there could be no offer of marriage if they were caught in a compromising position. Julian had obligations to the people who depended on him.

He needed to marry a proper countess and the very fact that Lainey had sneaked into his tent to have an illicit affair with Julian was more than enough proof she was not proper.

They lay together until sleep pulled at them. Then she left his tent for her own.

That first night, as she lay alone in her smaller bed, finally sated since they'd left the ship, she allowed a few tears to fall. For she wished things could be different. She wished things could be forever.

It seemed both of them had only this short adventure to create a lifetime of memories. And she wouldn't miss a single one.

WHEN JULIAN WALKED into the tent for breakfast the next morning, Lainey watched him searching for her. When he found her, he winked and offered that devilish grin she'd come to desire. She couldn't stop the answering smile on her face as he moved in her direction.

After so many years of avoiding Julian at balls and soirees, it was strange that her stomach fluttered with excitement whenever she was near him now.

"Good morning, Miss Bantham. I trust you slept well?"

"Yes, my lord. Very well. And you?"

He looked around as if to make sure no one was close enough to listen in before he leaned closer and whispered.

"I had a beautiful woman in my bed that needed tending so I barely slept a wink."

"Poor man." She pouted in mock sympathy and he let out a low groan.

"Don't put your lip out like that, Lainey, you are too enticing."

"But I should stay in my tent tonight so you won't lose sleep."

Another growl before he said, "Vixen," and went to collect his breakfast.

"I'm glad to see the two of you are getting along better," Uncle Henry said from behind her causing Lainey to choke until he slapped her back.

"I didn't realize you were there."

"I only just walked in as Lord Melville was walking away, but he was smiling, so you couldn't have been rude."

She laughed. "We had a misunderstanding before, but it has been addressed. I find it easier to be friendly now."

Friendly wasn't the correct word for the way she felt in Julian's presence, but it was the word she would use when discussing the situation with her uncle. She felt her cheeks grow warm.

"Are you well? You seem flushed."

She cleared her throat again.

"It is the desert, uncle. I'm simply acclimating to the warmer temperatures," she said, hoping she'd get better at keeping their secret.

JULIAN TRIED TO keep his distance from Lainey as others entered the tent for their morning meal. Even if Julian had wanted to sit with Lainey it would have been difficult with Comte Dumast taking up the seat next to her.

Rather than risk giving the man a piece of his mind, he left the tent to prepare. He wasn't very hungry as it was. Not with his stomach planning a revolt.

"Are you ready for your first day?" Lainey asked as they gathered their tools. She must have left the Comte sitting alone with his food. It might have brought a smug smile to his face, if he weren't so worried.

"No," he answered, trying to hide his nervousness, and failing.

She gave him an encouraging smile.

"You will do fine. I've trained you well and you won't let me down," she said with a smirk that made Julian want to drag her back to his bed.

"You trained me for the wilds of Scotland, not this..." He gestured toward the large monument that was thousands of years old.

"The basics are the same. You know what all the tools are and what they are used for. We start the day at the site on the west side of the pyramid as it is in shade during the morning."

"Outside the tomb?"

"Yes. There is next to nothing left inside the tombs. They've been looted many times over the years. However, the sand and wind cover things quickly here. It's common to find pieces of treasure outside of the tombs. Things that were dropped as the trespassers scurried away after taking their haul."

"I see."

"We spend the afternoon inside the tomb studying the paintings for clues of hidden chambers and interpreting hieroglyphics. Then we move to the site on the east side of the pyramid later in the day when the pyramid provides shade to that area."

He nodded. It seemed a perfectly reasonable plan.

"Here." She handed him a large canteen and a smaller flask. "Drink plenty of water. And use this."

He pulled the stopper and sniffed the stringent scent.

"What is this?" He winced.

"It is moringa oil, a native plant here that keeps pests at bay."

"I should poor it in my boots to ward off scorpions?" When she'd warned him to check his shoes before putting them on in the morning because of unwanted and incredibly large insects, Julian had almost wanted to run back home to Scotland. Almost.

"No. You should apply it to your skin every few hours. It's not as harsh smelling after a while."

She held up her arm and he leaned closer to take in the scent of her skin.

"Hmm. Perhaps we can help each other apply it." He leaned closer to her ear and whispered. "Everywhere."

She giggled. "Perhaps tonight. But for now, we must get to work."

"Yes, of course."

And work they did.

The next few weeks were filled with days spent sifting through sand, and nights spent making love to Lainey in secret. It was perfect. Even Ben was helping and enjoying himself.

Every once in a while, someone would call out when they found something. The group would gather round to watch as the treasure was revealed. It was exciting, even if the treasure turned out to be a bit of broken pottery or a scrap of leather.

Those simple discoveries thrilled him to no end and he and Elaina would discuss them as they lay in his bed together.

"Are you disappointed that we've not found anything of great value?" she asked.

"I have not been disappointed a single moment since stepping foot on the ship. I find myself trying to remember every detail. For these memories, they are a treasure beyond value."

She smiled. "I fear I have taken this life for granted for some time. Perhaps even resented it. But experiencing it with you has been wonderful."

"I can't imagine having such an opportunity. To do this for the rest of my life." He kissed her hair. "With you. I wish things were different."

"I wish your father had not been such a vile, heartless, bugger."

He laughed.

"I do love the names you come up with for him. It's most entertaining."

When their laughter died down, she fell silent for a little while. He could almost feel her thinking.

"What is it?" he asked when curiosity got the best of him.

"I was only wondering…" She paused. "No. It doesn't matter. Never mind."

"What is it?" he repeated, wanting to know what thoughts had stolen the lightness from their moment together.

"Would things be different, do you think? If your father had not made such a demand. That is to dictate that you marry someone proper?" She shook her head. "Please don't answer. It is silly. Of course, it wouldn't matter. You would still want someone proper as your countess regardless. I should go. I'm rather tired and I don't want to fall asleep here. We cannot be caught."

"Elaina," he said but she had already gathered up her things to leave.

She paused before her exit. "I know how you must feel, trying to remember every moment to recall later. I will treasure each memory I've made with you."

With that, she was gone and he was left alone to consider what she had asked, but not allowed him to answer.

If he could choose anyone to be his wife. If he could live the life he truly wanted...

He would most assuredly pick her and the life they had here.

Chapter Twenty-Six

THEIR TIME WAS passing by much too quickly. They would be returning to England the following week. They would arrive home by mid-April and Julian would be married soon after and Lainey… she would continue on as she had before.

Each night as she left his tent to sleep in her lonely bed, it became more difficult to leave him. She knew soon enough every night would be spent alone.

She tried to keep her sadness from ruining the time they had left, but it was there. A distraction she couldn't stop thinking about.

She secured her pack over her shoulders and set her foot on the first rung of the ladder.

It was mid-day, when the sun was high and they retreated into the cool darkness of the pyramid to complete etchings. She was already thinking of getting through dinner and retiring to her tent so she could sneak into Julian's tent when everyone was asleep.

She must have been too focused on what would happen once she was alone with him and not paying attention to her climb. Because near the top of the ladder, her foot slipped.

Gripping the ladder with both hands, she turned to bring her foot back up on the rung. Climbing a ladder was no time to be daydreaming about being with a naked Julian.

But before she could start climbing again the ladder shifted and began to fall. She only had time to scream before she fell to the ground. Pain shot through her head and neck. She raised her hand to touch the spot in the back of her head and it came away wet with blood.

Her head suddenly became too heavy to hold up. Her entire body became too cumbersome to move, and she allowed herself to drift away and let go.

⟫⟫⟫⟪⟪⟪

JULIAN'S HEART POUNDED as he raced to where Lainey lay in a pile of rubble.

"Ben, please go get Henry and Rose. Right now. Tell them Lainey has been injured," Julian said as he pulled Lainey's limp body into his arms and carried her to a nearby table that was covered in etchings and drawings.

Holding her against his body with one arm, he dashed away the papers and a few pieces of broken pottery, so the surface was clear and laid her out.

When he pulled back, he saw the blood covering his sleeve. Tilting her head to the side, he gasped at the blood staining her hair.

"Elaina? Can you hear me?" He moved her to her side, not wanting to set her on her back again. "Oh, God."

"What has happened?" Henry came in with Rose right behind him. "Is she…?"

"She is breathing. She fell and hit her head, there is so much blood."

"Dumast has served as a surgeon. Rose, find him and bring him to Lainey's tent. We'll take her there. She'll need to be stitched."

Henry made a move to lift her, but Julian intercepted him and picked her up instead. Julian needed to feel the warmth of her body and her breath against his neck to ensure she was alive.

Henry followed behind him as they made their way to camp and placed Lainey in her bed.

Against the stark white sheets, Lainey's skin seemed just as pale.

Julian turned to go find the Comte. He would carry the man to the tent as well, but he rushed in carrying a leather bag.

"What's happened?" he asked in French.

Julian explained how she'd been working on the wall and fell. He thought that was enough information, but he was asked additional questions. How far up was she? What did she fall on? Had she been awake at all after the fall?

He felt like a tiny boat at sea being hammered by the waves of a storm.

He tried to answer their questions, understanding why they needed to know, but he just wanted them to help Lainey.

"Please… help her," he finally said. "Her head."

"Wounds of the head bleed like the devil, but are rarely as bad as they seem," the man said in a calm tone that made Julian want to punch him, but doing so wouldn't help Lainey.

"It seems really bad, so can we make the bleeding stop? Now?"

The man let out a huff as if Julian was annoying him. He was about ten seconds from finding out how annoying Julian and his fists could be, but he pulled a needle from his bag and began sterilizing it in the nearby flame.

Julian thought he might need to sit down as the people in the tent began to blend together. He needed to be strong for Lainey. He couldn't swoon like a debutante with her laces too tight.

But strong or no, he did look away when the Comte began stitching Lainey's skin. There was no reason he needed to keep watch over that.

"When will she wake up?" Lady Darlington asked with tears in her eyes.

"She'll wake up when she's ready. The brain likes to protect itself by pulling away from the goings on out here. It could be a few hours or it could be a few days."

"A few days?" Julian snapped, revisiting his idea of punching the man now that he wasn't actively taking care of Lainey.

"It's perfectly normal when one gets a bump on the head. The bleeding has stopped. She just needs to rest now. Someone should stay with her while—"

"I'll stay," Julian volunteered immediately. He couldn't leave her. What if she woke and needed him? Even more probable was that he would worry himself into a fit if he couldn't see that her chest continued moving as she breathed.

"That isn't necessary," Lady Darlington said. "I will stay."

"I will stay with you," Julian altered his initial plan, knowing her aunt would want to see she was safe. "I insist. This is my fault."

"Why do you think that?" Henry asked with his brows pulled together.

"I set the ladder up. I should have made certain it was secure. I should have climbed it first myself to make sure it would hold." Suddenly the tent was too small and had too little air.

When Henry slapped him on the back, it forced him to draw in a big breath as he gasped.

"It was an accident, Julian. They happen from time to time on a dig. Everyone is aware of the dangers, including Lainey. There is no great science to setting up a ladder. I'm sure you did it well enough. Perhaps you would do better to come with me to get a drink."

"I must stay here," he said in his most earl-esque tone so it wouldn't be questioned. Hale often pulled out his "duke voice" when he didn't want to argue. Fortunately, Julian had been paying attention to how it was done.

"We'll all stay for a bit," Henry announced diplomatically and went to the opening in the tent to call for someone to bring more chairs.

The first hour passed in silence. Into the second, Lady Darlington began crying softly, which upset Lord Darlington.

"I would prefer she was screaming in pain as bad as that sounds," Henry said as Rose dabbed at her worried tears.

Julian said nothing, as he continued to watch Elaina's chest rise and fall with her breathing. He wanted to touch her, but despite seeing she was alive, he didn't dare reach out, in case her skin was cold instead of holding its usual warmth.

He'd surely touched every inch of her skin and knew the temperature it should be. But now, he twisted his fingers in nervousness and watched.

More hours passed and they waited. Lady Darlington dozed off and Lord Darlington ordered a cot be brought for his wife, knowing she wouldn't want to be removed from the tent.

Soon after, Lord Darlington began to snore where he leaned back in his chair.

Julian himself felt the weight of fatigue settle over him, but still he watched.

Up.

Down.

She was alive.

Up.

Down.

He might still get the chance to apologize.

Up.

Down.

He leaned close and without touching her, he whispered in her ear.

"Please, Elaina. Wake up now, sweetheart. We're all here waiting for you."

CHAPTER TWENTY-SEVEN

LAINEY KNEW SHE needed to wake up. She was surely late for something or had someplace she needed to be. But she was so comfortable in her bed.

Especially when Julian whispered to her.

Except when she focused on his words, she realized he was upset as he begged her to open her eyes and wake up.

Every few moments, his voice would take a hard edge as he demanded she wake up rather than asked her to.

If for no other reason than to remind him she didn't take orders from anyone, she attempted to open her eyes. It was more difficult than she'd expected and as she tried, she realized her head hurt a great deal.

She tried moving it from side to side and decided that was not a good thing at the moment. It seemed her head hurt on the outside as well as the inside.

And she was thirsty. It happened often in the desert. It was why she was always careful to make sure she drank plenty of water.

Had she not drunk anything today? The only way to know for sure was to wake up.

After it was decided, she made a valiant attempt to raise her eyelids. After a few attempts they opened enough for her to see the man sitting next to her bed.

Julian.

She knew something was wrong by his expression alone. He looked like he'd been awake for months. But somehow was as incredibly handsome even in that state.

"Elaina," he whispered, relief clear in his voice. "How are you feeling?"

"I'm thirsty and my head hurts." She knew it wasn't at all ladylike to complain, but he did ask.

In the next breath he was pouring her water and bringing it to her. As she gulped it down, she glanced around the tent to see Aunt Rose and Uncle Henry sleeping nearby.

"What happened?" she asked, unsure what had caused everyone to be in her tent. Clearly, she must have worried everyone.

"You fell from the ladder. I'm so sorry, Elaina. It is all my fault."

Seeing his hand clench in his hair reminded her of the time in Scotland when he'd worried himself into a panic. He was not far from that now.

"I am fine, Julian. And it is not your fault. You cannot be responsible for gravity. It happens."

"I should have protected you."

"Julian." She reached for him and took his hand in hers giving it what she hoped was a reassuring squeeze. "I do not blame you for what happened. Please stop blaming yourself. We all know the risks when we climb a ladder. Look at me," she said when she noticed he was looking everywhere but at her directly.

When his gaze met hers, she rubbed her thumb over the back of his hand.

"See? I'm fine."

He nodded unconvincingly.

"You say it. Say I'm fine," she ordered.

He winced and took a breath before nodding.

"Yes. You're fine. You must be for you are bossing me around as you always do."

She laughed as he laced his fingers through hers and raised her hand to place a kiss to the inside of her wrist.

"Better?" she asked.

"How horrible that you feel the need to tend to me when you are the one that was injured. How difficult I am, I'm so sorry, Lainey."

"You don't need to apologize for who you are, Julian. Not to me. Not ever."

"I did carry you all the way from the site to your tent in a rather heroic way," he said with that devilish smile.

She knew how he reverted to humor when he was uncomfortable and didn't know how to handle certain situations. She smiled.

"You are quite the knight in shining armor. I am so very lucky to have allowed you to come on this expedition so you were here to save me."

"Perhaps you would like to reward me with a kiss, my lady?"

They both glanced over to her aunt and uncle before leaning closer and kissing. He pulled away at the sound of shifting fabric. But Rose and Henry were still sleeping.

"You should know that your aunt and uncle saw me during one of my episodes after you fell."

His frown looked out of place on his always smiling lips. But of course, he was a human man. He couldn't be happy all the time. Regardless of what he showed the world.

It made her feel closer to him, that he would show her this other side. The real Julian.

"Don't fear. They wouldn't judge you for being upset."

"Oh, I don't worry that they are judging me. I think they are judging your sanity for agreeing to bring me on this trip."

It was said as a jest, but she heard the truth and worry behind his words.

"There is nothing wrong with you, Julian," she said with genuine rightness.

He glanced over at her with a different kind of worry.

"No, Lainey. Don't make me say it. I won't."

"Say there is nothing wrong with you."

"I just said I won't. I can't. It's not true."

"It is true."

"The way breath leaves my body but I can't seem to remember how to bring it back in? My heart pounding so fiercely I fear it might break free of my chest and flop about on the ground? The sweat that beads no matter how cold I feel on the inside? No. That is not normal. Saying so would be a lie."

"Very well. Perhaps, it's not normal. But you are not the only person that suffers such things. I feel similar whenever I hear horse's hooves and carriage wheels echo on the wooden planks of a bridge. And it makes no sense because I could swear I was asleep when the accident occurred. I only woke when we hit the water. So why would that sound evoke such a reaction?"

He shook his head, silently admitting he didn't have an answer.

"What we can do is accept it. Can you say you accept it instead?"

He studied her face for a moment before turning the question back on her.

"Do *you* accept it?"

"Yes. I've been this way since I was eleven."

Another small shake of his head.

"No. I meant… That is… Do you accept *me*?"

Her heart ached for this man who wanted only this simple thing. To be accepted. And to think his own father had refused this small request over and over. Causing these scars that might never heal.

How she wanted to help heal his pain.

She smiled and told him the truth of her heart.

"Yes."

He needed no more than that single word to bring the smile back to his face.

"Very well then, I will just have to hope your aunt and uncle don't throw you from the team for your poor selection."

"I doubt I will be dismissed. They do love me, you know."

"Yes, it is clear that they do." A hint of sadness returned to his words.

"I have been rather fortunate to have two families in my lifetime. Both with people who have loved me without me having to do anything. I've never even thought of it. It just seemed the way families behaved. But I am sorry you did not have that. I don't pity you, for you have turned into a fine man, a kind man, who deserves no one's pity. But I do wish you had experienced what I did."

"Perhaps if I had been doted on all my life, I would have turned into a right blighter no one could force themselves to withstand. Everything works out as it should in the end. Do you believe that?"

"Yes," she answered with a bit of hesitation. She normally did believe things had a way of working out for the best. Except, this man's destiny was written out, and it didn't include her.

She didn't know how that could ever be the right thing.

DESPITE HIS CONCERNS, Elaina was back working on the site the next day. Though Julian had at least managed to keep her off the ladder by pleading she would kill him if she fell again. He kept a watchful eye on her and enjoyed the faces she made when she caught him.

"I am fine, as I've told you several times," she said.

"And I worry for the smallest of reasons as you well know, so your assurances are a waste of your precious breath."

She smiled and looked around as if confirming they were alone. He had already done as much himself.

"Perhaps a kiss would go further to reassure you."

Julian pressed a kiss to Lainey's lips. A simple gesture of thanks for understanding him. Accepting him.

Kissing her, even in such a chaste way, seemed to make his

feelings for her grow even more so than when they were intimate. Not that they had been the night before. He preferred to just hold her after what had happened.

It was, perhaps, a different kind of intimacy. Not sexual, but more in some other way.

He'd never felt so connected to another person. So comfortable. He could tell her anything. Perhaps even things he should keep to himself.

But she never backed down from telling him how she felt either. He would give her the same courtesy.

And he felt…

Either he didn't know, or feared putting a formal word to it. Or maybe it was more powerful to leave it the way it was.

He *felt*.

He cared deeply for his friends. He'd felt a glow of warmth in his chest the first time he'd held Baby Verona. It had been the easiest thing to echo her parents' love and want the best life had to offer on her behalf.

He'd nearly had one of his attacks when Hale had asked Julian to be his daughter's godfather. It seemed a terribly difficult thing. But as he considered—for the three and half minutes it had taken him to reply—he knew he would see to her happiness. The rest of it would be dealt with, but he felt he had the most essential piece worked out already. Love.

So, he'd said yes. And then evoked a promise from the man that he would take care with his life so Julian wouldn't be called upon to take over.

That night Julian had wondered what had been wrong with his own father. For if it was so easily done to love a child, even one not of his blood, why couldn't his father have loved him?

Shaking away the maudlin thoughts and unanswerable questions, Julian pressed a kiss to Lainey's knuckles.

"Thank you, Lainey."

"You may not want to thank me yet. I have a bit of work lined up for you today." She offered her saucy grin he so much enjoyed when they were alone.

He appreciated the way she knew when to push him, and when to let the mood lighten.

"I am your humble servant. Please show me what heinous task you have set out for me."

She giggled evilly and rubbed her palms together in a sinister way, which made him laugh.

It was at that moment he admitted to himself that he was in love with Elaina Bantham.

"Please hold this lantern while I collect a sample of this engraving," she said while handing him the light. As if he would complain that holding a lantern was too lowly a job for an earl. She must know him better than that by now.

"Closer," she said, her breath caressing his ear because they were already quite close.

"I'm not sure how much closer you wish me to get, but if we don't stop now, I can't speak as to what might happen in this empty tomb with all the pharaoh's creatures watching us." He nodded toward the drawings of sphynx and gods in the form of dogs.

"Very well. Hold the light closer and allow me to finish this, so we will be free to sneak off later."

"Of course." He shifted so he could both hold the light closer as she'd requested, but also hold an edge of the paper she was using to create the rub.

It seemed an odd moment for an earl to be standing there in an ancient tomb thousands of miles from England so close to an untitled woman wearing men's breeches so he could do something so mundane as hold the light closer so she could work.

He absolutely loved every moment.

Julian had become quite comfortable with his tasks on the dig. He knew the most efficient way to use each tool and what each was called. But most importantly, he felt like he belonged.

He wasn't the least bit disappointed that they hadn't found many artifacts to uncover. The region had been ravaged for years, decades, and centuries. It was rare to find anything of extreme value. The occasional piece of pottery or painted stone. Ben had been elated to find some scraps of fabric and Elaina had even found a bone. But no golden statue or sarcophagus had been uncovered.

He wasn't surprised to realize he didn't care if he found anything or not. It was about the adventure of being here rather than discovering great riches.

After all, riches were measured differently for everyone and as he held the light and watched Elaina focus on her task so intently her tongue peeked out in concentration, he knew she was the greatest treasure of all.

And one he wouldn't be allowed to keep for himself. No matter how much he might want to.

✦

CHAPTER TWENTY-EIGHT

ELAINA OFTEN FOUND herself smiling for no reason.

Actually, there was a reason, and that reason was lying next to her asleep. Soon, she would need to slip from his bed to sneak through the darkness back to her own tent.

What it must feel like to wake up in his arms. To share that intimate moment of watching as he shifted from sleep to awareness. To earn his first smile of the day. But for the duration of their time together, they would be banished to a few sparse hours of the night.

But from the time she woke until she slipped from his bed, she was happy.

Their mornings were filled with happy greetings over breakfast before starting their task for the day. Julian had become more attentive since her fall, but she didn't mind in the least.

Because he hardly left her side, she picked up on his irritation with Comte Girard Dumast when the Frenchman flirted with her. She almost thought he might be jealous, but certainly he knew there was no competition. After all, she and Julian stole kisses at every possible opportunity.

They shared their mid-day meal as well as steamy glances with one another over dinner. As soon as everyone settled in their tents for bed, Elaina counted down the minutes until silence fell over the camp and she could join Julian in his tent.

He was always waiting as if he couldn't stand another second without having his body pressed up against hers. He kissed her frantically until their clothes were removed and they could touch skin to skin. They both groaned softly when they first joined and she thought she would never forget that feeling as long as she lived.

He stirred next to her and that familiar smile brought a rush of happiness as always.

"I am glad you are still here," he whispered.

"And I am so glad I agreed to let you come on this expedition. To think how lonely my nights would be," she said while his fingers trailed up her spine causing a pleasant shiver.

"I daresay, your nights wouldn't have been very lonely if you'd not wished it." He kissed the inside of her wrist, but she saw the flicker of unhappiness in his beautiful blue eyes.

"What do you mean?" she asked.

"Comte Dumast." He made the name sound like a curse.

"Girard?" She laughed. "No."

His low growl made her laugh again.

"The way you use his Christian name makes me want to bury him in the sand."

"I can't very well say 'Comte de Dumast' as we work together. It is quite a mouthful."

"Hmph," he offered a surly, Scottish sound.

"Regardless of whatever I call him, I have no interest in having him in my bed. Though I will admit it is interesting to see you ruffled by the thought. Honestly, I've never thought of him as more than a friend of Uncle Henry's until I witnessed your reaction."

"You should be careful of men like him."

"Because he might seduce me as you have done?" She fluttered her eyes at Julian until he broke out of his sour mood and smiled. But he turned serious again.

"You don't understand. I know what we have now must end when this expedition is over, and I want nothing more than for you to find happiness in your life after we part. But I can't bring myself to manufacture that happiness when I think of you with him."

"For now, we only have to think of me with you."

He nuzzled his lips against her neck just under her jaw in that place that made her heart race.

THE FIRST WEEK in March, everything shifted. As was common when the team moved from digging to crating and labeling the artifacts for transport. They wouldn't search for anything else on this trip.

They would make their trek across the desert and set sail for their voyage back to England before the season started. Lainey had never hated the process more than she did this time.

For when they returned to Egypt on their next expedition, Julian would not be with them. He would be married to his proper countess, and Lainey would be…

As she had been before. A spinster archaeologist with no prospects.

But she would be forever changed. She now knew a man's heated touch. The exquisite pressure of his claiming. The desire in his gaze, and the passion in those quiet moments after sex when promises were made.

Too soon, they were boarding the ship to return to London.

It wasn't just the pieces of pottery in cargo that were shattered, but her heart as well.

"OUR FINAL SUNSET. We will reach England tomorrow," Lainey said as they stood on the ship watching as the orange sun dipped into the sea.

"I don't want this to end." He responded as he had every

night for weeks. But this would be the last time he would have the opportunity to say it.

"Neither do I."

"I don't want to marry some giggling debutante or stuffy miss." He rested his forehead against hers. *I want to marry you.*

"You are going about it the wrong way. You see it as something you're being forced to do by the man who terrorized you all of your youth."

"Yes. That is exactly what it is."

"But you need to see it as an opportunity to find someone to share your life with."

He stepped back to look at her.

"Do you think I will find someone who will enjoy sharing tales of her travels around the world?"

"Well, probably not, as most women do not travel very far at all. Especially not proper young ladies."

"And I'm to find someone who will accept my attacks of self-doubt and talk me through them rather than swoon and break into hysterics?"

"That would only make it worse, I'm sure."

"As am I." The truth was he would never find anyone like her. She was quite clearly her own person. One of a kind. "I wish…"

He wanted to say so many things after those two words.

He wished he'd had a better father, that this wasn't his last adventure.

But most of all, he wished Elaina would pass his father's ridiculous requirements for a proper countess so he could spend the rest of his life making her smile.

"I do too," she said sadly, resting her hand over his on the rail. "I wish I was… suitable."

He didn't think he'd ever been angrier. And not with his father this time, but with himself. For somehow, he'd neglected to convince this woman he loved that she was perfect. To see her doubt herself… No. He wouldn't have it.

"You are perfect, Elaina. You may not have been trained to be a countess from the day you left the womb, but you are better for it. You aren't a simpering debutante who only wishes for a title, but someone who knows what life has to offer. Someone who follows her own path. I admire you. I…" *I love you.*

But he couldn't say that. Not anymore. To do so would just make this so much more difficult. She knew the truth. But they could no longer speak the words. Their time was over. They were forced to move on.

He didn't say anything because at that moment, the sun disappeared over the horizon.

"I guess that is the end."

He shook his head. "No. We still have tonight."

She nodded and offered a smile.

"Any suggestions on how we might make it one to remember?"

"I'm certainly going to do my best."

⇒⇒⇒✕⇐⇐⇐

THEIR NIGHTS TOGETHER in Egypt had been filled with urgency. After spending the days with him, Lainey was always so eager to touch him. It seemed he was just as impatient to remove her clothes. But tonight was unlike those other times. In fact, it felt almost the opposite.

After months of hurrying, they now wished to savor each touch. Each kiss.

It felt like many nights had passed before she was laid out next to him, her clothes tossed with his on the floor in his quarters.

She watched as his gaze searched her face and she knew he was trying to memorize everything about this moment just as she was. Their time was running out.

But they had this moment.

They kissed as if they had all their lives to do so. But other desires became insistent. She began making needy noises and their soft touches became desperate.

"Elaina," he said her name as a question. Always the gentleman making sure she wanted this but never doubting her answer.

"Yes."

When he slid inside her body he whispered in Gaelic, words she guessed were curses or promises.

"For as long as I live, I'll never experience anything as wonderful as the feeling when we join together. It is as if I've come home," he said as his body moved inside her.

Her hips rose with every thrust, meeting him, welcoming him. She was amazed at how perfectly they fit together. How right it felt to be with him in this way.

And then he reached between them to touch that place he alone commanded. He knew exactly how to touch her to make her world fracture and collapse in complete bliss.

The pressure built and broke, as echoes of delight surged through her body and into his.

"You are perfection," he said as he thrust into her as deeply as possible before pulling away completely as he gasped his release.

As much as she wanted to hold him closer at that critical moment, she understood the strength it took for him to protect her in that way. She was grateful if not also bereft from missing out on the connection.

He lay next to her, his heart pounding as quickly as her own.

When their breathing slowed, he shifted so he was looking down at her, his fingers stroking her skin softly. These moments afterward were a quiet pleasure.

"What are you thinking?" she asked, unable to help herself when he remained quiet.

His fingertips trailed lightly over her face, down her throat, and across her sensitive nipples. She thought he might not answer. When he did, his voice was rough.

"How much I hate my father."

She knew how she felt about the man who had injured Julian in the worst way without ever placing a hand on him. She hadn't ever met the man, but she despised him for the damage he'd caused.

Still, she didn't know why Julian was thinking of his father in that moment after they'd just shared themselves on a level beyond the physical. Perhaps these thoughts never left him.

"I have never hated him more than I do at this moment."

"Why?" she had to ask.

He blinked and focused on her.

"When I was young and I displeased him, he would punish me by taking away something I enjoyed. A book or a toy I showed favor to. It didn't take me long to figure out how to manipulate him into thinking I liked one thing more than life itself while hiding away the thing I truly cared for."

"You are so clever." She smiled and brushed his hair back from his forehead.

"I thought so." He offered a small smile that was gone too quickly. "But he has won this round, the most important one yet. He has managed to take the thing I favor most—rather the *person* I love more than life itself."

She felt the hot tears gather in her eyes and spill over on her cheeks.

It wasn't fair.

Part of her wished he'd never told her how he felt. It just added to everything she would have to give up. But knowing he loved her…

It was everything.

She leaned closer and kissed him softly. When she pulled away, she saw his eyes glistened in the lantern light.

"I love you, Julian. I know what we have must come to an end. But the love…" She shook her head. "He can never take that from us. Never. I will hold it in my heart for the rest of my days."

He nodded. "As will I."

CHAPTER TWENTY-NINE

J ULIAN SPENT THE last hour watching Elaina sleep. There would be plenty of time for him to rest later. For now, he wouldn't give up a second of her. Occasionally he'd lean close enough to brush his lips across her temple or touch her hair.

He worried he would forget the way the soft light made her curls look like burnished copper. Or the pattern of freckles across her nose and the one on the corner of her lips he loved to kiss.

He breathed in her vanilla and cinnamon scent knowing he would think of her anytime he smelled them in the future.

The future.

How could he marry someone else when his heart would always be with her?

He pushed away the familiar rage, not wanting the hatred to intrude on this moment and take away his final hour with her.

She would need to leave soon to go back to her room. If she was found here in his bed, naked and ravished, he would have no choice but to marry her to save her from ruin. He looked toward the wooden door, secretly wishing someone would come knocking, and find them there together.

To take the choice out of his hands.

There had to be a way to save the mines and have her. Some simple solution he hadn't thought of yet.

How would he give her up? How would he spend his life with another woman in his bed? A stranger that shared his name and bore his children, but who would never be Elaina.

His future wife would never truly know him. His insecurities and fears. She wouldn't know of his past. She would only see the charming smiles he would keep pasted to his lips until he was freed from his torture with death.

"You are thinking too much," Elaina whispered, startling him.

He smiled and kissed her as she blinked sleep away.

"I can't seem to help it."

"I know a way to make you stop thinking," she hinted, her lips pulling up on the corner where his favorite freckle teased him.

It was both the easiest and most difficult thing to sink into her warmth for the final time. Their fingers clasped together as if nothing could ever separate them.

They stared into each other's eyes as they moved together, giving and taking pleasure, sharing everything.

He kissed away the tears that slid over her temples into her hair as her legs pulled him closer. He smiled when he felt her body tighten and pulse around him. Proof of how perfectly they fit together.

As his climax grew closer, he briefly considered releasing inside her body, claiming her as his. A child would mean they'd have to marry. Another way to have the choice taken from him. But that way led only to guilt. He couldn't do that to her.

Pulling from her body brought tears to his eyes. And when she pulled him to her, he pressed his face into her hair already salted by her tears.

And his heart shattered.

JULIAN WAS STILL asleep when Elaina slipped out of his room. She'd been afraid to wake him for a final farewell. She worried what she might do or say in that moment of vulnerability, when she'd wanted everything with him.

She knew if she'd asked him to choose her, he would.

But later, he would come to resent her. When his mines were lost and the people working in them were forced to pay the price for her selfishness.

She couldn't allow that to happen, and yet she feared she wouldn't have been able to stop herself from asking.

Knowing she wouldn't be able to sleep with her heart so twisted in pain, she wrapped her robe tighter and went up on deck. With morning still hours away, the stars shone brightly in the night sky.

"It's late, I didn't expect to find anyone on deck at this time of night," Bentley said as he stepped up to the rail.

"I couldn't sleep."

In truth, she hadn't tried. She'd lay beside Julian, listening to his heartbeat wishing she could hear it every night as she fell asleep. She didn't know how she would give him up. But she had to.

"You don't want tomorrow to come." It wasn't a question. He spoke as if he'd heard her very thoughts.

The tears she'd kept tightly reined in when she'd been with Julian leaked from her eyes and ran down her cheek now.

Bentley offered a crisp handkerchief and she took it with a whisper of thanks.

"I don't want to burden Lord Melville with my feelings, but it is becoming ever more difficult to keep them restrained. If he saw me now, blubbering mess that I am, he'd surely be relieved to part ways."

She tried to laugh at her poor attempt at a joke, but it sounded painful.

"I've known him all his life and I can assure you, relief is the last thing he would feel in this situation."

Lainey nodded.

"Perhaps you wish to spare him seeing your pain?"

She swiped at the tears on her cheeks and nodded.

"What we wish doesn't matter. I am not proper and therefore we cannot be together."

"I believe there are many different versions of proper. I am not of noble birth, yet I touched a king's tomb. And I set out a finely dressed lord, if I do say so myself."

She laughed, grateful for his attempt to cheer her. Even if it wasn't working.

"I've thought myself dry of ideas," she admitted. "I considered asking my uncle to send me to finishing school." She laughed sadly. "At my age, could you imagine? But I would learn everything there was to know about how to run a proper household and be a countess if it would change anything."

"You speak of the scandal regarding your mother's legitimacy?"

She nodded. "My aunt thinks it a bunch of poppycock. They looked so much alike many people thought them to be twins. But then they also looked like my grandmother so that doesn't clear up anything now does it?"

"I think there are many people who would be surprised to find out their blood is not as pure as they think it is." He winked. "Servants talk."

She smiled briefly.

"Unfortunately, my legitimacy has been called to question publicly. And by my own grandfather." Though Elaina still wondered if the duke hadn't spoken out in anger at his daughter marrying a third son of a third son rather than the truth.

It didn't matter now. The damage was done.

"Even if I managed to learn the ways to act like a proper countess, there is no way to purge the suspicion of my birth. There is too much at stake. The person the late earl selected to make the determination would surely find me unsuitable and Julian would lose everything."

Mr. Bentley patted her hand.

"Your sacrifice speaks of your suitability, Miss Bantham.

Whomever is called on to make this fateful decision would be a fool to see anything unacceptable about you."

She offered a watery smile.

"Thank you. It means so much that you think so. Julian loves you as he would a true father. And I understand why. You want him to be happy, just as I do. It is my only wish that he be happy and loved. Doesn't he deserve that after everything he's endured?"

"Indeed, he does, miss."

Elaina nodded with a thread of thought that quickly wove into a plan.

She couldn't be with Julian, but she could help him find someone proper that would also make him happy and truly care for him.

He thought he would have a cold marriage, of duty only. But it didn't have to be that way. He could have happiness.

It might be the hardest thing she'd ever done, but it was the last thing she could do for him.

She would find the man she loved an adoring wife.

CHAPTER THIRTY

"A**BSOLUTELY NOT**," J**ULIAN** complained when Lainey shared her ridiculous plan to help him find a wife. She had waited until they'd arrived at the docks in London before apprising him of her ridiculous plan.

"You don't have to be saddled with just any snooty woman of the *ton* when we could find you someone you might actually care for."

"I don't want to care for anyone else." He may have sounded like a petulant child, but there was no helping it.

"You are being stubborn," she accused.

"Yes, and you know that because you know me so well. How am I supposed to stop loving you and start loving another? It doesn't work that way, Lainey."

Ben nodded that his trunks had been loaded and it was time to leave for his townhouse. This was the last moment of his adventure and he didn't want to spend it fighting with the woman he loved.

She let out a breath. "I don't expect it would happen so quickly, but it could happen. In time."

"No. If I cannot find a way out of this, I will marry the most proper woman who will accept my hand and be done with it. I will not attach feelings to a transaction my father has forced upon me. I won't do it."

"Please consider it when you are less upset."

"I will never be less upset."

She blew out a breath and he wanted so much to kiss her in that moment, but they couldn't continue in that vein. It was just causing more damage. Not to mention they were in plain sight of everyone.

"Please, Julian. For me."

"For you?"

"Perhaps if you allow yourself to be happy, I may be also."

He tilted his head in question.

"I thought myself unappealing for so many years because of what happened with Lord Dunnage. And perhaps because I carried around so much anger and suspicion, I frightened off anyone who might have otherwise shown an interest. But being with you, seeing the way you look at me, it has made me feel… beautiful."

"You are beautiful. Don't ever doubt that."

"I wasn't searching for a compliment, I was making a point that if I opened up, someone might offer for me."

The shattered pieces of his heart fell into his stomach. She was speaking of marriage. To someone other than him.

The vine of jealousy coiled around him, cutting off the air to his lungs.

He wasn't just going to lose the woman he loved. He would lose her to another man. A man who would touch her and make love to her as he had. Who would win her smiles as they grew old together.

And he finally understood what she was trying to do for him. Because despite the jealousy and hatred for the faceless man who would call her his wife, he knew he wanted that for her.

Happiness and love.

Of course, whoever the blighter was, he wouldn't deserve her. Julian knew he hadn't either. But if they could care for Lainey and allow her to be the person she was without judgement or trying to turn her into something proper or normal, Julian would praise the man until his final breath.

"Very well," he managed to say around the lump in his throat. He'd known the reality they were facing, but it hadn't seemed so real until this moment.

He needed to get away before he scooped her up and ran away with her. He only wanted to keep her for himself.

Julian greeted his dear friend as he entered the study at Roxburghe House.

Hale had always enjoyed town, but since he'd married his lovely wife who preferred the country, the duke and duchess spent most of their time at the country home he'd purchased for them in Scotland.

Except for a few weeks during the beginning of the Season.

"Where is V?" Julian asked after their daughter.

"Asleep. But you have only to wait a few minutes and I'm certain she will be awake yet again." If the man was attempting to complain, he did a poor job of it with the smile upon his face. "Come, tell me of your journey."

"First, I brought you something." He held out his small gift. A bit of rock with ancient painting on it. "I dug that from the earth myself."

"I will treasure it always. Thank you. Did you have a rewarding adventure?"

"Yes. Very rewarding."

Hale tilted his head.

"I don't think you could have said that with less enthusiasm. Was it not what you'd hoped?"

Julian stood and walked in a small circle. Hale frowned, no stranger to seeing Julian pace when he was distraught. He'd seen it many times over the years they'd been friends.

"It was everything I'd hoped and more. And I thought it would be enough to tide me over as I go forward with my father's plans for me, but instead, it made me realize how much I have to give up. *Who* I will have to give up."

"Who?" Hale was smiling now as he held out a glass of brandy. "Is this unrest over a woman, then? Have you fallen, my friend?"

"Do you remember when you said we weren't good at speaking of feelings and things of the like? Were you feeling things for the duchess before she was your duchess?"

"Yes. Are you in need of some advice? Because I daresay I will do a far better job of it than you did."

"At the time, I didn't really understand what you were going on about. But now… I think I do."

"You *think* you do?" Hale challenged.

Julian must have given more of his feelings away than he'd thought for the man to question him. Still…

"It doesn't bloody matter if I do or not. For I can't have her."

Hale frowned. "Is she already married?"

"No. But she won't meet my father's requirements of a proper countess, so I would lose the mines to Osborne if I married her and…"

"You want to marry her?"

Julian rubbed his temples with his thumb and index finger while nodding.

"Yes. I do. More than anything." Then he shook his head. "Except the responsibilities to those who depend on me."

Hale let out a breath and winced before he spoke again.

"I don't suppose she would be interested in being a mistress?"

Julian's fists clenched. "Speak of such a thing again and you'll find yourself across the field from my Wogdon pistol. I would never dishonor her in that way."

Hale held up both hands in surrender, apparently not wishing to duel one of his closest friends.

"My apologies. I meant no disrespect. But it is done when there is not another way."

Julian glared.

"By other people, of course," Hale added in an effort to appease him.

In truth, it wasn't that Julian hadn't thought of that option. But only briefly. What kind of future would that be for the woman he loved? He could not be so selfish as to keep her for himself while having nothing to give her in return.

"She will marry and have children and be happy. That is what she deserves. Nothing less."

"Perhaps I could loan you some money…" his best friend offered.

Julian sniffed. "It isn't just about the money. You remember the state the mines were in when I took them over. The children. The men missing limbs from accidents that could have been prevented. No. That is no answer."

"If I can't help in that way, perhaps I could at the least assist you in digging up your father and we could take a nice long piss on his remains."

Julian laughed at that.

"I appreciate the offer, but he's not worth the effort of digging him up."

"Fathers." Hale shook his head. "Every day when I hold Verona, I silently promise to be a better father than mine was."

"You already are."

"I didn't know I was capable of such love as what I feel for my wife and child. I almost feel sorry for my father for missing such a wonderful thing as I have."

"No regrets?"

"Not one. Remember, I was the wary bachelor like you. Trust me when I tell you, whatever I thought marriage would take from me, it has given me so much more."

Julian nodded. "You don't need to convince me. I want to marry her. But I can't."

"She's of good breeding, is she not?"

Julian nodded. "She is, unless you believe the gossips, that her mother was sired by a painter instead of the Duke of Renfrew.

But despite the rumors, she's also…" He smiled thinking of the woman who had stolen his heart. "Delightfully improper."

Hale's grin practically broke his face.

"The very best kind of wife."

Yes, Hale's duchess was rather unpolished. She was a horse-woman who probably rivaled Elaina for having as many pairs of breeches. But Hale hadn't been saddled with an ultimatum from beyond the grave that dictated whom he needed to marry.

"Life is too precious to spend it with someone you do not love. Find a way, Julian."

Julian nodded.

He'd been doing nothing but trying to find a way to have Elaina since before he'd even returned to London.

But time was running out. His thirtieth birthday loomed. It was time to admit defeat and give in to Elaina's plan to find a proper wife before it was too late to save the mines.

LAINEY WATCHED AS Julian danced with another debutante and another. Her stomach twisting in knots each time he graced one of the lucky girls with his distracting smile.

She couldn't even say it was jealousy that caused the pain in her chest, but rather heartbreak. She felt that Julian would have chosen her if he'd been able. But he could not.

Because she was not trained to be a proper countess. Her blood might be genteel enough, but her reputation was suspect. A spinster known to travel to remote parts of the world where she assisted with manual labor.

The Egyptian sun had tanned her skin and bleached her hair. Not to mention the freckles that no proper woman would have allowed. Her hands were not soft. They were calloused and scarred from working with tools. She didn't know the first thing about handling a household except to hire a housekeeper who could manage things with little input as her Aunt Rose had done.

She would not make the Earl of Melville a competent wife, but she was perfect for Julian in every other way. The man who loved adventure and wanted more from life than drawing rooms and port.

When the dance was over, he returned the young miss to her mother and fled in Lainey's direction.

"Might I have a word with you?" he said quickly.

"Of course." She followed behind him as he left the ballroom for the terrace.

After looking about to ensure they were alone he turned back to her with a pained expression.

"This is unbearable," he said. "I can't do this."

"Certainly, they can't all be unsuitable. They were selected because they were made for the duty of being a lord's wife."

He shook his head. "No. It's not them. It's you. Being here. I can't move on with any of these women when you are in the room. I look for you instead of being attentive to them. I wish for you. I want you. But I can't have you, which makes your being at these balls an unbearable torture. Please, Lainey. I beg of you to let me move on with this. Alone."

She was not hurt by his request. Possibly because she couldn't be in more pain and still walk under her own power. In truth, she would be grateful to have a respite from watching him move one step further away from her and what they'd had.

She'd known for months that this day would come and she would have to let him go. And now it was time to do just that.

Let him go.

"Very well, my lord. I wish you every happiness, truly."

"I wish the same for you, Lainey." He swallowed and looked about as if deciding if he should say something else. But rather than speak he simply bowed.

Tears stung her eyes as she curtseyed and returned inside where she found Aunt Rose and asked to leave.

They were outside waiting for the carriage to be brought

around when Lainey's last thread of control snapped. Tears streamed down her face and she struggled for breath.

"What is it, dear? Are you unwell? Has something happened?"

She knew what it must look like to Aunt Rose. She had reacted similarly the night of her come out, when that horrid boy had called her a stork and Julian had laughed.

"I will be fine, Auntie. I just want to go home." And stay there indefinitely.

But by the time she arrived home, she realized it would not be far enough.

She needed to go away where she wouldn't be able to hear of his marriage on the lips of their visitors. She needed to ensure she wouldn't see him with his new bride as she strolled in the park.

He had called the situation unbearable and it was an apt word.

"I am returning to Egypt," she announced the next morning at breakfast. "Today."

Her uncle's head snapped up as Aunt Rose gasped.

"But I will not be able to return until after the Season when the House of Lords is adjourned," Uncle Henry said.

"I understand. I wish to go alone."

"Why? What has happened? You were so distraught when we left the ball last night. Did someone say something to upset you?"

"No." She let out a breath, feeling the pain in her chest and considered her answer. "That is, nothing was said last night that I didn't already know. But it is of no matter and doesn't change the fact that I wish to return to Africa as soon as possible. It is surely no surprise to either of you to learn I am more comfortable in the desert than in a ballroom. Please. I beg of you to let me go."

"I shall go with her," Aunt Rose said as she rested a hand on Lainey's shoulder.

Her aunt must have seen her pain. Aunt Rose may not have been a mother herself, but she had cared for Elaina longer than her own mother had. Lainey was so lucky to have both her aunt and uncle. She now understood how they must feel for each other.

She couldn't be the reason they were apart for even a moment.

"No, Auntie. You don't want to leave Uncle Henry here alone. He needs you. I will hire a chaperone. Not that my reputation matters at all." Her chin trembled and her resolve to be stoic snapped. "Who cares if I have a proper chaperone when I am otherwise improper."

Uncle Henry looked at his wife in stark fear. "What is happening?"

But it was Lainey who answered before Aunt Rose could.

"What is happening is that Lord Melville is going to choose a bride and marry, but it can't be me, because I never attended finishing school. Instead, I was dragged about the world digging with my hands in the dirt and getting all these bloody freckles. Why couldn't you have at least seen that I wore a blasted bonnet in the sun so I might one day be a bleeding countess?"

To say she had shocked them was an understatement. They sat there in complete silence with mouths gaping.

She would need to apologize for yelling at them as well as accusing them of thwarting her opportunities. It wasn't their fault. She was grateful she had such kind people to love her after she'd lost her parents. Freckles or no.

"I'm going to pack," she announced. "I'll send word to Girard that I will be joining his team shortly. I'll see to getting passage on the next available ship." She left the room as more tears overflowed.

As expected, Aunt Rose entered her bedchamber a half hour later and sat in the chair by the window. She had probably been counting down the minutes in an effort to give Lainey enough time to calm down before approaching her.

"I'm so sorry, Aunt Rose. I shouldn't have shouted at you and Uncle Henry the way I did. I sounded like a spoiled, ungrateful child, but I'm most grateful for the two of you. Please forgive me."

"There is nothing to forgive, love. And nothing to feel grateful about either. Opening our home and our hearts to you was the easiest thing we've ever done. You are ours."

She stood and stared out the window down to the gardens.

"Do you remember how much Henry and I used to spoil you before your parents were taken from us?"

She shook her head as she tried to remember… before.

She'd been eleven when they died. Old enough to have many memories of them. But often she only recalled the night they died when she thought of that life.

But now that Rose mentioned it, she did recall the many times her mother and father ventured to Darlington Hall for Christmas. All the gifts waiting under the tree for her to open.

"You must know I am not leaving because of you or uncle."

"I know that, dear." Rose came and wrapped Lainey in her loving embrace. "I've known for some time how you felt about the earl. I could see it in the way you looked at him."

"He needs to marry a woman who will be a proper countess, and I do not qualify."

"It doesn't mean you have to leave. You may think running away will ease the pain, but there is no escaping a broken heart. At least here, you have us."

Lainey considered the suggestion but thought of how horrible it would be to see Julian after he married and know he could never be hers. At least if she fled England, she would be sure not to have to see him again.

She would surely be too busy to think of him.

It had to be easier this way.

※ ❖ ※

CHAPTER THIRTY-ONE

ANOTHER DANCE WITH another debutante. Julian forced a smile as he led her back to her hopeful mama.

Each girl he danced with was perfectly suitable. Perfectly elegant and poised. Able to carry on a perfect discussion of the ordinary topics, and smile in a perfect way. They were all perfectly… perfect.

But they were all a near replica of the last. True, their coloring might be different. Brown hair with hazel eyes, or blonde with blue eyes. They were lovely in their own ways. But none had the alluring combination of fiery gold curls and warm brown eyes a man wished to melt in.

It wasn't just Lainey's face he missed. It was her compelling conversation.

If ever she'd spoken to him of the weather, it had been to inform him of rainy seasons and draughts. Not the predictable drizzle of a London spring.

"It certainly is damp of late, is it not, my lord?" Miss Wendell said as he spun her around the dance floor.

"Yes, it is. I predict it will get increasingly warmer as we move from spring into summer," he answered with only slightly disguised sarcasm.

"Oh, yes. I hope you are correct."

The chit *hoped* he had decrypted known weather patterns for their geographical climate correctly? He might have asked, but there were at least six or seven words in that thought she possibly wouldn't understand.

Yes, Miss Wendell was lovely and she was no doubt competent in embroidery and playing the pianoforte as she'd been raised to do. It was an injustice the way noble families treated their daughters as if they were to be nothing more than frills. Substance was frowned upon. Miss Wendell would be a proper countess, just as any of them would be.

But she wouldn't be the perfect partner in life. Not for him.

He left the ball soon after and returned home. Bentley came in to assist him.

"Are you all right, my lord?" the man asked.

"No. In fact, I wish to change into something for the club," he said as Bentley hung up his evening jacket.

"Very well. I'm sure whatever is bothering you will be much easier to contemplate with a head full of whisky." The man didn't even attempt to veil his sarcasm.

"Why do I keep you, Ben?"

"Because I tell you the truth."

"I could do with a little less truth at the moment." The truth was time was running out. His thirtieth birthday was imminent. He needed to find his bride so there would be time to see to the wedding. But he couldn't bring himself to make a decision.

"Is there anything I can do?"

"Can you make Elaina Bantham a proper countess?"

The valet let out a sigh and shook his head.

"No. Though I daresay if she were a proper countess, you would probably not find her as alluring."

"You are probably right. I am between the proverbial rock and hard place. I need to do the right thing for the people who are counting on me."

"Which is not the right thing for you?"

"It isn't. The longer I'm away from her, I'm sure she is the only right thing for me."

"It is a difficult decision. I have faith that you will choose correctly."

Julian nodded though he didn't have the same faith.

The way he saw it, he had two choices. The honorable one and the selfish one. The honorable one led to a life of disappointment, and the selfish one was piled high with guilt.

At his club, Julian waved off invitations to sit with the other bachelors. They certainly wouldn't have any answers.

He was heading to a private booth when he spotted Lord Darlington sitting alone at a table by the window.

"Good evening. I didn't know you were a member here," Julian said, startling the man who offered a smile and gestured to the open seat in front of him. Julian sat and poured them each a drink from the bottle he had purchased.

"I rarely need to come. It is my place of solace when things at home are in turmoil."

Julian's heart rate picked up. "Has something happened? Is everyone well?"

He waved his hand in a soothing gesture.

"Yes. Everyone is of good health, if not good humor." He shook his head. "My wife is quite put out with me and my niece… Well, I'm not sure if she will ever forgive me. Apparently, I am at fault for giving her freckles and not seeing that she was proper enough, of all things." He rubbed his temples. "I thought I was giving her a good life with us. But perhaps I should have raised her like the rest of the young ladies of the *ton*."

"She is perfect the way she is."

"I thought so. And, of course, my wife agrees. But she also thinks I allow my dear niece to hide away from her problems. When her come out didn't go well, I allowed her to give up. But who can look into those trusting brown eyes and deny the girl anything she asks? A stronger man than I for sure, because I can't do it."

Julian laughed and shook his head. "Nor I."

"Lainey is in pain and since my wife cannot help her, she is blaming me. But things will settle now."

Hearing of Elaina's pain made his stomach clench. He was responsible. He shouldn't have even kissed her when he knew they couldn't be together. Everything they'd done, everything they'd shared, had given him an ample supply of memories. But what good are memories if they caused too much pain to recall?

"Time heals all wounds," Julian said though he wasn't sure he believed it.

Lord Darlington nodded in agreement.

"I suppose so. Maybe a little longer for a young woman in love." He shook his head. "I shouldn't have shared that, but I guess it wouldn't hurt for you to know, she fancied you. She was upset that she wasn't good enough to be a countess. Unrequited love is quite difficult to recover from."

Julian couldn't swallow. The weight of the man's words crashed around him.

Lainey thought she wasn't good enough to be his wife.

He knew well enough what that felt like—to not be good enough—and he wouldn't want anyone to experience such pain, especially not the woman he loved more than anything.

The woman who was perfect for him. The woman he realized he couldn't live without. No matter the repercussions. He would do whatever needed to be done, but he'd do it with her by his side.

"It isn't," he said quietly in answer to Lord Darlington.

"Oh, I daresay, it is. That thing about loving and losing or never having loved at all," the man attempted to explain unrequited love, but Julian was shaking his head.

"No. I meant it isn't unrequited. I love her, Henry. I thought I needed to follow my father's rules and marry a proper countess, but I can't do it. Not when I love her and want to spend my life with her."

The man blinked a few times before a wide grin split his face. "Rose was right. There will be no living with her when she finds out, but it will be fine with me so long as you can make my niece happy."

"I will do everything in my power to see that she is. In fact, I must go tell her right now. I can't let her think for another moment she isn't perfect the way she is."

He would find a way to take care of the miners and their families. He hadn't come up with a plan as of yet, but he had to believe he would find a solution as long as Lainey was by his side.

"Oh." Henry winced. "There is a bit of a problem." The seriousness in the man's words made Julian stop in his tracks.

"What problem?"

"She isn't here."

"Where is she?"

"Egypt. Or rather she is on her way."

As was his way, Julian began pacing in the small area near the man's table.

"She needed to get away and I allowed it." He tapped his chin for a moment then perked up. "She only left this afternoon. They will be stopping in Calais to load cargo. I can send a message to the captain to wait until you arrive. You could catch the ship there."

"Yes. Please. I have to catch her, Henry." And with that he ran out of the club much happier and determined than when he'd arrived.

He nearly bowled Hale over as the man was reaching for the door.

"There you are," Hale said as if Julian had been intentionally avoiding him.

"Yes, but I must go. Elaina is leaving for Egypt and I must catch her."

He turned to go, but Hale stayed him by gripping his arm.

"What I have to say will only take a moment, I promise and then you can track her down with a plan."

Julian glanced toward the street wishing to be on the move, but relented. Henry would hold the ship in Calais. Julian would catch up to her. And if he didn't, he would find another ship going to Egypt and find her.

"Go on."

Hale released Julian's arm and stood straighter.

"I will be purchasing the mines from Osborne when they are passed to him. I will then in turn sell them back to you."

Julian blinked and as the words filtered in, he shook his head.

"Osborne won't let them go for a pence. He'll want more than they're worth. I can't ask you—"

"You don't need to ask. It is what friends do for one another."

Julian rubbed his forehead as he thought it through. It would solve everything, but…

"The expense. It will be astronomical. I can't take food out of your family's mouths to help me."

"I spoke with Gia and she has agreed to part with a few of her horses to cover the expense. Besides, I've been doing a bit of reconnaissance, and I've learned of a dalliance between Lord Osborne and a certain Regent's mistress. If leverage is needed, I will go into the negotiations well-armed."

Julian felt his lips pull up in a grin. The first one since he'd given up on being with Lainey. If Osborne was fooling around with the Prince Regent's mistress, he surely wouldn't want anyone to find out. He would probably give up his own mines in the transaction in exchange for silence.

"I knew there would be a way. I had to trust I would find it."

"Well, I found it, actually." Hale brushed at his coat as his chest heaved with pride. Well deserved.

"I can never thank you enough for this."

Hale waved his hand in a dismissive gesture. "You can name your son after me and we'll call it paid." The man laughed to communicate he was only joking, but Julian thought Jeremy would be a fine name for his heir.

But only if he could find his wife first.

"I must go now."

"Yes. Go find her." Hale gave him a shove and Julian took off running down the street.

Back at his home he roused his servants and shouted orders

so he could be underway to Calais within the hour.

"Do you wish to come with me, Bentley? I know it is a long voyage and we've not been home very long."

"My old bones prefer the warmth of the desert, my lord. Besides… I go where you go. Always."

"Thank you."

"Now, let me pack so we can go catch your intended."

With a pat on the man's shoulder, Julian went off to his study to send off a few letters. He hoped to catch her ship, but even if he didn't, he'd catch the next one. He went to his desk and pulled out the bottom drawer where he kept his mother's ring.

He would find a way to take care of the mines. But first he needed to make sure the woman he loved knew his heart and how perfect she was for him.

CHAPTER THIRTY-TWO

AFTER SPENDING MOST of the night docked in Calais as they waited for cargo to arrive, they finally set sail at dawn.

Lainey stood on deck as the sky caught fire with the first of the day's light and remembered that evening weeks ago. The last sunset she'd shared with Julian.

The sun had set on their time together and now it rose on a new life for her.

This day would start like the rest of the days in her future. Without Julian.

As she did each time she thought of Julian, she pressed her fist to her chest and sniffed back tears. The pain seemed to grow worse instead of easier. She didn't know if she would survive it.

Her aunt and uncle had been supportive of her retreat from London. Though Aunt Rose warned her there was no escape from a broken heart, and so far, she seemed to be correct on that. But in Egypt, Lainey would be able to focus on her work and not have to think of Julian's marriage.

"Beautiful, is it not?" a voice said from behind her. She froze for a moment thinking she'd conjured up his voice, but when she heard his footsteps approaching, she couldn't help but turn to see.

He was really there. Walking toward her with a devilish grin, looking slightly rumpled. Julian was there.

"What...?" She swallowed and tried again. "What are you doing here?"

"You are here, and I want to be where you are."

She shook her head.

"But you need to return. Time is running out. Your birthday is in just a few weeks and you must find someone to marry."

"I have already found the person I want to marry. It is the reason I am here." He kneeled before her and offered up an exquisite emerald ring. "Would you do me the honor of becoming my wife, Elaina?"

"I would love nothing more but marrying me will mean giving up your mines. I can't do that."

He stood again and sighed.

"I have found a way. Or rather Hale has. He is going to purchase the mines from Osborne after the transfer and sell them back to me. It may be a while, but I'll pay him back."

"But you shouldn't have to lose them at all. I can't allow you to make such a sacrifice."

"It is not a sacrifice at all to get my own way."

He tilted his head to the side and winked at her with his normal boyish charm. Her heart, raw and broken, seemed to heal as if it had never been injured. How did he do such a thing?

"But later you might—"

"Be so deliriously happy with my choice I won't care that our coffers are not overflowing. We will not be destitute, love. I promise I can provide for you and our children. We might not have excess, but we'll have each other. We'll make it work." He blinked and his grin faded. "Unless it matters to you."

She smacked him in the arm.

"Of course, it doesn't matter to me. I love you, not your money or your title. And I don't need extravagance. I'm certain whatever we have will be enough to keep me in breeches."

"Do you love me?"

"Yes. So much I left London rather than have to see you marry someone else. As you said, it was unbearable."

"I love you, Elaina. I can't marry anyone else. I don't want to marry you to rebel against my father's wishes, though it is a welcome incentive. I want to spend my life with you, Lainey."

He kissed her and she felt her resolve melt away.

"Marry me? Please? We will be happy, I promise. Say yes."

"Yes," she answered. There was no other answer. She wanted him too much.

Seeing him smile, she knew it was the right thing. No matter what happened, they would face it together.

He kissed her, but just when it started to lead somewhere he backed away.

"One thing. What do you think of the name Jeremy for our firstborn son?"

She laughed, vaguely remembering hearing the Duke of Roxburghe's given name was Jeremy.

"It's beautiful."

"Good. Then stay here. I'll be right back," he said before stealing another kiss and rushing off.

"Where are you going?" He'd just asked her to marry him and he was leaving? Not that he could get far since they were out at sea.

Instead of answering, he called out for the captain who appeared too quickly to have been very far away. Bentley was also there.

"What is this?" she asked as he came to take her hand again.

"The captain of a ship can perform a marriage ceremony."

"We are marrying *now*?" she whispered rather than ask loud enough for the others to hear.

"Now that you've said yes, I don't want to wait another minute. Besides, my birthday is coming quickly and I must be married after all. Does now suit you?"

She couldn't argue because she didn't want to wait either. With a smile on her face and no trace of doubt in her heart, she nodded and said, "Now sounds lovely."

JULIAN SMILED INTO his bride's eyes as they said their vows in front of the crew and his longtime friend. The captain gave an efficient ceremony and when he prompted Julian to kiss his bride, he didn't need to be asked twice.

He managed through an impromptu wedding breakfast, but when they'd finished eating, the weight of the journey to rendezvous with the ship began to catch up with him.

"Husband, I think I should take you to my room and allow you to rest."

"Yes. Take me to your room, and I'll give you a reason to need rest as well."

She offered a naughty smile and took his hand to lead him below.

As he closed the door behind them, Lainey remembered the last time they'd been together. How sad it had been to have to leave him afterward that final night.

But this night held no trace of that heartbreak as he removed her gown with a sense of urgency that came from being apart and thinking they would never know such happiness ever again.

"Wife," he said, but this time it wasn't a question, her new title was said with sheer joy.

"Husband," she answered and he groaned as he thrust inside of her.

"We never have to be apart again," he promised.

Those words alone were enough to bring her pleasure, but her new husband went out of his way to make her cry out his name as she reached her climax.

But this time, he didn't pull away when he found his release. Instead, he thrust deeper as he pulsed inside her body matching her own tremors. It was more than she'd ever expected.

Her happiness overflowed her eyes and ran down her cheeks.

THAT EVENING AFTER another round of love-making with his wife and a generous nap, Julian and Elaina went up on deck to watch the sunset.

It gave him peace like he'd never felt before to know he would share a lifetime of sunrises and sunsets with her.

He wound his arms around her and kissed her neck. He was about to suggest they go back to their quarters when someone cleared their throat behind them.

Julian turned to see Bentley waiting patiently with a knowing smile on his lined face.

"I'm sorry to interrupt, but I wasn't able to give you your wedding gift this morning."

"Your being a witness to our ceremony was gift enough, Mr. Bentley. I'm so glad you agreed to join Julian for this journey," Lainey said while squeezing his valet's hand.

"As am I, but if you will permit me a moment of your time."

"Of course, Ben. What is it?"

"Perhaps you should read it for yourself." Bentley held out a letter.

As soon as Julian opened it, he noticed the handwriting as belonging to his father. The familiar tension pulled his fingers into fists.

"I received it when we returned from Egypt and was instructed not to open it until after your wedding."

Julian began pacing as he read the letter, but Lainey stopped him so she could read it as well. He held it out so they could both see.

Dear Friend,

I know you have always had a soft spot for my son, but I must ask you to do your duty since I will not be there to see to the matter myself.

I have instructed my solicitor to give away the mines if my son is not married to a proper countess by his thirtieth birthday.

He defies me with his every breath, but he will have no

choice in this if he wants to continue in the lifestyle he is accustomed to.

I need you to ensure his wife is acceptable. Of good breeding, without scandal, a woman of grace who will bear the next Melville heir. You know the type of woman I would pick for him if I'd been there, and I ask that you judge the woman as I would myself.

This is the final request of a dying man. I know you will see to my last wish to the letter, old boy.

Earl of Melville

He and Lainey shared a glance and then turned as one to face the valet. The anger in Julian's chest was for the man who had written the letter. Who had placed such a burden on Bentley.

Elaina's lip trembled when she looked up at him.

"I'm so sorry."

He shook his head, rejecting her apology.

"No. We knew this is how it would be. It doesn't matter. We are happy and we will find a way." He turned to Bentley and patted the man on the shoulder. "I'm sorry you had to be involved in this. I don't blame you in any of this. I know you are only doing your duty."

The valet looked between them with a crease between his brows.

"Do you really think I would give you such a thing as a wedding gift if it was not good news?"

Julian and Elaina waited in silence.

"I approve," he said.

"You approve?" Elaina said with the surprise he felt.

"Of course."

"But my father said—"

"Pfft." The older man waved his hand. "Your father left the decision up to me. He wanted to ensure you selected the perfect countess, and I can say without a doubt you have. As far as I know, there is no scandal attached to your name. Your grandfather was a duke so your breeding is commendable and you are the epitome of grace, my dear. When the two of you are blessed with an heir, I am certain you will raise him with love and honor."

He swiped his hands together as if the matter was settled before he continued.

"Those were the man's requirements and as I see it, they were well met. When we arrive in Cairo, I will send word back to the solicitor to let him know you have passed this ridiculous test, and that the mines will remain part of the Melville estates."

"Thank you, Mr. Bentley," Elaina said with tears running down her cheeks. Julian might have given Ben the riot act for making his wife cry except Julian himself was having a bit of tightness in his throat.

"There is nothing to thank me for, my lady. I should be thanking you for making Julian so happy and showing him what it is to be loved unconditionally. I feel not a trace of guilt with my decision since the man who wrote this letter, failed to love his son in the same manner as you do."

Julian hugged the man who was more like a father to him than his sire ever was.

"I'll see you are well compensated for this, my friend."

Ben laughed. "I would be willing to forgo compensation so long as I might stay in Egypt during the winters. I do prefer a warmer climate."

With a promise to do just that, and a few more hugs, Ben excused himself to allow them privacy.

"I told you everything would work out. You should have trusted me," Julian said with a wicked smile.

"I fear if I agree you were right, I will not be able to live with you." She leaned up and kissed him before pulling away to add, "I do trust you, Julian. Completely."

That feeling of acceptance he'd searched for all his life wrapped around him, and he knew he was where he belonged.

EPILOGUE

Dalkeith Castle, Scotland
One year later…

L AINEY SMILED UP at Julian as they stepped outside to greet the carriage coming down the drive.

"Are you warm enough?" he asked as he wrapped his arm around her shoulder. "Is our little prince warm enough?"

Julian had taken to marriage and fatherhood in the same way he took to most things, with a great amount of worry. Lainey knew it was the way he cared for those he loved and didn't mind having to reassure him.

"We are fine."

She placed a kiss on their son's head. Wee Bentley had been born in Egypt in February and, much to their relief, was an intrepid traveler. Julian called him their little prince as he'd been born in the Valley of the Gods. And despite his promise to the duke, they named him after Ben since he claimed the man was the true hero.

"I don't recall it being so chilly in Scotland in May," Julian said and rubbed her arm. "I've grown as weary of the cold as Ben."

Julian's former valet had stayed behind for this visit, but had sent a letter that he'd found a bit of treasure in a preserved papyrus.

The carriage stopped and before the coachman could open

the door, Aunt Rose was hopping down and bustling up the stairs.

"Oh, there he is. My great nephew." She turned to yell over her shoulder. "Henry, you must see how precious he is."

"I'm coming, love. I prefer not to jump from the carriage while it's still moving."

"Let us go inside so no one takes a chill," Julian suggested.

When their guests were seated in the drawing room by the fire, and Aunt Rose was holding baby Ben, Julian stood behind Lainey and wrapped his arms around her waist before leaning down to press a kiss by her ear.

"Perhaps we could sneak away while they're all distracted," she whispered causing him to laugh.

Years ago, that sound had broken her, and set her heart to anger and vengeance. But now, it was treasured proof of her husband's happiness.

"As much as I would like to do just that, I'd also like to stay here a moment longer and enjoy being part of a loving family."

She leaned back to kiss him and he squeezed her tighter.

It was still a mystery to her why his father had been unable to love this very loveable man. Fortunately, Julian had no issues showing his love for her or their child.

She often wished the rotten man could see Julian now and know how happy he was despite the old earl's plans. Julian rarely ever spoke of his father. Perhaps that was the best revenge. Allowing the man's memory to drift away into nothing.

"I have basked in this happy moment enough for now," Julian said. "Let us give the grandparents time with their grandson, shall we?" He took her hand to lead her toward the stairs. "I don't know if anyone has ever told you how convenient it is to kiss someone of your height." He gave a saucy wink. "Among other things."

About the Author

One very early morning, Allison B. Hanson woke up with a conversation going on in her head. It wasn't so much a dream as being forced awake by her imagination. Unable to go back to sleep, she gave in, went to the computer, and began writing. Years later it still hasn't stopped.

Allison lives near Hershey, Pennsylvania and writes Highlander Historical and Scottish Regencies.

Catch up with Allison on any of her social media platforms here:

Website:
allisonbhanson.wordpress.com

Facebook:
facebook.com/BlueRidgeRomance

Twitter:
@AllisonBHanson

Instagram:
@allisonbhanson

Goodreads:
goodreads.com/author/show/9860589

BookBub:
bookbub.com/authors/allison-b-hanson